THE
AMERICAN CRYPTIDS ™

Volume One: Blood County

by Yuman Sun

THE AMERICAN CRYPTIDS

Volume One: Blood County

Created and Written by Yuman Sun

Illustrated by Rodriguez Brothers of Ink The Tea

Book Cover by Muhammad Waqas

Published by Franklin Publishers

Printed in the United States of America

For permissions, inquiries, or additional copies, contact:

Franklin Publishers

www.franklinpublishers.com

DEDICATION

This book is dedicated to my beloved husband, who fights monsters in his dreams.

TABLE OF CONTENTS

CHAPTER ONE

THE HANGMAN

It was a dark night without an inch of moonlight. An owl hooted in the distance above Camp Moonlit Smiles.

Camp counselor John Webber woke up after midnight to check on the Boy Scouts. He came out of the Recreation Center where he lived and walked towards the cabins behind three redwood trees where the scouts were asleep.

As he walked through the redwood trees, he shined his flashlight towards the cabins. As soon as he looked over, his eyes opened wide, with horror written all over his face. He could not believe what he saw with his own eyes.

John rubbed his eyes, hoping what he saw was only an illusion from not getting enough sleep. After all, he had been working nonstop for the last week since the Boy Scouts arrived.

But it was not.

In front of him, there were what looked like bodies hanging from the roofs of the cabins. He walked a little closer, praying to God this was merely a prank by the boys.

Ropes were tied with bowline knots. John remembered seeing the scouts learning to tie these bowline knots yesterday. On each of the hanging bodies, a bloody bag was seen on top of the head.

Blood was still dripping on the floor from the bottom of the bowline knots. John pinched himself. It hurt. In the middle of this silent night, every drop of blood sent a chilling reminder that this was not a dream.

A cold gust of wind suddenly blew John's hair apart, covering his eyes. He brushed his hair from his eyes quickly so he would not miss anything in front of him.

John took a deep breath before he removed the bag from the body in front of him. In his mind, he hoped to hear a "Got you!" from the boys.

Inside the bag was a bloody, skinned face of a boy. The reek of iron filled John's nose, his stomach lurched, and he stumbled back choking on bile. The night seemed to tilt around him, every shadow now alive with menace.

That was 30 years ago.

In present day, the full moon above shines through dense redwood trees, giving the abandoned campground the limited light that it desperately needs.

A white van is seen driving on the road leading to Camp Moonlit Smiles.

Inside the van, a guy named Cole Carter with a long curly beard is driving. He is a veteran who survived the Iraq war and acts as cameraman and driver for this ghost chasing group on TheyTube and Teek Took called SpiritScouts.

Cole vapes while he drives. He only vapes in coffee flavor because it keeps him awake during these long nights of shooting.

Through the vaping smoke and coffee smell, a girl named Mei He is busy typing scripts on her laptop. She has long black hair and wears a shirt and a pair of jeans. She is the original creator and host for the TheyTube and Teek Took channel. She looks through notes made earlier today about the haunted campground when they interviewed John Webber, the camp counselor who discovered the Boy Scouts' bodies.

"30 years, and no one dared to come here," smirks Joseph Wilson, who acts as sound engineer, is a high school art teacher, an avid Halloween enthusiast, and a bit sensitive about his waistline.

"Yeah. This whole serial killer thing scared the locals." Miguel Garcia, the video editor and gaffer, shows a piece of newspaper with the front-page reporting that 14 Boy Scouts were found dead overnight.

"Okay, we are here," says Cole as he removes his vaporizer for a second and puts it back for another vape before the shooting begins, "Let's do this." Cole steps down from the driver side door. His military style boots disappear in the knee-high weeds.

Joseph, Miguel and Mei get off the van from the sliding door and see that they have arrived at the entrance of Camp Moonlit Smiles. The wooden sign of the campground is now half eaten by termites and barely hanging on to the poles it once was securely nailed to.

Swimming through the weeds, the crew takes the camera, microphone, and light out of the van into the campground.

The crew like to film haunted areas without scouting the target because they think it gives audiences a live experience of fear, excitement and exploration.

Cole gets the camera rolling. Joseph grabs the microphone and points it at Mei. Miguel shines light on Mei and then the campground.

"Here we are at the entrance of Camp Moonlit Smiles," Mei begins her narrative, "where 14 Boy Scouts were found dead overnight 30 years ago. Ever since that night, locals have been saying that this campground is haunted."

"Let's walk towards the cabins where the boys were hanged. John Webber, the camp counselor we interviewed earlier today, told us that the cabins are behind three redwood trees." Mei continues, "He did warn us not to come to this location. But we are SpiritScouts. We are not fearful of haunted places."

"As you can see, this campground has been closed for over 30 years," Mei talks and walks, "and that's why there are weeds everywhere. I see the three large redwood trees ahead. We are getting closer to the cabins."

The crew walks by the trees towards the cabins. It is a windless night. Leaves and weeds look stale with light shining on them. As the crew moves through the weeds, a narrow road is created behind them.

"We are at the cabins." Mei points at the roofs, "The young boys were found hanged on the roofs of these exact cabins, with ropes tied in bowline knots, and bags on their skinless faces."

Cole and Miguel move the camera and light towards the roofs, following Mei's fingers. The roofs of cabins are seen with spider webs and fallen leaves, worn by sun, wind and rain.

"Who would have committed these horrific, senseless killings? The locals say the serial killer still lives among us. It could be your neighbor, your mailman, or your school principal." Mei narrates, "And ghosts of the Boy Scouts have been seen crying and tying bowline knots on their necks at midnight. Tonight, we will see if we can find them."

Mei continues to walk into the cabin and opens the door. Spider webs are everywhere, so Mei has to break them in order to walk into the door. In the process, Mei cuts her fingers on a rusty nail, "Ouch."

The crew go in with Mei. Cole films the bunk beds inside the cabin.

When the light points towards the wooden floor, Mei notices something carved onto the pieces of wood. "Wait, what is this?" She wipes away the dust and leaves on the floor.

"The carvings look like Latin characters," Mei says, as she uses her hands to touch each character on the wood. Some blood from her fingers is left on the carvings.

Suddenly, the crew feel a strong gust of wind blowing past them. The light goes out. At this exact moment, the full moon becomes completely covered with thick clouds.

"What happened?" Mei gasps. Something feels like Deja vu. She remembers a time when she broke her skin on a nail in a haunted house, and heard a distant whisper in her ears, "Leave." She shakes off the goose bumps on her arms and the fear she remembered.

Miguel shakes his head and uses his hand to bang on the light that went out, "I'm not sure why the light is not working. I checked beforehand, and it was fully charged." Then he takes out his phone to use its flashlight as a make-shift light source for filming, but the flashlight does not turn on. "Weird!" Miguel exclaims.

Cole continues to film. The camera has a light too, but it is not functioning, just like the other lights.

"Luckily, the camera has night vision," Mei says to the camera.

"Where's the microphone?" Mei realizes the microphone is no longer there, and neither is Joseph.

Cole, Miguel, and Mei look around for Joseph.

The moon has come out of the clouds. Some moonlight shines into the cabin through the broken roof pieces and windows.

"Joseph? Where are you?" Miguel calls out with a shaky voice, hoping to hear a response.

And there is nothing. No response except for Miguel's heavy breathing due to his growing fear. He thinks to himself, "I should not have taken this job. Remote work sounds perfect right now." He only started to work for this crew a little over a month ago after he turned down a remote work opportunity.

An owl hoots on one of the redwood trees.

"Something is touching my foot!" Mei shouts as she feels something on her left foot.

Cole and Miguel rush over to Mei's side. Miguel is too scared to do anything, so Cole uses his left hand to sweep through the ground surrounding Mei while holding the camera on his shoulder with his right hand.

Cole feels something.

It is the microphone that Joseph was holding. It must have fallen on the ground.

Joseph never lets that microphone go. For it to be lying there alone means something had torn it from him. Cold dread prickles across their skin.

Mei, Cole and Miguel look at each other under the moonlight. They know something is not right.

Miguel says, "Maybe we should stop filming."

"But the night vision from the camera might help," Cole says.

"Let's just continue filming. We need to stick together and find Joseph." Mei agrees with Cole.

Mei is worried about Joseph. But she is also hoping to film something extraordinary so that the number of followers for the channel can be increased. "Joseph will be fine, he always is." Mei thinks to herself, "Maybe he really needed to pee and walked away."

Mei, Miguel and Cole walk slowly outside of the first cabin. Now they are under the roof. Because they do not have light other than moonlight, the range they can see is limited.

"What's moving?" Miguel says.

Cole points the camera to the floor where the movement is heard. He sees a rat the size of a medium dog crossing by.

"Rat," Cole says.

Miguel feels a bit relieved.

Mei continues to walk past the first cabin to the second cabin. As she goes up the steps, she bumps into something.

Cole points the camera towards Mei. In the camera, behind Mei, he sees Joseph's shoes.

"Joseph?" Cole asks.

Mei steps away to look at what just bumped into her. Suddenly, a thunder flashes in the sky, making everything visible.

Then a scream is heard throughout the campground. "Ahhhh!"

Mei, Miguel, and Cole all realize what exactly is in front of them: Joseph has been hanged on the roof of the second cabin! The body they see in front of them wears Joseph's clothes. The height of the body is the same as Joseph's, as well as the waistline.

Cole comes forward to the body and removes the bag on the head. It is a skinless face like the rest of the 14 Boy Scouts hanged 30 years ago.

"Help!" Miguel panics, starts to shout and tries to run back to the van.

Cole grabs Miguel and says, "We need to stay together! The killer is still around!"

Miguel pauses to listen, but before he could speak, a rope bites into his throat, yanked tight by claws the size of meat hooks. His cry chokes into a strangled rasp as terror seizes his eyes.

Cole throws away the camera and attempts to grab the giant hands with all his strength, but he cannot compete with the strength of this creature. He then holds on to the bowline knot on Miguel's neck, hoping to stop the creature from dragging Miguel away or suffocating him. But the strength of this creature is so significant that nothing Cole does stops it. Both of his hands are cut and bleeding from the rope.

Miguel keeps yelling for help, desperately.

The creature uses its claws to pull on the bowline knot with much more strength than previously. The force is so strong that it decapitates Miguel.

Cole can barely take his hands out of the knot before it closes.

Mei is devastated. She kneels next to Miguel, and tears fall down her cheeks uncontrollably.

Cole grabs Mei and says, "Run!"

Under the bright moon, Mei and Cole run as fast as possible, through the cabins, through the redwood trees, through the picnic tables, into the Recreation Center.

They close the Recreation Center's double doors and lock them with chains they locate on the side of one door. Finally, they can breathe for a little while.

The Recreation Center is dark inside. There's a reception area and a gift shop. On the right is a swimming pool, and on the left a large hall. Behind the hall is a kitchen.

Cole and Mei tip toe inside the Recreation Center, walking past the gift shop, past the swimming pool, and past the hall. In the gift shop, they pick up two baseball bats as weapons.

That's when they see light leaking through the kitchen door.

Mei whispers to Cole, "Why is there light in the kitchen? It's been years since this campground was occupied."

Cole says, "Maybe they left in a hurry and forgot to turn off the light years ago? Let's go check it out."

"One, two, three, open!" Cole says to Mei. They open the kitchen door quickly, holding their baseball bats up. Cole stays in front of Mei to protect her.

As the door opens, Cole sees a creature with black fur, black claws, and black pointy spikes on its spines turn around. The creature is around 5 feet tall and wears a camouflage long sleeve with turtleneck and a pair of jeans. In its right claw is what looks like a half-eaten lamb chop.

Cole immediately strikes the creature with his baseball bat, and the creature deflects with its claws.

Another creature is seen sitting at the round table near the kitchen counter. This creature looks huge. It is more than 6 feet tall with brown fur all over its body. A red flannel shirt, tan colored pants and a blue baseball cap are worn by this creature.

Mei enters the kitchen and waves the baseball bat towards the brown-furred creature that is walking towards her. The creature grabs her baseball bat and opens its mouth, "Lady, calm down."

A third creature is seen flying from the stove towards the kitchen entrance. The creature's face looks like a giant moth with two antennae. It has giant powdery wings and wears a flight suit.

"What are you? Why did you kill Joseph and Miguel?" Mei asks in shock after seeing the three creatures in front of her. She knows she will die today. But before that, she wants to know who will kill her and why.

The brown-furred creature says, "Don't worry, lady. We won't harm you. I'm Big Joe."

The black-furred creature says, "My friends call me Chupa. Have you heard of Chupacabra before? That's me!"

Chupa smiles, "Big Joe was called Sasquatch by people, and this one," he points at the creature with wings and winks, "was called Mothman."

The moth-looking creature says, "I'm Saxon."

Big Joe rumbles a laugh that seems too deep for the small kitchen, "Humans call us cryptids. We've lived with that name long enough, so we took it for ourselves. But you'll find we're not the monsters you think."

Chupa and Saxon both laugh at the last comment made by Big Joe.

"So, how can we help you?" Big Joe asks.

Just as Mei is about to respond, the kitchen door is broken into with such force that the entire door comes off from the hinges nailed to the door frame.

Dust and debris fly hectically in the air.

Big Joe, Chupa, Saxon, Mei and Cole look towards the entrance and see a demon-looking creature enter the kitchen. This creature has a rope with a bowline knot on its neck, multiple horns on its head and shoulders, and long claws. The creature's face is skinless, which means the red muscles and eyeballs are just hanging out without any cover.

The creature immediately takes a leap to attack Mei and Cole as if they are the only living things it sees in the kitchen. Big Joe, Chupa and Saxon jump in to help shelter Mei and Cole.

The creature has such strength that Big Joe, Chupa and Saxon must use their full strength to grab its arms, claws, and the bowline knot to stop it from attacking Mei and Cole.

Big Joe yells, "You two, run!"

Mei and Cole start running out of the kitchen, out of the Recreation Center, through redwood trees and into their van. Luckily, Cole still has the vehicle key with him. He starts the engine and drives out of the campground at full speed.

It rained outside when they were inside the Recreation Center. The roads are slippery.

Finally, Mei and Cole can breathe, thanks to Big Joe, Chupa and Saxon. They grieve the loss of Joseph and Miguel and wonder why the demon-looking creature is so keen on killing them. They also wonder about Big Joe, Chupa and Saxon. They said they help humans. How do they help? And are there more of them?

But before they can take a break from fear and horror, Cole notices something running fast behind the van in the distance. He speeds up, hoping to lose it.

The creature is getting closer and closer. Cole and Mei look in the back mirror, and their nightmare returns. It is the same demon-looking creature charging at the van!

On the wet, whiny road of the hills outside of the campground, Cole makes fast turns and hits on gas whenever he can. The creature laughs as it gets closer to the van each time, and then Cole speeds up to lose it.

In front of Cole is a sharp turn, so he must hit the brakes. The creature speeds up, takes a huge leap, and lodges itself onto the van.

Now Cole and Mei feel hopeless. The creature probably killed the cryptids just now and is about to kill them.

Just when the creature uses its claws to swipe on the roof to gain entrance to the van, Cole sees something else in the back mirror.

A creature that is more than 6 feet tall with brown fur and a creature that is about 5 feet tall with black fur are running towards the van.

When Mei looks up, she sees another creature flying on top of the van.

"Big Joe, Chupa and Saxon are not dead! They are here!" Mei feels hope rising from the dark, cold ashes of desperation.

Saxon flies down, uses gravity to kick the creature, and then swipes the creature with his sharp claws.

Big Joe and Chupa both jump on the van and fight the creature at the same time. Big Joe hits the creature with blunt force, punch after punch. Chupa utilizes his long claws to swipe at the creature, turns around and uses his spikes on the back to further scratch the creature.

The creature is now fighting three cryptids on top of the van at the same time. It becomes ruthless. Black blood is seen pumped into its bare eyeballs. Its arms are full of large thorn-like veins. Its strength is unmatched.

Big Joe, Chupa and Saxon see that there is a large cliff ahead. Big Joe and Chupa both grab the bowline knot on the creature's neck to tie the knot onto the side mirror of the van.

Saxon flies down to signal Mei and Cole.

Cole nods and opens the driver side door. Mei opens the passenger side door.

Cole steps on the brake, hard.

Big Joe, Chupa and Saxon give the creature final punches on its head, then Big Joe and Chupa jump off, and Saxon flies off the van.

At the same time, Mei and Cole jump off the van from the doors they just opened.

The creature is seen falling off the cliff, with its neck tied to the side mirror, struggling to climb up, bumping against boulders, and eventually being swallowed up by soaring waves of the Pacific Ocean.

Mei and Cole are drenched in rainwater, dirt, blood and sweat after jumping off the van and rolling on the ground. Luckily, no major damage was done. Mei twisted her wrist, and Cole scraped his left arm.

"Thank you for saving our lives!" says Mei.

"You are very welcome, ma'am." Big Joe responds.

"By the way, what's your name?" Chupa asks.

Mei and Cole chuckle and introduce themselves, "I'm Mei He." "My name is Cole Carter."

"Nice meeting you!" Saxon says.

Big Joe, Chupa and Saxon invite Mei and Cole back to the Recreation Center of the campground. In the gift shop, Mei and Cole pick up some new clothes and shoes to replace their torn-apart ones. They go to the shower room of the swimming pool to take showers, change, and gather with the cryptids in the kitchen afterwards.

"Whatever you are cooking smells good!" Cole says.

"Do you want to try some of Chupa's world-famous goat chops?" Saxon invites Mei and Cole.

"Oh, that's what Chupa was eating when we first met. I thought it was a lamb chop." Cole replies.

"Yep, I only eat goat chops. They are the best. Lamb chops are no comparison." Chupa replies and serves Cole some goat chops.

"How about you, Mei?" Chupa asks.

"I'll take some!" Mei replies, "I sure feel hungry after all the running."

"Great! Let me know what you think." Chupa serves Mei a plate of goat chops.

Mei and Cole bite into the goat chops. They are very well-seasoned and cooked to perfection. Medium-rare perfection. "Hmmmm, this is good," Mei says, and Cole agrees.

"So, who are you and why are you here?" Big Joe asks.

Mei explains that they are part of the crew for a social media channel, and that they are here to film paranormal activities after the murders of Boy Scouts 30 years ago, and then they were attacked by this creature and lost Joseph and Miguel.

Big Joe says, "This creature seems to be one of the demons we've been tracking."

"Yea he definitely has some of the same features." Chupa chimes in.

Mei asks, "Do you think he's dead?"

Saxon says, "It's hard to tell. Some demons we met were very resilient. I'm not too optimistic."

Mei gets nervous, "You mean the demon can come back?"

Big Joe says, "Yes, some of the demons we fought before are extremely powerful. They can only be defeated in specific ways."

Cole asks, "Why does the demon want to kill us? It seems that the same demon killed the Boy Scouts 30 years ago."

Big Joe speculates, "Some demons have triggers that irritate them. We can investigate what happened 30 years ago and compare that with what happened today to find out the pattern."

Now the sun is out, shining brightly above Camp Moonlit Smiles. Another day has begun.

The cryptids, Mei and Cole, are ready to investigate the killings that happened last night and 30 years ago after a good night's sleep.

They start from the cabins.

In daylight, the campground looks different, with birds chirping and a wide variety of plants growing and competing for sunlight.

Mei and Cole try to locate Joseph's and Miguel's bodies to no avail. There is blood everywhere, but somehow the bodies are no longer there. Mei and Cole grieve the loss of their coworkers. What is sad is that they cannot even give them proper burials.

Cole locates his camera, which is beyond salvaging. He finds the SIM card and saves it in his pocket.

They walk into the cabins and examine everything in sight. Mei shows the cryptids the Latin characters carved on the floor with her blood smeared on them.

Big Joe reads the characters and says, "This is a demon named Hereticus. Someone had written these Latin letters to summon him. Maybe it was the Boy Scouts."

Mei says, "That makes sense. But why would they do that? And how do they know Latin?"

"Not sure. Nowadays, not a lot of people know Latin. And to know this demon's name is even harder." Big Joe says.

"Let's keep searching," Cole says.

To Mei and Cole, Big Joe, Chupa and Saxon seem well-trained in investigations. They are combing through every inch of the cabin, paying attention to every little detail, whether it's a loose nail, a crooked piece of wood, or a bent door handle.

"Hey, come here!" Chupa finds something interesting. Everyone gathers around.

Chupa points at a shorter piece of wood under one of the bunk beds. He puts his claws on it and gives it a little shake. The wood piece gets loose. He then uses his claws to pry the wood piece open. After all, it helps to have long, strong claws. Chupa raises his eyebrows, looks at Mei and Cole, and says, "Long claws, makes it easy to pry things open."

As the wood piece opens, a journal falls to the ground. Dust flies in the air and then settles. Mei sneezes.

"This person must have something secretive to hide," Chupa says and then picks up the journal.

He hands it to Big Joe, "Long claws, hard to turn pages."

Big Joe opens the journal. The pages are yellow, and the edges are soiled and have water damage.

"July 11, 1994. Monday. First day of Boy Scouts. I was so excited for today, but it turned out to be disappointing. Two big boys picked on me. I am too scared to tell. Hopefully, tomorrow I can stay under the radar." Big Joe reads.

"Aww, poor boy," Mei says with sympathy.

"July 14, 1994. Thursday. I hope I can survive tomorrow. We have an exploration, and Sam and Adam might try to do something to me." Big Joe continues.

"July 15, 1994. Friday. They put me in a cave. They blocked the entrance with trunks of fallen trees. THEY NEED TO PAY. I found some Latin characters written on the cave, which can summon a demon named Hereticus. I WILL MAKE THEM PAY. They make fun of me for being nerdy. I bet they don't know Latin and the characters I'm about to carve onto the floor! I SHALL MAKE THEM PAY!" Big Joe reads.

"The boys were found hanged on the dawn of July 16, 1994, Saturday, according to a local newspaper," Cole says.

Saxon says, "Unfortunately, the owner of this journal succeeded in summoning the demon."

Chupa says, "There's a price for everything. And he paid with his life and 13 other lives that day."

"And Joseph's and Miguel's lives as well," says Mei with sadness, "They were taken too soon."

The cryptids, Mei and Cole, decide to find the cave in the hills. Before they do, the cryptids bring out some weapons and let Mei and Cole choose their own. This is precautionary, just in case they run into the demon again.

"What weapons do you use?" Mei asks.

Big Joe takes up an axe and says, "This is my camping axe. I like using a heavy weapon. All the weapons here have been blessed with Holy Water and can be used against demons effectively. See the symbols on the weapons? They glow in the dark when the weapons are used against demons."

The symbol, complete with a crucifix cross and what looks like ancient characters, is engraved on each of the weapons.

Mei and Cole learn that Chupa uses a rope, and Saxon uses a bow and arrows.

Mei chooses a sword because she has no fighting experience, and a sword seems lighter and easier to use. Cole takes a gun. He's good with guns after being trained by the Iraq War.

With weapons in their hands, the cryptids, Mei and Cole, are ready to search for the mysterious cave mentioned in the Boy Scout's journal.

"According to John Webber, the camp counselor, the Boy Scouts usually have activities near the creek. Perhaps we can start our search there." Mei says.

"Should we split into three teams, with Saxon taking the route from above, Cole and Chupa on the north side of the creek, Mei and I on the south side of the creek?" Big Joe suggests.

"Sounds good. Signal when you find the cave." Chupa says.

They search along the creek on both sides and from above. The overgrown trees and weeds do not help. Bugs and animals are everywhere. The good thing is they still have daylight.

Saxon notices an area with large rocks that has some weeds stepped down. Unless there is a mountain lion nearby, it might indicate that the demon was recently there.

He whistles to signal the rest of the team. Cole, Chupa, Mei and Big Joe hear the whistle and rush over.

Saxon points at the area. The team agrees that this is an area of interest.

Big Joe reminds the team, "Let's be cautious. This might be where the demon lives. He might be inside."

The team acknowledges his reminder, and everyone raises their own weapon and stays alert.

Big Joe moves in. It is a cave made in volcanic times. He brings out the flashlight he keeps in his pocket as it gets darker.

The rest of the cryptids, Mei and Cole, follow Big Joe inside. As they walk deeper into the cave, it gets harder to see.

"Look, writings on the wall!" Mei sees something and points.

Big Joe shines the flashlight towards the direction of Mei's right hand, and everyone gathers around while Chupa stands guard.

"Latin characters." Big Joe says, "These are the same characters as those carved in the cabin."

"This confirms that this is the cave that the boy was trapped in," Mei says.

Big Joe says, "Yes, we are at the right place. Everyone, please be on high alert as the demon might come to us at any time. Let's go in and see if there's anything else notable."

The group goes further inside the cave. Along the way, there are dried bones scattered everywhere.

As they reach the end of the cave, they prepare to face the demon again. Quietly, they move. Big Joe turns quickly along the last corner and holds his axe up, ready to fight. There is nothing in front of him, except for a bigger round opening where more dried bones and skulls are scattered around. Along the round opening, there are more Latin characters.

Big Joe signals everyone to follow him in and reads the Latin characters. These characters describe the origin story of Hereticus.

"It says that Hereticus the Hangman was created in the Hell dimension known as the Demonus Realm. He kills people that summon him and those around them." Big Joe reads.

He continues, "He is a low-level demon."

"Does it tell you how to get rid of him?" Mei asks.

Big Joe says, "Let me see. Here is something else. It reads, 'By way of summoner's blood, words of summons shall return summoned home.'"

Big Joe barely finishes reading the sentence when everyone hears a loud roar. They look back at where the roar comes from and see the demon charging towards them.

Hereticus is visibly irritated and angry. He must be mad that they pushed him down the cliff and tracked him down to his cave. His veins are large and pointy. His strength is beyond anyone's comprehension.

Big Joe, Chupa, Saxon, Mei, and Cole use their weapons against Hereticus. The axe, rope, bow, arrows, sword, and gun are glowing a blue light and moving around in the cave as the group fights Hereticus. Because Holy Water is on the weapons, the group is able to scratch Hereticus' thick skin with small, non-life-threatening wounds that hurt the demon. But the wounds will not allow them to send Hereticus back.

Big Joe signals to the rest of the group that they need to retreat to the beginning of the cave, where the words of summon are carved on the cave wall. In his head, he is trying to make sense of the last sentence he read at the end of the cave about how the demon can be sent back. Chupa pulls the rope to force Hereticus to move towards the cave entrance. Hereticus gets even madder because Chupa is using his signature bowline tie to tie him up.

The rope burns a line on Hereticus' neck because it has Holy Water on. But Hereticus was so ferocious that he used his thick claws to break the rope.

Big Joe walks backward towards the cave entrance while facing and fighting Hereticus. Chupa, Saxton, Mei and Cole follow Big Joe's lead. Chupa uses his rope to double up and form another bowline tie and throws it onto Hereticus' neck.

As they reach the first Latin writings on the wall, Big Joe stops and signals the group to fight Hereticus there while he concentrates on figuring out how to send the demon back. The summoner died 30 years ago. Who can send this demon back now?

That's when it dawns on Big Joe. The reason why Hereticus keeps attacking Mei and Cole is because Mei ran her fingers against the Latin words and accidentally smeared blood on the letters. And that made Mei the new summoner. Her blood is needed on the Latin words to send Hereticus the Hangman back to Hell.

Once he figures this part out, Big Joe gradually moves towards Mei. In between fighting Hereticus and protecting Mei, he mentions, "You are the new summoner. Your blood needs to be smeared onto the Latin words to send him back."

Mei understands the assignment, but she is busy fighting for her life and cannot move towards the wall.

Hereticus also hears the conversation and figures out that the cryptids have figured him out. So, he focuses his efforts on attacking Mei.

Now the cryptids and Cole are protecting Mei against Hereticus. Cole uses his gun to fire the last round of bullets against Hereticus' head, but the bullets only make small holes in the head, far from disabling him.

As Big Joe, Chupa, Saxon, and Cole are fighting Hereticus to help Mei, she tries to move her sword to cut her skin on her left hand. But it is hard to do between defending herself and attacking Hereticus. Chupa notices and says, "Let me help you." He retreats to where Mei is and uses his claws to break the skin on her hand. Now blood is coming out of Mei's hand. All they need to do is have Mei go near the writings on the wall.

Hereticus sees the situation in his eyeballs and moves himself to cover the writings on the wall. Mei tries to put her bloody left hand on the wall, but is forced to back out because of Hereticus' constantly fierce attacks.

Now Big Joe, Chupa, Saxon, and Cole surround Hereticus with Mei in the back of the circle of the cryptid team. Mei desperately wants to help them as they are getting injured by Hereticus. Big Joe's brown fur is dyed with his own blood. Saxon's flight suit is shredded. Chupa's head and arms are covered with blood. Cole's chest and back are both bleeding.

Mei decides to utilize her body size to squeeze herself through the circle and smear her blood onto the Latin characters carved on the wall.

Mei takes a deep breath, gets her left hand ahead of her, and squeezes through the group.

At this point, Big Joe's hands are pinned on Hereticus' left arm, and Chupa's claws are holding on to Hereticus' right arm. Saxon is punching Hereticus's head, and Cole is hitting Hereticus on his gut. But this moment of advantage does not last long. Just as Mei comes inside the circle and reaches out with her left hand to the wall, Hereticus gets his right arm loose and uses his claws to swipe at Mei.

Mei's arm is swiped deeply by the demon.

Blood comes out, splashing everywhere, including the wall.

A few drops of blood touch the writings. The Latin characters turn bright red with thousands of beams of red lights shining out, lighting up the whole cave with the color of blood.

To stop Mei from making him return, the demon digs his own grave.

"Hereticus the Hangman, I hereby banish you back to Hell," Mei says.

Hereticus is seen rising in the air and being sucked into the bright, bloody light.

Now, the demon is gone, back to where he came from.

Big Joe, Chupa, Saxon, and Cole rush over to Mei.

"Is he gone?" Mei asks as Cole picks her up from the ground.

"Yes, he is gone. Great job, Mei." Big Joe replies with a tiny smile on the left side of his mouth.

"Let's go back to have some goat chops! I'm starving." Chupa says. The rest of the group laughs at Chupa's comment.

"Alright, let's go." Saxon agrees.

The cryptids, Cole and Mei, walk slowly back to the Recreation Center.

As they enter the kitchen, they see four creatures sitting at the dining table and eating Chupa's world-famous goat chops. The first creature is a little shorter than Big Joe, has horns, pointy ears, claws and wings with more horns on them. He wears an American flag T-shirt, and bulky muscles are sticking out of the T-shirt. The second creature has grey skin and looks like an alien with a huge brain. He wears a military bulletproof vest. The third creature has pale white skin, long silver hair, long fingers and long claws. He does not wear a shirt but wears a pair of black pants, goggles and a black beanie. The fourth creature looks like a crocodile with a large mouth. She wears a scuba diving suit and has thick green skin, a long, pointy tail and strong claws.

Seeing Big Joe, Chupa, and Saxon walk in, the creature wearing the American flag T-shirt greets them, "So, what did we miss?"

CHAPTER TWO

THE HEAD

"A lot." Big Joe smiles and responds, "These are our new friends, Mei and Cole."

Mei and Cole greet the four creatures.

The creature wearing an American flag T-shirt says, "I'm Noah, the New Jersey Devil. Nice meeting you."

Then Noah points at the grey-skinned creature, "This is Grey, the Alien Hybrid. He doesn't talk." Grey waves.

The creature with long hair and pale skin says, "My name is Rake. They call me the Pale Walker."

The creature that looks like a crocodile says, "I'm Nessie. People call me the Loch Ness Monster."

"So, where have you been?" Noah asks.

Chupa says, "Just fighting a demon called Hereticus the Hangman. He's the one responsible for the death of 14 Boy Scouts 30 years ago at this campground."

Mei chimes in, "And he killed my colleagues Joseph and Miguel."

"Oh wow. My condolences." Nessie says.

"Thank you, Nessie," Mei says.

"I'm starving. Let's talk while we eat. I'm going to have some goat chops. Are there any left?" Chupa can't wait to eat.

"There are still plenty of them," Rake says.

Everyone sits around the table and starts eating goat chops.

Nessie chomps down three goat chops at once and says, "I missed these chops."

Big Joe asks, "How did the lead go?"

Noah says, "Yea the junkyard in New Jersey was haunted. The owner, Ed, is blind, so we were able to talk to him directly on what happened without blowing our covers."

Two weeks ago, the cryptids received a tip about paranormal activities around a junkyard in New Jersey. Noah, Rake, Grey, and Nessie teamed up and went to investigate.

Noah continues, "When we arrived at the junkyard, it looked gloomy and sad without any activities. The whole place is filled with silence and, of course, useless junk."

Nessie says, "Yea. There was nothing else, no life. We could not even see a bird fly by or hear a cricket."

Rake says, "We met Ed at his office. He told us that he was born blind, so his hearing is better than other people. He is a nice elderly guy, living a lonely life."

Noah chimes in, "Ed described what happened. He said that he kept hearing screams at a distance late at night. But when he went out to find out what happened, nothing seemed to be around. In the meantime, local news stations broadcasted about several missing person cases around the junkyard area. He thought these cases might have been connected. But since he did not have any evidence, the local police did not take him seriously. That was when he turned to someone well-connected to find investigators like us."

Mei asks, "How did you investigate?"

Rake says, "When we arrived, we did a surveillance of the junkyard and its surrounding area. The junkyard is in the rural area. There are farms around it."

Nessie says, "Unfortunately, we did not find any clues as to where the screams came from."

Noah says, "Yea we had to camp in the junkyard to find out more. That first night was very quiet. Nothing happened. Second night, nothing. Then on the third night, we heard something at midnight."

Rake continues, "We rushed out of the tents, figured out the direction of the noise, and ran towards the noise."

Noah says, "Guess what we found? A wolf was stealing a goat!"

Chupa laughs, "That's my specialty!" Then he bites into the goat chop.

Everyone laughs with Chupa.

Noah says, "Yea it was disappointing. I thought we found the demon."

Mei asks, "Did you find something the fourth night?"

Nessie nods, "On the fourth night, right after midnight, we heard a distant scream. It was very distant, but Noah was able to recognize it."

Rake says, "We followed Noah's lead. Noah figured out the direction of where the scream came from."

Noah says proudly, "I just kept using my ears and sense of smell to identify the direction. Soon we ran to the farm nearby."

Noah continues, "I could hear the noise, but it did not come from the farmhouse. Where could it be?"

Rake says, "That was when I thought about a TheyTube video about underground bunkers. I said, 'What if it's under the farm?'"

Rake continues, "That was when it all made sense. Everyone thought it must be above the ground, so no one thought about it being underground! We located the door right after we figured out it was underneath."

Noah gets excited, "Yep! That was when we kicked the hell out of the door. The wood just shredded to pieces with our force. No one can mess with these." He flashes his huge muscles.

"Impressive!" Mei says. She is a good interviewer and knows that compliments can encourage people to talk more.

Nessie continues, "We went downstairs from the broken door. We were only halfway down when a demon charged at us."

"Everyone reacted and used their weapons. Noah's spear, Grey's sniper rifle with a laser blade, Nessie's flail, and my dagger." Rake says.

Noah says, "This demon's gut looked like it was cut a long time ago, with scars in the shape of fire. He was half naked, wearing blue cargo pants, and he had a black spiky dog collar on his neck."

"After we surrounded him, he became desperate and started hissing at us. His long claws became a bright red and orange color as he was making a hissing sound." Nessie continues.

"That was when I gathered my strength and beat the heck out of him." Noah is visibly excited, "And I pierced my spear into his gut."

"So now he's gone?" Saxon asks.

Noah, Grey, Rake and Nessie exchange a look.

"What's going on?" says Chupa.

Rake says, "We didn't want him to do it, but he insisted on bringing it back."

Noah stands up, walks towards a backpack on the kitchen counter, reaches inside, and pulls out something and says, "See?"

Noah drops the object onto the table with a thud. The stench of rot hits them first. Then, as the light shifts, Mei sees what it is: a severed demon's head, its mouth curled into a mocking grin. The demon's head has an animal-looking nose, pointy ears and four horns.

Mei immediately starts to gag, wanting to throw up.

Just as everyone's attention is being grabbed by Mei, the head starts to talk, "You morons seriously think I am dead?"

Chairs screech against the floor as everyone leaps back. Mei gags, hand clamps over her mouth. Cole's eyes widen in shock. Even the cryptids' hardened faces twist in disbelief.

Everyone jumps away from the table and looks at the demon's head.

"How are you still alive?" Noah asks.

"Haha! I just don't die like this," the head says.

"Okay, now we need to go back and find the body and destroy them together." Big Joe says, shaking his head, thinking he cannot believe he has to do everything himself.

"Do you know where the body is?" Chupa asks.

"It should still be in the bunker." Rake replies, "We can find it and destroy both the head and the body."

"Hello? I'm right here!" the head says, smirking, "And I am happy to report that my body walked away. Haha!"

Noah feels embarrassed and becomes angry at his own mistake. He grabs his spear and pokes the head in the eye. "Tell me where the body is!" Noah yells at the head as he pushes the spear further in.

"Ouch! Oh, I'm so afraid!" the head says sarcastically.

Noah turns the spear, "Where?"

"I don't know. Even if I know, I won't tell you," the head says.

Big Joe says, "Noah, that's enough. He's not going to tell us right now. We need to go back to the junkyard and find the body." He turns to Mei and Cole, "Do you want to tag along?"

"Sure, we are invested at this point," Mei says.

"Yep." Cole agrees.

At night, the cryptids, Mei and Cole, patch up their wounds and sleep in the cryptids' underground structure. The entrance is inside the walk-in fridge of the kitchen. It is a huge structure with sleeping quarters, a large meeting room, a weapon room, a prison, a chapel, and other rooms.

Noah puts the head inside the fridge. The head complains about being cold inside the fridge when the fridge door is being closed. Noah shouts, "Shut up! New Jersey is cold in winter, and you should be used to it!"

The next day, the cryptids show Mei and Cole their RV. It is a beaten-up RV with scratches and bumps everywhere. But it is big, so they all can fit in.

And then, the road trip begins.

Big Joe drives.

Chupa asks Mei and Cole, "How do you know each other?"

Mei says, "When I was little, I saw a little boy climbing onto my bed. I was very scared and tried to kick him off my bed. I yelled, and my parents came over, turned on the light, and there was nothing. Ever since then, I have been obsessed with paranormal activities."

Mei pauses and continues, "When I was in college, my friends encouraged me to start a TheyTube channel to document my findings. That was when I came up with the name SpiritScouts. When Teek Took became popular, I opened my channel there too."

Mei drinks some water from a water bottle and continues, "Cole is a friend of a friend. He is a veteran. He also believes in spirits, as many of his mates have passed away. We talked and clicked immediately. When I gained more followers and the channel started to generate some income, he came to work with me on the channel as a cameraman and driver."

Cole agrees, "I don't have special abilities, and that might be why I don't see anything when I'm awake. But sometimes I talk to my mates in my dreams. That's why I believe in these paranormal activities. Now with the Hangman and this," he points towards the head, "I have seen them with my own eyes."

Rake says, "Man, I'm with you. Some of the stuff we have seen, no one could have imagined."

"Haha, you think this is strange, wait until you see what's coming!" the head smirks.

"Shut up!" Noah shouts to the head, "You want to be in the fridge? It's a lot smaller than the one at the campground!"

The head rolls his eyes. Somehow, his eye that was poked by the spear regenerated overnight.

Mei asks, "How do you all know each other? Where did you grow up?"

Nessie smiles, "That's a long story!"

"We are stuck in the RV and have all the time in the world," Mei says.

Chupa says, "Big Joe is the first to start the group. He is the glue that holds us together."

Big Joe drives, as the road leads him through memory lane, a long, long time ago.

Growing up in the forest, little Big Joe always knew that he was different from the rest of the animals. He was one-of-a-kind. He did not have a mother nor a father. The earliest memories that he had were of him picking berries and drinking raindrops from leaves. The forest was a dangerous place. But he knew how to hide and run from various dangers. Life continued as he adapted through an abundance of predators' attacks.

He had to survive on his own. No one was there to rescue him, comfort him, or offer help to him.

One summer when the creek was singing and running, it dawned on him that the wolves, tigers and bears he had seen recently seemed to have walked away instead of trying to chase after him like they used to.

He walked towards the creek, looked down on the surface of the water and saw his own reflection. His face and body were no longer that of a naive boy, but were those of a teenage boy, handsome and tall. He noticed that he was much bigger than most of the animals he saw in the forest.

That was when he started to rule the forest.

Behold, the prey had become the predator.

He ran around chasing after animals, tearing them apart with his bare hands, and eating their flesh and bones. In this way, he took revenge for years of him being hunted and having to hide to survive. Now that he was the biggest and strongest, he needed to be the baddest. He did not even blink when the animals that he was about to kill pleaded for their lives.

Why would he have any empathy when none was given to him?

Big Joe terrorized the forest. Occasionally, he ran into human beings hunting, and he would chase after them for invading his territory. The locals called him "Bigfoot" or "Sasquatch" and deemed him extremely dangerous. They put signs up to caution other human beings of this mad creature.

He had so much anger. He felt like there were shadows within him that constantly produced anger. And he needed to release the anger somehow, with wild animals being easy targets.

However, everything changed in one fateful day.

It was a beautiful morning in the fall. Young Big Joe was expanding his territory by walking through the forest along the creek flow when he spotted a beautiful white bunny. The sun was shining on its white fur, making the bunny look holy and innocent. It was eating grass along the creek. What was interesting was that the bunny had a piece of red and white plaid cloth that formed a bow around its neck. To Big Joe, he had never seen a bow before. So, he thought this bunny looked strange with the weird cloth thing on it. Naturally, he chased after the bunny and picked it up.

Just when he was about to tear the bunny apart and devour it as his morning snack, a human being's voice was heard saying, "Please stop!"

Big Joe looked up from the bunny and saw an elderly woman with wavy grey hair flowing down her shoulder. Her hands were out towards him as if she wanted to hold the bunny. He did not understand what she said.

The woman continued, "This is my pet bunny, Isabella. Please give her back to me." Realizing Big Joe might not understand her, she approached him slowly, put her hands around the bunny, and gently pushed his hands off.

Big Joe would have been mad if it were some other human beings. Somehow, he was not angry at this lady. Instead of killing her like he would do to anyone else, he became curious about this woman. She had a warmth and calmness in her that soothed Big Joe's dark and angry heart.

The woman smiled at Big Joe. She held the bunny in her left hand and used her right hand to hold Big Joe's left hand, and made him pet the bunny with smooth, gentle strokes.

The woman looked at Big Joe in his eyes for a while when Big Joe petted the bunny and signaled him to follow her.

And he did.

Somehow, Big Joe was captivated by her beautiful, deep blue eyes and the peacefulness he felt around her.

She brought him outside of her cabin near the creek and called out, "Alex, look who I brought!" An elderly man wearing a blue flannel shirt came out and looked at Big Joe. Unlike other human beings who would have yelled in fear, Alex did not panic when he saw Big Joe. He simply said, "Ashley, you brought home a guest for dinner? Great!"

Big Joe did not understand what Ashley and Alex were talking about. But from their expressions and body language, he figured they were not scared of him and were friendly towards him.

Ashley put the bunny down and gently put her right hand on Big Joe's left arm, with her left hand inviting him into the cabin.

Big Joe had nothing to worry about. He was much bigger than both Ashley and Alex combined. So, he stepped inside the cabin and at Ashley's signal, sat down at the dining table.

It felt like home. For the first time in his life, Big Joe knew what home felt like.

And Big Joe never left since that day. He was at the dining table with Ashley and Alex every day, chatting, laughing, learning to speak and write in English, wearing flannel shirts that Ashley tailor-made for him, hugging, making Thanksgiving feasts, opening Christmas gifts, and simply enjoying time spent with each other.

Ashley and Alex took him in as the son that they never had. They nicknamed him Big Joe.

Ashley brushed his dark brown fur and took out leaves and dirt trapped inside. She played with Isabella the bunny and taught Big Joe how to be gentle and loving towards small animals.

Alex took him to hunt and showed him how not to treat prey cruelly. He taught Big Joe the wheel of life, about how when predators die, they become dirt that grows grass, which is then eaten by prey.

The Father loves the Son and has given all things into his hand.

At night, when the weather was nice, Ashley, Alex and Big Joe often lied on the grass and looked up at the starry, starry night. Ashley and Alex taught Big Joe about the Great Bear constellation, the Little Bear constellation, the Orion constellation, the Canis Major constellation, and the Cygnus constellation. Ashley and Alex told Big Joe that when they die, they would become stars in the sky and look down upon Big Joe and protect him, just like their ancestors were protecting them right now.

Gradually, Big Joe became less angry about the world and more compassionate towards humans and animals.

He remembers Ashley and Alex used to tell him, "With great wisdom comes great responsibility. You are meant to do something great."

And he remembers the world he now carries on his shoulders. His face looks serious as he drives.

"Big Joe, are you okay?" Chupa asks Big Joe, which brings him back to reality from memory lane.

"Yea, just remembering something." Big Joe says.

Chupa continues, "Big Joe and I met in the 1920s. Then we met Noah, Rake, Saxon, Grey, and Nessie."

Mei asks, "Wow. I guess you folks don't age much?"

Chupa says, "We do age, but very differently from humans."

The head smirks, "We demons don't age at all. We are immortal! Haha!"

Rake says, "You are forever stuck in the miserable state of 100% evil, and that's not something to brag about."

Noah just says, "Shut up! We are not having a heart-to-heart with you."

And so, the road trip continues. They stop for bathroom breaks, leg stretches and grilling sessions for Chupa's world-famous goat chops.

After what feels like forever, the RV arrives at the junkyard.

Noah, Rake, Grey and Nessie chat with Ed first, asking him if anything strange happened after they left. Ed confirms that he has not heard any screams after midnight, and the local news channels have not mentioned any more disappearances.

The group goes to the bunker that they found the demon in. There seems to have been a fire that burned the bunker down. Saxon flies under and sees that everything has been burnt to ashes, leaving nothing noteworthy behind.

Noah asks the head, "Now there are two ways we can do this, the easy way, or the hard way. Which way would you prefer?"

The head is not intimidated, "Come on, you know I enjoy torture. I can regenerate my body parts in no time."

Hearing this, Noah brings out his spear and aims to penetrate it through the head's ear.

The head says, "Okay, okay. Let me tell you where my body might have gone to. But believing it or not is your choice. It might be a trap, or not." He laughs evilly.

"Okay, we are all ears, no pun intended." Rake says sarcastically.

The head says, "There's a church nearby."

"A church, of all places?" Rake says.

"An evil priest helps me, believe it or not," the head says.

The cryptids, Mei and Cole, look at each other and discuss. They do not fully believe the head. But since they don't have any other leads, they have decided to give it a try.

The RV drives past the church and parks on a street two blocks away. They split up, scouting the church. From the outside, the church looks normal.

Mei and Cole walk into the church, asking to talk to the priest.

Father Devin comes out, "How can I help you?"

Mei asks, "Father, we are investigating some demonic activities. Have you noticed something strange recently, like screams at night, or the disappearances of people around town, or the strange fire in the bunker?"

"Well, I have heard of the strange disappearances. Prayers to those people for their safe return. But I haven't really seen anything unusual. Sorry." Father Devin says.

"Okay thank you, Father," Mei says.

"May God bless you." Father Devin says.

Mei and Cole walk away, looking at each other. They know something is strange about the father. He did not even flinch when he heard about the bunker fire. Not everyone knows about the bunker, not to mention the fire.

The cryptids, Mei and Cole, decide to follow Father Devin around and see what he does after meeting Mei and Cole.

It is Friday, a day without meat. After church, Father Devin drives to a local farm and picks up four chickens.

"That is strange. He's not supposed to have chickens today." Noah says. Noah is a man of faith and knows the dos and don'ts about Catholicism.

"Maybe he is not a true Catholic?" Rake says. Rake is a liberal hippie. Noah and Rake are best friends, but they argue about politics all the time.

Then Father Devin is seen driving around town, and it seems like he is trying to confuse whoever might be following him. Big Joe is good at following at a distance, and Saxon starts flying above to ensure they don't lose the priest.

Finally, after turns and turns, Father Devin arrives at an abandoned factory. He brings the chickens in.

Big Joe says, "That's it. Let's go in."

The cryptids, Mei and Cole, grab their weapons and surround the factory.

Noah kicks open the factory door. Everybody looks inside.

There it is, the body, with a teeny tiny head, eating raw chicken that is cut into small pieces by Father Devin. The small head has a small mouth, so it makes total sense for the chicken to be cut into bite pieces before the demon can consume it.

The demon sees the cryptids, immediately grabs the priest and throws him towards the cryptids.

The cryptids push the priest away and use their weapons against the demon. The evil priest runs away during the fight.

Big Joe's axe, Noah's spear, Chupa's rope, and Rake's dagger are making new wounds on the demon.

The rest of the cryptids, Mei and Cole, come in. Everyone fights the demon.

Even though the demon only has a tiny head, his movements are not to be underestimated. He is strong and feisty. The cryptids are able to hurt him, but not able to fully incapacitate him.

Noah flies up and signals to Big Joe and Chupa.

Chupa uses his rope to tie the demon's hands up. Big Joe gives the demon's gut a strong swing of the axe, opening it up from the old fiery scar. Then Noah puts his spear inside of the demon's small head.

The demon is incapacitated, again.

Now the problem is: the demon regenerates fast. They can see his wounds healing already. How do they destroy the demon?

"You think it's time?" Chupa asks.

"Yes. We should." Big Joe says.

The cryptids gather around. Big Joe turns to Mei and Cole, "Folks, just watch."

Mei and Cole watch the cryptids form a circle. The cryptids close their eyes. A bright light starts to shine among them, and a biblically accurate angel starts to appear.

The angel has an abundance of eyes to see past, future and present, with thousands of feathers surrounding him.

"My children, why have you brought me here?" the angel says.

Big Joe says, "Bariel, we are seeking guidance on how this demon can be banished back to Hell. He regenerates fast, so we need a quick solution. Please help us."

Bariel the angel says, "Let me check my book." He turns his eyes, "The demon is called Zorzulith. He can be banished by Hellfire or Heaven's Light."

Then Bariel teleports a sword with Hell Fire to Big Joe.

"Thank you, Bariel," the cryptids say.

As Bariel disappears, he says, "Farewell, my children."

"Do you want to do the honor, Noah?" Big Joe gives the burning sword to Noah.

"Happy to." Noah takes the burning sword and cuts Zorzulith's body and small head in half, "I hereby banish you back to Hell."

This time, both the small head and body disappear as the sword with Hell Fire burning cuts through.

"How about the head?" Mei asks.

"Let's get rid of it too!" Noah laughs.

The group heads back to the RV to banish the head. However, the head is nowhere to be found. The fridge door on the RV is open.

Somewhere in the forest, the severed head has sprouted a grotesque body. It scuttles through the trees on stunted limbs, laughter rattling from its throat like broken glass, "Stupid small-headed body, I am the head, and I am the only Zorzulith. And I always get away!"

44

CHAPTER THREE

SONG OF THE SIREN

48 miles from Camp Moonlit Smiles, there lies a quiet and foggy fishing town with the name of Oasis Moon Bay. It holds a beach full of white sand. The ocean is at times peaceful, at times rampant, but never dull.

Right now, it is peak fishing season. Fishermen of the town gather at the town's pier, waiting for a long day of towing, haling nets, baiting, and setting lines. Everyone is sleep-deprived and exhausted.

It is dark and cold during dawn, and the fishermen stand under the yellow streetlights that shine down.

Among the fishermen is Sam Sinclair, a 22-year-old local high school graduate. He has a girlfriend named Judy Miller who works in the local cafeteria. He is working extra hard this fishing season to save and buy an engagement ring for his pregnant high school sweetheart.

Sam sees his captain, Bill Lobby, arrive in his truck, and follows him with fellow fishermen Dan Sanders and Mike Johnson.

They work on a small fishing boat called "Seaduction". Bill came up with this name and is proud of the sound of it, saying it reminds him of the mystery of the sea.

It is just another long day of fishing. Bill is driving the boat into the deep sea. Judging from the color of the water ahead, he is hoping to find a large school of fish.

The ocean is peaceful, with small ripples running alongside a gentle breeze. Sam is feeling a bit cold, so he closes his jacket to feel warmer.

The steady slap of waves dulls into silence. Then, cutting through the mist, comes a woman's voice - haunting, lilting, as if the ocean itself has learned to sing. The melody wraps around them like a net, tugging at grief they have never spoken aloud. This female voice is singing a mysterious melody that sends chills through Sam's whole body, causing his goose bumps to come out from hiding.

Sam says, "Bill, are you hearing that?"

"Yea. Not sure what that is. We are at the deep sea. There shouldn't be anyone around." Bill says, while turning off the engine, to hear more clearly.

Sam, Dan and Mike look around from the boat and cannot locate any person or boat nearby.

Dan yells, "Anyone out there?"

Nothing. Nothing except for the sound of the sea.

Bill says, "Let's go on then. It's probably nothing to be of our concern."

Just as Bill turns the engine back on, the female voice starts again, singing another sad melody that makes the fishermen dig deeply buried sorrow out of their rusty hearts while weeping and wailing.

"What is happening?" Bill says, looking at his fishermen who cannot help but have tears fall down their cheeks.

"I'm not sure." Sam says, "But I feel very, very sad. My heart hurts as if someone is pulling the muscles and veins away, piece by piece." Sam puts his arm on the left chest, where the constant pain comes from.

It is as if all the scars from one's past are cut open, much deeper this time than before, with seawater splashed on, over and over again, until flesh and blood become dark and rotten.

At the climax of the pain for the fishermen, the moonlight comes out from the dark clouds it was hiding in, shining brightly and sharply on the sea.

Bill, Sam, Dan and Mike look under the moonlight. And they notice a woman with long, wavy brown hair floating in the sea.

"Hey! Do you need help?" Bill shouts.

"Yes, please," the woman says, weakly and shakingly, as if she has been floating in the freezing water for days without rescue.

Bill stops the engine again, goes out of the wheelhouse, and says, "Dan and Mike, get the life buoy and rope. Sam, bring some blankets from the bathroom downstairs."

Bill, Dan and Mike tie the rope on a life buoy and throw it into the water.

As they are doing this, Sam walks down the stairs to the bathroom. It is not exactly a well-kept bathroom, so Sam has to look hard to find clean towels for the lady in the water.

When Sam comes upstairs with towels, no one is on board. He looks around, but cannot for the life of him find Bill, Dan, or Mike on board. He then looks into the water and tries to find the lady in water. But he sees nothing. The lady is no longer in the water.

How can there be nothing? He clearly saw them earlier.

The emptiness is worse than any scream. No splash of water, no shadow of a body, only the boat rocking to the slow breath of the sea, and Sam alone upon it. He rubs his eyes frantically, trying to see more clearly. But still, he sees nothing in front of him. Nothing in front of the fishing boat that is floating up and down with the ocean's inhales and exhales.

He starts to scream, "Bill? Dan? Mike? Anyone?" There is not even an echo nor the sound of a wave.

Sam is freezing in this quietness, both inside and outside.

Sam starts to scream, "Help!" But no other boat is around him either.

Later, the U.S. Coast Guard rescues Sam out of the abandoned fishing boat, with Sam shivering uncontrollably on board. When questioned, he is not able to comprehend or explain what happened to the rest of the crew.

At the same time, the cryptids, Mei and Cole, have returned to Camp Moonlit Smiles from New Jersey.

Mei and Cole are processing what happened in the last month and discussing what to do going forward. Now that they know there are cryptids and demons out there, it is hard not to change the course of their careers.

Mei asks Cole, "Cole, what do you think we should do next?"

Cole responds, "Honestly, I don't really know. I think we need to figure out what our new direction is, if there is a new direction."

Mei says, "Do you still have that SIM card from the broken camera?"

Cole replies, "For sure. I kept it in my pocket." He searches around and finds it, "Here."

"Let's look at what we were able to capture before the camera broke. Maybe Big Joe can lend us a computer." Mei says.

"Big Joe, do you have a computer you can loan us? We want to look at what we filmed from a month ago." Mei finds Big Joe and asks.

"Oh, sure. Let me find one." Big Joe goes to the meeting room and locates a laptop, "Go ahead and use this one. Passcode is 444."

Luckily, the SIM card is not damaged, and Cole is able to play the video of what was captured. He fast-forwards the video to when the demon appeared, and the camera caught a glimpse of the Hangman!

"Wow! We have something to show." Mei is glad.

Just as they are about to discuss how to edit the video, Big Joe comes in and says, "Mei and Cole, we just received a call for a lead from the Coast Guard about a possible sighting. Do you want to tag along?"

Mei and Cole look at each other and say, "Sure!"

Big Joe takes Nessie, Chupa and Saxon to this mission.

The group starts the RV and drives to the Oasis Moon Bay. It is a beautiful coastal drive. The ocean is bright-blue-colored, reflecting white cotton-candy-like clouds.

When they arrive at Oasis Moon Bay, they locate Sam and Judy's house. Mei and Cole step outside the RV and knock on the door. They are both wearing hidden microphones that transport voice signals back to the RV so that the cryptids can hear the conversation.

Judy opens the door and asks, "How can I help you?"

Mei says, "We are from TheyTube channel SpiritScouts. Is Sam Sinclair home? Can we ask him a few questions about what happened at sea?"

Judy says, "Yes, Sam is home. He's shaken up, but he can talk."

Mei and Cole step in the house. It is a nice and cozy farmhouse. Sam is sitting at the dining table, with a bowl of tomato soup in front of him. He's just stirring the soup with a spoon and not really eating much.

Judy says, "Sam hasn't had much of an appetite after he came back."

Mei introduces herself to Sam, "Hi, Mr. Sam Sinclair, I'm Mei He, a TheyTube content creator and investigator on paranormal activities. This is Cole Carter, my colleague."

Cols says hi.

Sam raises his head and says, "Hi, Mei and Cole. More questions about what happened?"

Mei says, "Yes, unfortunately. You must have answered the same questions repeatedly. But if we know more details, maybe we can help resolve the situation."

Sam says, "Okay. I wish someone could find Bill, Dan and Mike. And that lady."

Mei asks, "Could you please share with us what happened that day? Please don't leave any details because sometimes the devil is literally in the details."

Sam says, "Sure." He takes a deep breath and begins, "It was a normal day of fishing. We were up early and had been working hard these past few weeks, so everyone was exhausted. Bill drove the boat to the deep-sea area we normally would go to. Everything was normal until we heard a female voice singing the most mysterious melody that made us so sad that we wanted to kill ourselves."

Mei is intrigued, "What about it that makes one want to kill themself?"

Sam shakes his head, "I don't really know. Just the sadness inside, I guess. I felt like all my sufferings had been pulled to the surface instead of buried inside."

Mei asks, "What happened then?"

Sam continues, "Then we saw this woman with long hair floating in the sea. It was her that was singing. Bill asked her if she needed help. She said yes. So, Bill asked Dan and Mike to bring a life buoy and a rope and asked me to bring towels."

Sam takes another deep breath and says, "When I found the towels and came back upstairs, I could not find anyone. It seemed that everyone disappeared, including the woman in the water."

Mei asks, "No other signs?"

"Nothing. Just quietness surrounding me and the boat." Sam sighs.

Mei and Cole thank Sam and Judy, then walk back to the RV.

"What do you think?" Mei asks the cryptids.

"Definitely a demon," Nessie says.

"Then what's our plan?" Mei is kind of excited to investigate further.

"I think we need to go on the boat. The same fishing boat that Sam was on." Nessie says.

Mei says, "That should not be hard to find. I know the name of the boat is 'Seaduction'."

"Okay. Nessie, you know how to steal a boat?" Big Joe asks.

"Yes, I know everything about a boat," Nessie responds.

The group sneaks into the fishing boat at night. Nessie turns on the engine and starts driving the fishing boat to deep sea.

The coldness of dark water reminds Nessie of where she grew up.

Nessie's first memories were of the swamp she lived in. She remembered how incredibly cold it was at night. She was all alone. All she had was dark shadows in her heart, trying to eat her alive every day.

Every morning, she woke up trying to figure out which shelter was better to live in at night and where she could get more food.

At first, she practiced hunting small animals for food. When she got good at hunting fish and frogs, she upgraded to hunting snakes, then buffalo, cattle, and horses. Her appetite got bigger while her hunting abilities got better. Eventually, hunting animals was no longer a challenge for her.

Nessie wanted more. She had grown up to be fast and strong. She was capable of anything. She wanted to prove herself.

One time, Nessie was resting when she saw a lost tourist along the swamp. She chased after him, but he was smart and escaped from her claws. So, she decided that her next set of targets would be human beings, who seemed more intelligent and versatile than other animals she had killed before.

With human beings on her mind, Nessie started to scout new areas where they could be found. Boats were good targets where human beings were isolated without any help from onshore.

Nessie usually swam quietly to the boat, climbed up, then charged at the human beings onboard, tore them apart, and ate them alive. She enjoyed everything: the screams, the fighting, the blood, and most importantly, the mighty feeling of control over others' lives gave her a sense of power over intelligent beings. She felt invincible.

And after all, human beings and animals were the same. Humans would eat her if it were the other way around. It had always been a dog-eat-dog world. An eye for an eye and a tooth for a tooth, that is the only rule.

Nessie continued to do this for years and years, until one day, she ran into something different.

It was a small boat that she climbed into. She went inside the wheelhouse and was prepared to attack whoever was there. But the guy at the wheelhouse was already dead. She scouted the boat for other human beings, but did not see anyone else, "Disappointing."

Until she heard a little coo.

Nessie looked around and saw a bassinet. She was not sure what that was. So, she walked a little closer and saw a little, tiny, monkey-looking human being.

The little human being saw her. Instead of crying, the tiny little thing smiled. Planning to slash its head, Nessie put her claws inside the bassinet. Suddenly, the thing grabbed her claws. The little human being's grip was strong.

Nessie felt something she had never felt before. It was a small, tiny crack of warmth in her heavily shadowed heart. It felt kind of good, a different good than when she killed.

She grabbed the bassinet. "Maybe I'll have a snack later," she thought.

But she never killed this little thing.

She tried to feed it fish and insects, but it did not have teeth to chew. She went back to the boat to find something helpful and saw a milk bottle. She brought back the milk bottle and put the tip inside the little human being's mouth, and it immediately started to suck on it. Whew!

Nessie named the little human being Doris, which means gift of the ocean. She cared for her, changed diapers for her, fed her, and taught her how to hunt.

Nessie built a raft house tied to the boat that she found Doris in. She learned how to drive a boat, with the intention of protecting and teaching Doris when she grew up.

And how they had bonded over the years. They were best friends. They were mother and daughter. They were everything love and warmth meant.

For the first time in Nessie's life, she felt nurtured. Nessie nurtured Doris while the love between them nurtured Nessie's heart in return. The shadows that were once growing inside of her slowly moved on, replaced by the bright sunlight of warmth and love. She no longer needed blood to fill the emptiness that the shadows carved in her heart. Her heart was full of Doris' gorgeous smiles.

Nessie thought she was invincible before, until her heart was captivated by Doris, little by little. And eventually her whole heart belonged to Doris.

Ever since Nessie met Doris, she could not bear the thought of eating humans again. She reverted to eating animals.

As Doris grew up, Nessie noticed that when they passed by different neighborhoods, Doris would often hide behind bushes and watch other kids play in front of their houses. The kids were playing with toys, laughing and running around.

Nessie felt bad. In her mind, whatever the other kids had, Doris deserved more. So, Nessie went and stole a bunch of toys, wrapped them up with papers she found as neatly as her claws allowed her to, and surprised Doris. Doris was happy to unwrap the toys and played with them for a few days, but then continued to watch other kids play whenever she had a chance.

That was when Nessie realized that what Doris needed was not toys. It was companionship from little kids of her age.

But how could Nessie give her that experience? There was no way any human parents would say yes to a playdate proposed by Nessie, a monster in their eyes.

That was when Nessie reluctantly looked at the cruel reality. As Doris' mother, Nessie could not provide any normal human interactions that Doris needed as a kid. Doris would probably grow up lonely and spend the rest of her life alone in their raft house. What if Nessie died? Then Doris would be like Nessie before she found Doris, all alone.

Nessie started to observe all parents with kids around the neighborhood. She watched from afar how parents interacted with kids, how parents interacted between themselves, how parents interacted with neighbors, and how parents interacted with strangers.

One family that lived on Ocean Avenue seemed to be kind and caring with their kids. They paid attention to their kids, played with them, and comforted them. Most importantly, they were patient and did not scold their kids like the other parents constantly did.

Nessie made the most difficult decision of her life.

One day, she put Doris on the front door of the family on Ocean Avenue. Doris thought she was going to play with the kids and then go home with Nessie. What Doris did not know was that Nessie planned to leave her with this nice family that Nessie carefully and painfully chose with all the hopes and well wishes for Doris' future.

The parents opened the door and saw Doris standing in front of the house. But no one else was around. Doris started to cry and turned around to run towards where Nessie was hiding, but the parents held her and said, "Little girl, are you lost? We can't let you run away and get hurt." The mother glanced at where Doris was trying to get to and saw a strange-looking creature staring at her. Nessie's eyes were full of tears when she looked at the mother and Doris. There was so much emotion in Nessie's eyes that the mother understood what had just happened.

Then Nessie turned around without ever looking back. Her tears flooded out of her eyes. Her heart broke into a million pieces.

The parents on Ocean Avenue would then adopt Doris as their own. Every year, Nessie came back on the anniversary of when she found Doris on that boat, stayed where she was hiding, and looked at the house from afar. Sometimes, Doris would be inside her room reading. Sometimes, Doris would be outside playing with her siblings. Every year, Doris grew taller. Every year, Doris grew more beautiful. Every time Nessie saw Doris, she was even more perfect than the year before.

"We are at the coordinates where the fishing boat saw the woman," Mei says.

Hearing Mei's words, Nessie is brought back from her memory. "Do you see anything?" she asks.

Big Joe, Chupa, Saxon, Mei and Cole look around. They don't see or hear anything.

There's just quietness. The moon is shining brightly down, making the moving edges of waves in water visible.

Out of nowhere, a boat slowly floats into their view. The lights are on, but no one can be seen on board.

"That might be another victim boat." Big Joe says.

Saxon flies over the boat, and Nessie swims and climbs up to the boat. They confirm there is no one onboard the boat.

"Interesting. Lights on, but no one on." Mei says.

Cole says, "Yes, sounds way too similar to what happened to Sam."

Saxon and Nessie come back to the boat. At that exact moment when they get together with the rest of the team, the moon is blocked by a dark cloud and a woman's voice is heard singing a melody.

It is the same song that forces waves of sadness and despair into the heart of each listener. The team is consumed by sorrow.

It is as if the desperation from dark shadows of sadness paralyzes everyone on the boat.

Big Joe fights back tears and tells the rest of the team, "Let's be on high alert. Bring out your weapons."

Everyone brings out their weapons while struggling not to be absorbed into the gusty wind from the mysterious hurricane of misery.

The moon comes out of the dark cloud. The woman's voice continues. The group is able to see the profile of the woman in the water. Wavy long hair, floating on water. Just like what Sam described.

All of a sudden, the singing stops, and the woman turns to the group. Her cheeks glisten with tears, but her lips twist into a smile too wide, too jagged, as though grief itself has curdled into mockery. Her expression is twisted beyond imagination.

Then she swiftly flies onto the boat and attacks everyone onboard.

The demon utilizes multiple fishhooks attached to her hair simultaneously to attack the cryptids, Mei and Cole. One hook grabs Big Joe's axe, the other hook knocks Saxon out of arrows, another hook catches on Chupa's rope, another one grabs onto Nessie's flail, another swings the sword out of Mei's hand, and the other hook grabs onto Cole's gun to stop him from firing.

Big Joe cuts the hair using his axe, but another hook shoots towards him and wraps around his arms. Nessie swings her flail with great force and breaks the demon's hair with a fishhook on it, but another set of hair with a fishhook comes for her immediately after, forming a hair net that tangles her flail inside. Everyone is fighting tooth and nail against the demon's hooks and hair.

Feeling trapped by the cryptids, the demon lets out a high note while continuing to use her hair with fishhooks to tie up the cryptids. Her voice is so powerful and high-pitched that a gigantic wave is sent out into the ocean. The cryptids, Mei and Cole, are knocked out by the sound wave of the demon's high note. Then the fishnet is thrown to wrap them up, and they are seen being dragged away.

It feels like ages before Nessie wakes up. She looks around.

The cryptids, Mei and Cole, are all tied in fishnet onto dining chairs surrounding a dining table. They are inside what looks like a pirate ship with spider webs and dirt everywhere. The dining chairs and dining table are rusted with deep scratches.

As the rest of the cryptids, Mei and Cole slowly wake up, the demon comes in, dragging fishhooks with her long hair and wearing fishnets as her clothing.

"Oh, my sleeping beauties. You are finally awake," the demon says, "Are you ready for dinner? Hope you are hungry."

As the demon finishes her sentence, her hair shoots out to the kitchen area. The long hair then pulls back, with each hook carrying a giant plate.

The stench of salt and rot rises with the platters. What lie upon them make their stomachs turn: fingers shaved thin and pressed onto rice like obscene sushi, arms flayed into sashimi, garnished with seaweed and scallions as if cruelty were a delicacy.

All the plates contain dismantled human parts.

This is the most gruesome scene that the cryptids, Mei and Cole, have seen so far.

Mei starts to throw up uncontrollably.

The demon laughs after seeing the shocking reactions of the cryptids, Mei and Cole. She says, "Impressed, I see. Indeed, I am a very good chef."

She turns to Nessie, "Nessie, you have tried this before, many, many times. Don't you just miss the taste of raw, fresh human beings?"

Nessie's animal instincts are woken up by this bloody scene. She cannot help but remember how good it felt when she hunted human beings and ate them alive.

Big Joe says, "Nessie, don't listen to this evil demon, you can do better! Resist! Don't give in to your temptation!"

Chupa says, "Yes, Nessie, you have come a long way! Don't let this break your sobriety!"

Nessie starts to sweat as she's resisting the temptation of fresh, tender, bone-in human sashimi.

The demon uses one of the fishhooks to pick up a piece of thigh meat and slowly chews it, "Hmmmm, delicious human meat. You can just taste the freshness. Incredibly tasty."

Now Nessie is drooling and holding on to the chair and sweating bullets. Her animal instincts want this so bad. She feels like a shark that is drawn to blood in water with an urge that is impossible to fight off.

But Nessie keeps thinking about Doris, her gift from the ocean, and the love of her life. She can see Doris' disappointing face if she starts consuming human beings again. She pictures Doris's wide, trusting eyes, the laughter that has once broken through her shadows. To give in now will mean betraying the only light she has ever found.

Nessie resists.

The demon persists. She picks up a piece of finger and starts chewing on it close to Nessie's mouth. The crunchy sound of bones breaking in the demon's mouth is impossible to ignore. Nessie starts to drool uncontrollably as she bites the air with her pointy, sharp teeth.

Nessie is hangry. She has not had any food in a long time, and her stomach is growling. She has been eating animal meat only, which provides less energy than human meat does.

With an abundance of hunger and anger in her, Nessie finally explodes and bursts out of the fish net.

"Aren't you strong. Help yourself to these human..." the demon says.

Everything happens so fast. Before the demon realizes, Nessie has her mouth on the demon's shoulder, chewing away with her sharp teeth. The demon is shocked and fights back with fishhooks, but at this point, nothing can stop the hangry, starving, drooling Nessie.

Nessie is so hungry that she consumes half of the demon's body without ever stopping.

Chupa says, "Well, that's one way to end a dinner conversation."

Big Joe says, "That's enough, Nessie."

Nessie hears Big Joe and comes back to her senses. Now that she's eaten half of the demon, she resumes her usual self.

She helps untie everyone with her claws.

Chupa ties up what's left of the demon. Big Joe says, "Let's search the ship to find out how we can send the demon back."

The group spreads out in search of Latin characters or weird symbols.

It is a very old pirate ship. Mei finds the rice cooker that the demon used to cook rice with. Chupa finds numerous old skulls that have grown mold. Nessie goes to the wheelhouse and finds some more fishnets and fishhooks. Cole goes to the deep side of the ship and finds some Latin characters. He calls everyone here, "I found some Latin writings and symbols!"

The group gathers around. Big Joe reads, "This demon's name is Annyachet. This is her sigil."

Mei asks, "How do we send her back?"

Big Joe says, "There are no writings about how. We need to search the ship more to find a way."

Saxon notices an old, rusted chest box in the corner. But it has a lock on it. Chupa uses his claws to open the lock. Inside the chest box are gold necklaces, gems and silver dinnerware, all covered with seaweed.

Chupa picks out the jewelries with disgust, "Like we need these. They are probably cursed or something, just like the TV show 'The Ragoon Pirates' that we watched."

After the chest box is emptied, Chupa notices something strange about the bottom of the chest box. He knocks on the bottom, and it sounds hollow, "There's a hidden compartment on the bottom!" He pries the bottom open with his sharp claws, and there lies a book that is torn and barely bound together.

Big Joe picks the book up and reads the Latin words on the cover, "The title of the book is 'Book of Evils.' Let me see if there is any description of how to send the demon back."

Big Joe continues searching inside the book, "Here it is, on the last page. It says human blood, when put on the sigil of the demon, can send the demon back."

Cole asks, "Human blood? Let me try." He borrows the sword from Mei and cuts his arm, then smears his blood on the sigil.

Nothing.

The group waits for 10 minutes. And nothing happens.

"Let me try. Maybe it needs female blood." Mei says. She wipes Cole's blood off the sigil with her shirt, then cuts her finger and smears blood on the sigil.

The blood and sigil light up, and blood-colored light shines everywhere. Annyachet's remaining body is lifted by the light, then it disappears, leaving the rope that was tying her up loose on the floor.

"Well, at least we know Mei's blood works," Saxon says.

Just as the group is about to leave the ship, everyone hears a duet of female voices singing the same sad song by Annyachet at a distance.

Big Joe, Chupa, Saxon, Nessie, Mei, and Cole look around the pirate ship, but they cannot seem to find anything. The sadness of the voices pulls their heart strings and brings everyone's deeply buried sorrow out. Before they realize, pearls of teardrops fall out from their eyes. The teardrops are pulled into the ocean, with every drop hitting a somber note.

At the climax of the song, the voices subside, leaving the ocean waves alone, singing mystifying songs of the sea.

CHAPTER FOUR

The Fire

Big Joe, Chupa, Saxon, Nessie, Mei and Cole drive back to the campground.

Now that they have some time to rest, Mei and Cole start to edit the video they captured for the Hangman. Even though they only captured a part of the Hangman's face and body, and the image is blurry, the video material should still be able to attract new viewers and subscribers.

Mei and Cole review the edited video and post it online. Then they discuss what to do next.

Mei says, "We should invest in body-mounted cameras. If we're ever chased or forced into a fight, we need continuous footage that proves what we're facing."

Cole agrees, "That's a good idea. Both of us can wear cameras so we have videos from multiple angles."

Mei says, "Of course we need to cut the part where the cryptids are filmed. We just need to leave the demon part."

Big Joe overhears the conversation and says, "Thank you, Mei. We'd appreciate you not exposing us."

Mei says, "Of course."

Big Joe asks, "Do you need a lift to get new cameras? Noah and I are about to stop by a gas station for some gas. You are welcome to join. We can drop you off at the store."

"That'd be nice. Thanks!" Mei says.

"Let's go!" Noah says and jumps on the driver seat of the RV.

Big Joe says, "You are driving?"

Noah replies, "Yep."

"Okay." Big Joe gets in the passenger seat. Mei and Cole sit in the back.

Mei and Cole pick up two cameras, and the group heads to the gas station.

On the way to the gas station, they notice yellow tape surrounding a burnt fire station.

This piqued everyone's interest. Why would a fire station be burnt? It seems unusual and ironic, given that the fire station usually helps others put out fires.

They look at each other and wonder the same thing: Is this another paranormal activity?

"What are the chances, a fire station is burnt down!" Mei exclaims.

"I say something's not adding up!" Noah says.

"Cole and I can interview the Sheriff and obtain some details," Mei says.

Big Joe says, "Appreciate that. Noah and I will scout the outside of the fire station while you do that."

"Sure!" Mei says.

Noah and Big Joe drop Mei and Cole off at the Sheriff's Office and then drive back to the abandoned fire station.

Mei and Cole look at the Sheriff's Office. It is a regular government building with mostly grey-colored walls. On the door, it reads "San Cara County Office of the Sheriff".

Mei and Cole walk into the Sheriff's Office. Two people are waiting in the reception area. Maybe they are waiting for fingerprint services. Mei and Cole see a window with a deputy sheriff behind bulletproof glass.

Mei starts to talk to the deputy sheriff, "Hi officer, I'm a TheyTube channel content creator. I would like to interview the Sheriff about what happened at the fire station."

The deputy sheriff says, "Sure. Let me talk to the Communications Officer about this media request. Please take a seat."

Mei and Cole wait at the reception area for about 20 minutes when the deputy sheriff calls their names, "Mei He and Cole Carter, it's your lucky day. Normally, media requests require advanced notice. But right now, Sheriff Hampson is available. Follow me."

Mei and Cole follow the deputy sheriff through the door, into the elevator, to the third floor, then to the office of the elected official, Sheriff Gary Hampson.

Sheriff Hampson was elected recently after the previous Sheriff had a scandal and was forced to leave the post.

Mei believes that the new Sheriff wants a good press impression, and that's why he agreed to see them fast.

"Nice meeting you, I'm Sheriff Hampson," the Sheriff greets them.

"It's a pleasure meeting you, Sheriff Hampson. I'm Mei He." Mei says.

"I'm Cole Carter," Cole says.

"We are content creators for a TheyTube channel. Do you mind if we film this interview?" Mei asks.

"Sure, no problem." Sheriff Hampson says.

Mei and Cole both turn on their cameras.

"Would you please let us know what happened at the fire station?" Mei asks.

"Of course." Sheriff Hampson says, "Last Friday, we received a 911 call about the fire station being on fire."

Mei asks, "Is this normal, a fire station on fire?"

Sheriff Hampson replies, "No. This is the first time we have seen it. There are multiple firefighters in the station. If there's a fire, they should be able to put it out from inside in a short amount of time."

"Then what happened?" Mei asks.

Sheriff Hampson says, "We tried contacting the firefighters in the station, but the phone calls were not picked up. As a result, we sent other firefighters from the neighborhood."

"Wow. No one from the station even responded." Mei says.

"Correct. It was very strange. And when the other firefighters arrived, they put out the fire with water through fire hoses. Some firefighters went inside the collapsed building, but they never came back out. It seemed that whoever went in was consumed by the fire." Sheriff Hampson says.

"I saw some crime scene tapes around the fire station. Is this an indication of foul play?" Mei asks.

"Yes, we are investigating this event as a suspicious case. Even the FBI has been involved." Sheriff Hampson replies, "The initial evidence gathering has concluded. The clean-up phase will begin today. Because this is an active investigation, I cannot share the findings with the public right now."

"Thank you so much, Sheriff Hampson. We appreciate your help in providing information." Mei says.

Mei and Cole both thank the Sheriff, and the deputy sheriff walks them out of the office.

By then, Big Joe and Noah have completed scouting outside of the fire station and are waiting in the RV outside of the Sheriff's Office.

Mei and Cole get inside the RV and let them know what the Sheriff told them.

"Demonic activities," Noah says, after hearing more details.

"Yea that's what I think too. Firefighters should be able to stop the fire from inside the fire station, unless something's causing all of them to be incapacitated." Big Joe says.

"Let's drive back to the fire station and investigate," Noah says, before starting the RV.

By now, it is dusk. Noah, Big Joe, Mei and Cole arrive at the fire station. They park the RV far, then walk over to the fire station. Big Joe tells everyone to bring their weapons just in case.

What they don't notice is an unmarked car following their RV and parking a block away.

The yellow tapes are gone, like Sheriff Hampson mentioned. No one is seen around the fire station. The group walks into what is left of the fire station. The place is full of burnt dust and collapsed structures.

Noah looks around and remembers what the aftermath of fire smells like, especially the smell of burnt humans.

He used to enjoy the feeling of burning humans alive. He would hiss fire out and grill human beings, and then eat their meat while the fire is still burning. He called it "farm fresh BBQ".

Back in New Jersey, little Noah lived in the forest.

He remembered being tiny and vulnerable. He had wings, but they were not strong enough to fly. He hissed fire out of his mouth, but the fire was small and flickery. He had horns, but they were not sharp enough to puncture through anything.

He was constantly picked on by the bigger animals in the forest.

Noah remembered one time, a hawk flew down and used its long claws to grab him. The claws broke into his tender skin, and it hurt like hell. He hissed fire at the hawk, only burning a few feathers. The bird shrieked, but its claws dug deeper into his skin. Weak as he was, Noah thrashed wildly, knowing that if he didn't fight, he would be eaten alive.

He would never go down without a fight. Eventually, his skin broke, causing the hawk's claws to lose him.

He started to free-fall. He looked down at the forest he lived in, looked at the beautiful canopy that was green and full of life, looked at the lake that was blue and vibrant, looked at the hills that were tall and dynamic. He wanted to rule the forest. He wanted to survive this and take control of the forest like a king. So, he started flapping his wings like never before. He flapped his wings like his life depended on it, and it did. He was determined to live and rule. He was going to become the king of the forest. There was no way he would let go.

He had not lived. He had not seen. He had not felt. He had not hurt. He had not healed. He had not hoped.

And he succeeded. He flew, for the first time in his life, in the sky.

That day, he flew everywhere. He saw frogs eating mosquitoes, he saw snakes eating frogs, he saw owls eating snakes, he saw coyotes eating owls, and he saw wolves eating coyotes. He saw the whole food chain, and he wanted to be on top of that. He knew he could be on top of everything.

The next day, he woke up and was ready to practice his fire. He hissed at the grass with fire, but the grass did not burn. He took a deeper breath and hissed at the grass again, and this time, the tip of the grass burned. He tried to figure out what caused his fire to be big or small by practicing everywhere. He hissed at berry trees, flowers, rabbits, and anything that was on his way. After practicing hissing all day long, he became very tired. At this time, a lion came charging at him. He remembered feeling desperate and angry. Then he hissed with all his strength that he had left and hoped for the best. This time, to his surprise, it was a bigger fire that burnt the lion's eyebrows. The lion backed off.

From then on, he became unstoppable, the king of the forest. He could eat any animal he wanted. He set fire to hundreds of trees just for fun. He reveled in the terror reflected in the animals' eyes as fire devoured the forest around them, their screams fueling his growing hunger for power.

One day, he got bored, flew to the edge of the forest and hissed fire at one dead tree that was dried up. It was windy, so the fire spread quickly to other trees. Before he noticed, the whole forest was on fire.

Then he heard this loud and high-pitched noise from afar. Flashing lights approached the fire, and out of the weird box thing came a bunch of human beings in firefighter suits. They started to use water to put out the fire.

The fire was Noah's masterpiece. How dare they?

He was not happy about what these human beings were doing. So he flew over them and started hissing fire at the firefighters, burning them alive. The fear in the firefighters' eyes before they died satisfied Noah's already enormous ego. He took the bodies of firefighters and ate them, which made his ego even bigger.

Grilling and eating human beings became his new hobby. The dark shadows covering his heart rewarded him with an ego that became larger and larger every time he ate a human being. He felt all mighty. He felt invincible. He felt indestructible. He felt like a god.

One day, after he grilled a house including the humans inside near the edge of the forest, a bright heavenly light was seen, encompassing the whole forest.

A voice was heard from the light saying, "Stop. You need to stop what you are doing."

Normally, if someone tried to stop Noah from doing what he wanted, he would be furious. But somehow, he felt peace and joy hearing the voice from the light.

The voice continued, "You have a higher purpose. Find your purpose."

Then the light slowly disappeared.

Noah stood there with his mouth open. He wondered why he felt peaceful, a feeling that he had never felt before, and a feeling that brought joy in his shadowed heart.

"What is my purpose?" He asked himself. He did not have an answer. He started to look back at what he did over the years and somehow did not feel good about himself.

Then he got sick. Really sick. He was so out of it that he could not move any part of his body. He barely had any strength left in him. He laid there, starving, ill, unwell.

He started to hallucinate. He saw all the human beings he grilled walking towards him. He started to get defensive. He crouched his back and opened his mouth, ready to burn them alive all over again. But the human beings smiled at him. They did not hurt him. Instead, they reached out with their friendly hands. They comforted him, cared for him, and fed him.

Then his creator walked over. He smiled at him. He nurtured him. He mentored him. He guided him.

The next day, Noah woke up, feeling rejuvenated. He left the forest.

He had lived. He had seen. He had felt. He had hurt. He had healed. He had hoped.

He had found faith.

The old has passed away; behold, the new has come.

"Noah, what's that on your side?" Mei asks.

Noah is pulled back to reality from the past. He looks around and sees a floorboard on his right. But underneath the floorboard, there seems to be something bright. So, he uses his right hand, picks the board up, and throws it on the other side.

There is dust everywhere from the board being picked up and thrown away. When everything settles, Noah, Mei, Cole, and Big Joe look to see what is under the board. But the brightness is no longer there.

They look around and see the brightness moving fast across the fire station. Everyone chases after the brightness. Noah flies up and grabs it.

The brightness is what looks like a fire imp. It is small. And its body consists of burning fire.

"Good thing your skin is fireproof, Noah." Big Joe says.

"Yep." Noah holds on to the fire imp and asks, "What are you?"

The fire imp moves its fire of a body around, trying to escape. When it realizes it cannot escape from Noah's grip, it refuses to talk and looks the other way.

"I see. You don't want to talk, huh?" Noah says with a smirk, "That's easy."

Noah looks at Big Joe, "Do you have Holy Water with you?"

Big Joe says, "I keep a bottle in my pocket. Here you go." Then he opens the water bottle and hands it to Noah.

Noah uses his left hand to grab the bottle and splashes some Holy Water onto the fire imp.

"Ouch!" the fire imp says, with its face all fired up.

"You like that, right? Here's some more!" Noah continues to pour Holy Water onto the fire imp.

"Okay, okay! I will cooperate." the fire imp cannot take the painful shower anymore.

"Good. Now talk." Noah says.

"Talk about what?" the fire imp says.

"You want more Holy Water?" Noah yells.

"What are you?" Big Joe asks.

"I'm a fire demon," the fire imp says.

"I don't think you are a full demon." Noah laughs.

"Well, I'm in training," the fire imp replies and lifts his fire chin.

"What happened here?" Mei asks.

"Well, don't you see what happened? It got burnt, like everything should be!" the fire imp says with a smile.

"We know it got burnt. Don't you dare stalling. Who did it?" Noah pours some more Holy Water on the fire imp.

"Okay, okay. I did it," the fire imp says.

Big Joe asks, "You did this all by yourself?"

"Yep," the fire imp says, proudly.

"I don't believe him," Noah says to Big Joe.

At this moment, Mei looks back at the entrance and sees something else that is bright. She points in that direction and says, "Look! What's that bright thing that's moving?"

Everyone looks at the entrance, and it looks like that bright thing is trying to escape.

Noah flies up immediately with his right hand holding the fire imp. He uses his left hand and catches the other bright thing. It is another fire imp.

"How many of you are out there?" Noah asks.

"I don't know," the first fire imp says.

"Who's your boss? There must be a leader if there are many of you." Big Joe asks.

"We don't know. We are lower-level fire demons," the second fire imp says.

"That might be true." Big Joe says.

Just after Big Joe's comment, the sky above the fire station is lit up.

Noah, Big Joe, Mei and Cole look up. There are about thirty fire imps in the sky, falling fast to the fire station.

Noah, Big Joe, Mei and Cole fight the fire imps with their weapons. The weapons light up. The fire station looks bright like daytime.

Noah's spear pokes holes in the fire imps.

Big Joe's axe hits the fire imps and splits them in half.

Mei's sword cuts the fire imps into pieces.

Cole fires shots towards the fire imps, grabs the Holy Water bottle, and splashes the rest of the Holy Water towards the fire imps, causing them to cry out loud in pain.

While everyone is occupied with the fire imps, Furus, the real fire demon, jumps inside the fire station.

He has one giant yellow eye, spikes on top of the eye, pointy ears, a long, big mouth with sharp teeth, a mustache, long claws and a long pig tail. On his back are three humps that squirt out fire that turns into fire imps.

Furus' legs start to stretch longer, and he gets taller. He uses his right hand to shoot out fire at the group. The fire imps become stronger as Furus' flames touch them, making them harder to defeat.

Noah flies up and starts hissing fire through his mouth at Furus, and Furus points the flames from his hand towards Noah. The two flames meet mid-air and start to eat at each other. Noah's flames have blue edges, and Furus' flames have red edges.

Noah and Furus both use their inner emotions to drive the flames. Noah uses his sense of purpose. He reaches inside his heart for the calmness, love, and kindness he stored over the years from the Great Creator. He feels trees, breeze, waves, and sunshine behind him while he is hissing fire. Furus uses endless miseries and vengeance from the darkness of Hell.

Noah gradually gains momentum with his blue flames, while Furus' red flames are losing inches.

Noah draws on a strength deeper than fury, a fire fueled not by vengeance but by purpose. His blue flames surge, swallowing Furus' rage until only ash remains.

Furus is defeated by Noah. The fire imps immediately become incapacitated and lie on the ground.

Big Joe takes Chupa's rope out of the RV and hands it to Noah to tie Furus up. Noah then throws punches at Furus' face.

Big Joe says, "Noah, that's enough. The demon is captured. Blunt force is no longer needed."

Noah is not happy about the sound of that, "You don't get to boss me around. I'm as much the leader of the group as you are."

Big Joe says, "I'm not bossing you around. And I'm not saying you are not a leader." He pauses to calm himself down, "Right now, we need to focus on finding the sigil for this demon to send him back."

"Great job, Noah. Let's look around for the sigil." Mei says.

The group spreads around and looks for anything suspicious. Big Joe looks at a fallen piece of wall and has a gut feeling that something is under it. He lifts the wall, and there it is, a sigil in black ink, written on the other side of the wall.

He gathers everyone around and takes out a bottle. It is Holy Water. He says, "I think we should try to see if Holy Water can send this demon back."

Big Joe pours Holy Water onto the sigil, and the sigil lights up with bright white light.

As the sigil lights up, the fire demon Furus and the fire imps he created immediately cry out in extreme pain. The cryptids, Mei and Cole wait, but the white light does not lift them up or send them back.

"I guess Holy Water hurts them, but won't send them back," Noah says.

Mei says, "Let me try." Mei cuts her hand and smears her blood onto the sigil, "I hereby banish you to Hell." The sigil lights up with red light, lifting Furus. The red light intensifies, and the fire demon is absorbed into the red light and gone, together with his fire imps.

"Who keeps summoning these demons?" Mei asks.

"We need to investigate who is behind all this." Big Joe says.

The group walks back to the RV. Noah starts the engine and notices the unmarked vehicle one block away.

Noah looks at Big Joe and signals him to be on alert. Big Joe looks at the back mirror and sees that the car behind starts its engine right after they do.

Noah starts driving the RV slowly. The car behind them drives slowly as well. Noah suddenly speeds up and makes irrational turns, and the car behind does the same.

Now they are sure that the car is following them. Who sent this car to spy on them and why? The cryptids, Mei and Cole are curious to find out.

CHAPTER FIVE

THE VAMPIRE

Noah continues to drive the RV while being followed by the unmarked car. He stops abruptly in the middle of the road and flies out of the driver's door. Big Joe quickly moves over to the driver's seat.

The unmarked car realizes its cover's been blown. It speeds up, trying to get out of the encirclement.

Big Joe drives the RV and follows the unmarked car closely. Noah flies above the unmarked car, tracking it so they don't lose it.

The unmarked car moves quickly through the main road and drives onto a narrow side road, hoping the RV will not be able to follow through. But whoever is driving the unmarked car underestimates Big Joe's driving abilities. Big Joe follows the car, swerving left and right to avoid hitting parked cars on the narrow road.

Noah flies in the sky between tall buildings, avoiding AC units and fire ladders that are sticking out. He gets bored with the car chase and says, "Enough with this!" Then he flies down in front of the unmarked car, grabs onto the car mirrors and blocks the driver's view.

The car cannot see what is in front and hits a tree on the side. Noah flies to the driver's door. Big Joe stops the RV and comes out with Mei and Cole, holding their weapons.

The driver has nowhere to go and starts to shoot bullets. The cryptids, Mei and Cole, dodge the bullets by hiding behind the RV and using their weapons to deflect the bullets.

When the driver runs out of bullets, Noah grabs the driver's door and opens it, breaking the hinges. Big Joe drags the driver out with his left hand, using his right hand to hold the axe in case the driver attacks. Cole cuffs the driver. Mei blindfolds the driver.

Cole then searches the car. It looks like an unmarked law enforcement car with a radio. There is no personal item inside.

With the driver of the unmarked car in hand, Noah drives the RV back to Camp Moonlit Smiles.

They put him in the underground prison and interrogate him.

"Who are you? Why are you following us?" Big Joe asks.

The driver resists, "I'm just a regular guy driving. I'm not sure why you were chasing after me."

"Okay. You want the hard way." Noah says while punching the driver.

The driver, with a broken nose and bruised cheek, stays firm.

"You shot bullets at us. We found a police radio in your car." Cole says.

The driver's left eye twitches.

Noah says, "Talk! You want your arms and legs broken, too?"

"Okay, okay, I'll talk. I'm a deputy sheriff. My name is Jason Sims," the driver says.

Mei asks, "Are you under Sheriff Hampson's orders to spy on us?"

"Yes. He told me that the media request seemed suspicious, so he ordered me to follow you." Deputy Sheriff Sims responds.

"What's suspicious about the media request?" Mei asks.

"I take orders. I don't ask questions." Deputy Sheriff Sims says.

Noah wants to punch him again with his fist raised up, but Big Joe uses his hand to hold Noah's arm, "Noah, that's enough. Let's debrief in the meeting room."

Big Joe, Noah, Mei and Cole talk about what to do next in the meeting room.

"I want to investigate Sheriff Hampson. Maybe we can find a lead for who is summoning these demons." Big Joe says.

"I'll go with you," Noah says.

Chupa walks in with a smile, "You want some goat chops? I just made a fresh batch."

"Food sounds great! I'm starving." Noah says.

Noah, Big Joe, Mei, and Cole follow Chupa into the kitchen. Saxon is eating a goat chop already.

Everyone digs into the juicy, tender, and well-seasoned goat chops. The world-famous chef means no joke.

"Noah and I will go investigate the Sheriff in town. There might be something there about who is summoning demons." Big Joe says.

"Oh, okay," says Chupa, "Saxon and I received a tip about some activities in the temple on M street. We plan to go there afterwards."

"What about the temple? I visit there with my family sometimes." Mei asks.

"There was a mysterious disappearance of a monk," Saxon says.

Mei says, "Can I tag along with you to the temple? That place holds a lot of my fond memories, and I want to make sure nothing demonic is there."

Chupa says, "You are welcome to." He turns to Cole, "Cole, are you coming too?"

Cole says, "Affirmative. Maybe we can record some materials for the channel, too."

"Wait, how do we go to two different places at the same time with one RV?" Mei asks.

"Oh, we have an SUV too, and Big Joe and I can take that," Noah says.

So Big Joe and Noah take the SUV to the Sheriff's Office.

Chupa, Saxon, Mei and Cole take the RV to the temple on M Street.

The temple on M Street has light yellow walls, tall red beams and dark yellow roofs. Every first and fifteenth of the month, according to the Lunar Calendar, Buddhists come to the temple to pray.

It just happens to be the fifteenth of the month. When Chupa, Saxon, Mei and Cole arrive at the temple, there are probably more than a hundred people in the temple. The temple provides visitors with free plates of vegetarian food.

Mei and Cole take plates of food for themselves as well as for Chupa and Saxon back to the RV.

Chupa tries to pick up a piece of bean curd with chopsticks, but he does not know how to use them, and the bean curd is like a slippery fish that keeps escaping from a fisherman's hook. He gets frustrated and uses his claws to pick up the bean curd, "Who needs chopsticks when you have long claws? They are practically curvy chopsticks." To his surprise, the piece of bean curd tastes good. "Wow, I didn't think vegetarian food would taste like anything. But this is not bad."

Cole tries and agrees, "I'm usually a steak guy, but they made these bean curds tasty."

Saxon also likes the taste, "Simple bean curds, but they made them taste like meat."

Mei is glad they like the food, "When I was small, my parents and grandparents brought me here to pray to Buddha. Afterwards, we would eat a plate of food each just like this."

"They are Buddhists?" Chupa asks as he picks up a piece of tofu.

"Yes, they eat vegetarian food every first and fifteenth of the month. According to the Lunar Calendar, of course." Mei replies.

"The tofu is not bad either. There's a tenderness to it." Chupa says.

"You are going to give up your goat chops and go vegetarian?" Saxon laughs.

"Hold your horses! I can't let my world-famous goat chops go extinct." Chupa laughs as well.

"I vote for your world-famous goat chops." Cole laughs.

By now, it is after dusk, and the crowd has subsided in the temple.

Mei says, "Let me go talk to the monks about what happened."

"I'll go with you," Cole says.

Mei and Cole wear hidden microphones so that Chupa and Saxon can hear their conversations from the RV. This has become standard practice for them, which makes them feel like FBI agents.

They walk towards the entrance, and Mei sees Shifu Kong'an, one of the older monks in the temple.

"Shifu Kong'an, how are you? Do you remember me?" Mei catches up to him.

"Of course, Mei. Long time no see." Shifu Kong'an says.

"How have you been, Shifu Kong'an?" Mei asks.

"I've been old and steady. Hope you are doing fine?" Shifu Kong'an says.

"I'm doing well. But I heard something strange is going on here at the temple?" Mei says.

"You have heard about it, I see." Shifu Kong'an says.

"Do you mind telling me what happened? I am a TheyTube producer, and it would help with my channel." Mei asks.

Shifu Kong'an says, "Okay, sure. The Sheriff's Office has come to investigate already. But we have not heard from them since then."

He continues, "Recently, we noticed that Kongguan did not show up for the morning prayer session. So Qingyuan went to check on him. But he was not found in his room. One morning, Guiwu was sweeping in the bamboo forest and saw someone standing behind the bamboos. When he went closer, he saw it was Kongguan, with his face pale like paper and eyes open wide. When the Coroner's Office came, the coroner told us that all the blood in his body was mysteriously gone."

Chupa hears this conversation in the RV. The sound of a possible vampire sighting gives him flashbacks.

The first memories that little Chupa had were of him drinking water from a lake. He remembered that the water was fresh and crisp. He drank it like he did not have anything to drink for days. But his stomach started rumbling. He was still hungry and thirsty. Thirsty for what? He wondered. He had plenty of water to drink.

What could he eat? He was small and furry. His claws, spikes and teeth were not that sharp. He could not even jump. He tried to chase after rabbits and squirrels, but he was not fast enough.

That night, he was wandering around the edge of the forest when he noticed a farm. He climbed over the fence and saw a barn. Through the gap between the wooden pieces of the wall, he saw there were around ten goats inside the barn.

At this very moment, Chupa saw three bats flying through the gap into the barn. They latched gently onto the sleeping goats and began sucking blood.

Something clicked in his brain. He followed the bats' lead and quietly climbed into the barn through the same gap that the bats used. He was small, so he could fit. He approached a goat that was sleeping, showed his sparkling fangs, and launched them into the neck of the goat.

Then he tasted blood, metallic, hot, and frighteningly perfect. By dawn, the goat was a husk. After that night, the barns went quiet wherever he passed.

At first, it was all about survival. Chupa needed the blood to fill his immense hunger from years of malnutrition. His dull fur started to become shiny and smooth. His teeth, spikes and claws grew sharper and stronger.

Then it was another kind of hunger that he tried to fill. His hunger to kill.

He killed even when he was full. Not for hunger, only to watch the struggling stop.

The hunger caused by dark shadows in his heart was fulfilled when he enjoyed the sufferings and struggles of goats.

The local farms were terrorized by Chupa. The farmers put up tall wire fences with pointy spikes on top to deter the Chupacabra, but he jumped over them easily. His agility was unprecedented.

The farmers hated him. They set up night watch shifts just to catch him. There were a couple of incidents where he was seen by some of them, but they were not able to apprehend him.

One night, Chupa was out looking for new victims of the night when he noticed a poorly kept farm. The fence boards were rotten, and the barn was surrounded by tall, outgrown weeds.

He slipped through a rotten door, and steel teeth closed on his foot. The chain held. He yanked once, twice, and the bone popped. The shouting came next.

At this moment, around ten farmers holding farm tools ran inside. They were ecstatic that they finally caught the Chupacabra that had been haunting the farming community for years.

They pinned him to a cross and opened his veins. The barn smelled of rust.

"An eye for an eye and a tooth for tooth," the farmers said. They wanted him to die after all his blood dripped out.

Chupa felt weak. He felt like his life force was dripping away slowly, drop by drop. He started to hallucinate. He saw a nice, fluffy lawn with numerous goats on it, lining up patiently for him to kill. Their little goat beards danced up and down in the cool breeze.

As his blood kept dripping, he felt that his hope was fading away. After all, he did not make any friends in his life. Why would anyone save him, a convicted felon who killed hundreds, if not thousands, of goats?

It was dark. No one was around except for an owl that hooted in the distance.

That was when he saw a giant creature.

In Chupa's view, this huge, fluffy, furry brown creature was glowing like an angel. It must have been a dream, but he thought that he saw the fluffiness look him in the eyes and say, "I'm going to get you out of here, don't you worry." The fluffiness approached him, used its bare hands to take out the nails on his hands and feet, then carried him on its shoulder. The shoulder was warm and sturdy.

For a moment, he thought the light itself had a face. Then he blacked out.

He dreamed of a white field where silent goats drifted past like clouds. They bowed their necks, and the world went red. Blood flowed through his mouth nonstop.

All of a sudden, heaven turned upside down. The goats fell into a dark ocean. Rain came down hard. Chupa opened his eyes. His face was covered with water.

The fluffy creature had splashed water from the lake on Chupa to wake him up.

"Finally, you are awake," the creature said, "I'm Big Joe. And you are welcome. Here, eat some grilled rabbit."

Chupa looked at Big Joe and saw that he was indeed a big furry guy, holding a grilled rabbit leg.

Chupa grabbed the rabbit leg with his claws and took a bite. It didn't taste bad. It was different from the raw blood he was used to eating.

"Drink some water." Big Joe handed him a water pouch made of some kind of animal skin.

Chupa drank all the water inside the pouch as he had been dehydrated from loss of blood. But some blood would have been better. He missed the thick and smooth texture, the metallic scent and the messiness of blood.

Big Joe said, "I've been observing you for a while. Why did you kill so many goats when you did not even need or want to eat them?"

"Because I could."

"And when they bled you? That is how they felt," Big Joe said.

Chupa had no answer.

For the first time in his life, he thought about how he felt when his blood was dripping away, and how the goats must have felt before they died.

The night was long. Chupa and Big Joe fell asleep.

The next day, Big Joe woke up. He looked at where Chupa was sleeping, but Chupa was no longer there. Chupa had escaped.

Great. Now Big Joe had to figure out a way to capture him again.

Big Joe tracked Chupa. His footprints stopped when they reached the forest. Chupa could not have walked far as his feet were injured from being nailed to the cross, and he lost a lot of blood; thus, he was very weak. Judging from his experience yesterday, Chupa would probably avoid barns for a while. But his raw instincts could still lure him towards goats.

So Big Joe stole two goats from a nearby farm, held the goats up by his shoulders, and walked through the forest. The goats let out mehhhh sounds intermittently because they were scared of this fluffy furry creature who was holding them.

Chupa was resting on top of a giant tree. He was feeling weak and exhausted. When he heard the mehhhh sounds of the goats, he thought he was dreaming again. He looked up and saw two goats moving among the foliage in the forest. He tried to fly over there because he thought he was dreaming, but that did not work. So, he climbed down from the tree and started walking towards the goats. As he got closer, he opened his mouth, getting ready to plug his fangs into the goats' necks.

That was when Big Joe grinned, "Hello, stranger!" At the same time, Big Joe grabbed Chupa. The two goats ran away.

Chupa got mad, "Hey, I don't know what you want from me, but I'm tired of being lectured by you."

Big Joe said, "You have so much potential. I would hate to see you waste your time with killing."

"What else can I do? That's all I know." Chupa said.

"For starters, you can use some lessons on how to hunt properly." Big Joe said, "Drinking goat blood is not honorable. And I did save your life. You owe me at least this."

"Okay. I'll try. But I can leave anytime I want." Chupa said, reluctantly.

"That's fair." Big Joe said, extending his right hand for a handshake.

"What's this?" Chupa was confused.

"Give me your right hand." Big Joe said.

Chupa extended his right hand. Big Joe took his hand and shook, "This is called a handshake. Two parties use this as a sign of agreement. You are essentially agreeing to learn from me."

Big Joe took Chupa to hunt rabbits, deer, and wild boars. Big Joe taught Chupa to be humane and not to treat prey cruelly, just like how Alex taught Big Joe years ago. They would eat together every day, chatting and laughing, just like what Ashley and Alex used to do with Big Joe.

For the first time, Chupa felt more than hunger. Big Joe's guidance filled a void he hadn't known he carried, replacing cruelty with the strange, fragile warmth of trust. He felt a sense of brotherhood and a sense of friendship when he hunted with Big Joe.

Big Joe nicknamed him Chupa, short for Chupacabra.

"Chupa, let's go!" Saxon says.

Chupa is brought back to reality with Saxon's voice, "Where are we going?"

"Mei and Cole said that the temple is empty now because the monks are resting. Let's go investigate." Saxon replies.

It is midnight. The full moon is shining down the red beams of the temple, and the beams give out an illusion of being covered with fresh blood.

Chupa and Saxon meet Mei and Cole at the bamboo forest of the temple.

They inspect the bamboo closely. But nothing catches their eyes. Bamboos are extremely versatile, and they cannot locate any damage from when Kongguan was found killed.

"Someone's coming!" Cole warns the group.

Chupa, Saxon, Mei and Cole hide behind the corner of the temple and observe.

They see Guiwu walking along the eaves of the temple. He checks that the gate is locked, then goes towards the back of the temple, probably to check the back gate.

At this very moment, a red flash appears for a second, and Guiwu disappears.

Chupa, Saxon, Mei and Cole come out of where they are hiding. They run towards where Guiwu disappeared. They do not find anything, except for the flashlight that Guiwu carried rolling on the ground.

A red flash licks the bamboo. Something moves with a dry, papery hiss. Guiwu sags in its arms. Then the creature turns: a bat-faced demon in Qing robes, fangs sunk deep.

The demon sees the group, takes his fangs out of Guiwu's neck, and starts charging towards Chupa, Mei and Cole. Guiwu falls on the ground and is unconscious. Saxon uses his bow and arrows to shoot the demon. The arrows hit the demon, and the demon lets out a sharp chirping sound. The sound wave hits Saxon like a heavy punch, and Saxon drops off from the sky.

Chupa throws his rope towards the demon, and the noose settles on the demon's shoulder. Chupa tightens the rope. The demon struggles, trying to stretch out of the noose. The demon then uses his hands to hold on to the rope and gets close to Chupa. Fangs slide into his neck. Chupa bites back, gagging on tar-black blood. "Wrong vintage." Chupa uses his claws to push the demon away. The demon's fangs come out of Chupa's neck.

Mei uses her sword to cut, slash and stab the demon. Cole shoots multiple bullets at the demon.

The demon is getting weaker due to cuts from the weapons with Holy Water. Every time the demon is injured by the weapons, his energy level lowers a bit. Saxon, Chupa, Mei and Cole receive cuts and bruises from the demon as well.

But darkness never prevails.

The dawn is upon them. The cryptids, Mei and Cole, are gaining the advantage over the demon. Eventually, they are able to capture the blood-sucking demon with Chupa's rope wrapped around him.

"Quick, before the other monks wake up, we need to find the sigil and send the demon back," Chupa says.

Chupa keeps watch on the demon while Saxon, Mei and Cole look for the sigil. Saxon flies around the temple, while Mei and Cole run through the inside of the temple. After searching, Saxon locates the sigil behind the main plaque of the temple and calls Mei, Cole and Chupa to gather around.

Chupa says, "This demon's name is Wangliang."

"Same ritual, with human blood?" Saxon asks.

"We can try. From our experience, human blood works." Chupa says.

"Cole, do you want to try your blood again?" Mei asks.

"Sure!" Cole answers and borrows Mei's sword to cut his finger. He smears the blood on the sigil, hoping something will happen.

But the demon looks fine. Nothing is changing or happening.

Mei wipes Cole's blood out of the sigil. "It's time for me to try," Mei says, cuts her finger, and smears her blood on the sigil.

Mei's blood works like magic. "Wangliang, I hereby banish you back to Hell," Mei says. The sigil lights up with beams of red light, raising the demon in the air, and then the demon disappears into the thousands of beams of blood-colored light.

"There must be something special about your blood, Mei." Chupa says, "Do you come from a powerful bloodline?"

Mei laughs, "Not that I know of. My parents are normal people with normal jobs."

"Weird." Chupa says, "I wonder why your blood is the key to sending demons back. Maybe we can investigate it later."

"Well, let's leave before the monks wake up," Saxon says.

"Yes, just like superheroes leaving after they defeat villains." Chupa smiles.

"I'm getting hungry now." Cole says, "Do we have some of the leftover goat chops at the camp?"

"For you? I'll cook you a fresh batch, bro," Chupa says.

The cryptids, Mei and Cole, get into the RV and drive away from the temple.

Back in the temple, Guiwu wakes up. He realizes that he is lying on the ground. "Was that a dream?" he asks himself. His fingers run through his neck and feel something wet. He brings his hand up and sees blood. At this point, he believes that he was indeed attacked by a vampire last night, but someone must have saved him from the same fate as Kongguan had.

"Amitabha." Guiwu puts his hands together and kneels to the Buddha in the temple. The statue of Buddha smiles mysteriously.

CHAPTER SIX

THE SUCCUBUS

"Aura!" Chupa says, "Welcome back!"

In comes a beautiful lady with long, braided dark hair, reindeer horns and pointy ears, wearing indigenous clothes. Her eyes look tired but determined.

"Hi, my friends," Aura says. She looks at Mei and Cole, "You must be the TheyTubers that I heard so much about. My name is Aura, and people call me the Skinwalker."

"Yes, and nice meeting you, Aura. I'm Mei He." Mei says, extending her right hand. Aura extends her right hand as well for a handshake. Mei sees that Aura has beautiful, long fingers with long, well-maintained nails.

"Nice to meet you, Aura. My name's Cole Carter." Cole reaches out for a handshake too.

Chupa, Saxon, Rake, Nessie, and Grey give Aura hugs.

"How have you been, sis?" Chupa asks.

"I've been grieving. Dezba passed away." Aura says, with tears circling in her eyes.

"Oh, I'm so sorry to hear that!" Chupa says, and the rest of the group sends their condolences.

"Do you mind sharing what happened?" Nessie asks, while comforting Aura by holding her hand.

"Actually, that's why I have come back." Aura says, "I need your help."

"Whatever you need, we are here for you," Chupa says, and the rest of the group agrees.

"A demon named Vanet is responsible for Dezba's cancer. She shape-shifted to look like me and slept with my husband, intentionally transferring cancer cells to him in the process." The pain of losing her husband makes Aura tear up, but the rage towards Vanet makes her other six arms come out. Each of the six limbs has long, sharp nails, ready to poke into Vanet's eyes.

The rage also brings Aura back to the dark days of her past.

It was a cloudy day. Little Aura was playing in the playground when she noticed a nice-looking little boy. The little boy noticed her and came over to play. She whispered, "I can become anything," and her skin shimmered into the boy's own likeness. Instead of wonder, his face twisted in fear. He screamed, calling her a freak, and ran. Aura's chest burned as if he had torn something from her with those words.

Aura was mad. She was furious at the little boy. She trusted the little boy enough to show him what she could do, but he threw her trust away, like it was a piece of useless apple pit. Shame, anger, and darkness conquered her heart.

As the little boy was crying to his parents, he looked back at Aura.

Aura looked like the little boy still, but with his eyes taken out. There was nothing in the eye sockets except for emptiness and dark blood.

The little boy freaked out even more and started screaming.

The parents looked at Aura, and Aura let out a creepy smile, showing the squashed eyeballs in her mouth.

That was when Aura realized human beings were stupid and not trustworthy. In her mind, humans became prey that she would hunt.

Little Aura played tricks against humanity to get her way. She would go to supermarkets and look for her target. She pretended to be a lost little girl and told the old lady pushing a shopping cart that she thought her mom had left the store without her. The old lady was kind enough to take her out to find her mom. When they walked into an alley, Aura showed her true self with multiple limbs and horns. The old lady was shocked and scared. Aura captured the old lady and ate her alive.

As Aura grew taller, she realized that it was getting harder for her to pretend to be a little girl. So, she looked for other ways. She posed as an old man and an old lady, but they did not work as well as posing as a little girl.

One time, she changed herself to look like a beautiful young lady and walked inside a bar. People were hanging out, having drinks. She followed suit and ordered a beer like the guy next to her. Before long, the guy started flirting with her. She led him on and accepted the offer from him to drive her home. When they were inside the car, the guy leaned in for a kiss, only to be met with multiple limbs stabbing his eyes and organs with sharp nails. Aura devoured the guy alive and felt satisfied that she had found another easy way to lure prey into her calculated death trap.

One rainy night, Aura walked inside a bar named Urban Oasis. She looked beautiful as always, wearing a dress with long stripes, showcasing her curvy body. She sat at the bar, ordered a Bloody Mary, and observed the room while looking for a good target. She liked challenging targets where she had to work for their attention.

Across the bar, Aura noticed another beautiful blond lady wearing a red dress. The blond lady was gazing at her. Their eyes met. Aura had a weird feeling that this lady was doing the same thing as her: Hunting. She became intrigued.

The blond lady smiled at Aura and walked towards a handsome guy sitting at the table. She talked with him for a little while and started walking towards Aura. She looked Aura in her eyes and said, "Hi, beautiful, I'm Vanet. What's your name?"

Aura was shocked at Vanet's direct move. But she was not easily intimidated, "My name is Aura. It is interesting that we have the same plan."

Vanet smiled, "Yes, it is. Good luck!" As she finished her remarks, she turned around with her blond hair swinging in the air. She went back to the guy she was flirting with, and together they left the bar.

Aura was more than intrigued at this point. She has never met anyone like Vanet before.

Over time, Aura and Vanet became frenemies. They competed on how many prey they were able to capture and eat, and through competition, motivated each other to be better at choosing targets, obtaining attention, and trapping targets.

Life went on. Aura and Vanet became more and more competitive. More men disappeared each night. The dark shadows within Aura felt satisfied with all the innocent lives consumed.

However, everything changed in one summer night.

That night, Aura and Vanet were in a bar called Moonlit Tree Brewery. There sat a good-looking fellow at the bar.

Vanet walked over to talk to the guy. She tried to flirt, but he mentioned that he just wanted to enjoy his beer. This was the first time Vanet's shape-shifting charm did not work. She was rarely defeated.

Aura took interest in the situation. She looked at the guy closely. He looked like an indigenous guy. He had long hair, strong, masculine jawlines, and a toned body. He wore a white T-shirt and blue jeans.

For some reason, Aura wanted to talk to him. She went inside the bathroom, changed her clothes to a red T-shirt and blue jeans, and walked out.

Aura made sure the guy could see her when she walked past him.

And the guy did. He did not move his eyes from her.

He walked over.

Aura had talked to guys thousands of times before, but this time, she felt nervous. There seemed to be butterflies fluttering in her chest. With each step he walked towards her, her heartbeat rate doubled. She could feel her face flushing.

"Hello, do you mind if I sit here?" the guy asked.

"Sure," Aura answered.

"My name is Dezba Nez. Nice meeting you." Dezba said.

"Nice meeting you, Dezba. My name is Aura." Aura replied.

Dezba was charming, straightforward and honest. He told Aura that he was a Native American Navajo. He told her that she was beautiful and that he would like to see her again. He was not like any other guy she had seen before.

For some reason, Aura trusted him. She trusted every word that came out of his mouth. She wanted to see him again, instead of eating him.

The next day, Aura and Dezba went out for a date, then another date, and another. One year later, he proposed, and she accepted. They got married and lived happily ever after, until Dezba was diagnosed with cancer.

Vanet was furious about Aura and Dezba's relationship. She thought it was stupid of Aura to fall in love with a mere human being. She also thought that Aura had betrayed her identity and lived in a fantasy world with Dezba that was built on lies. By hiding who she was, Aura was not being authentic or being her true self.

Maybe there was a hint of jealousy too. Vanet had never experienced love before. All she had seen was lust, betrayal, and sin.

Vanet believed that her own purpose, thus Aura's purpose as well, was to kill human beings: to kill the greedy guys that did not care about anything else other than what was in their pants, the men who wasted no time betraying their wives when approached by Vanet and Aura.

Vanet needed to kill Dezba and free Aura from the lies Dezba must have promised. She made this goal her sole purpose after Aura married Dezba and told her that she would never kill again.

Vanet tried, for years, to seduce Dezba. But nothing worked. She was desperate after years of attempted seduction to no avail.

Vanet studied Aura and Dezba's routines in secret. Vanet found out that Aura was away from Dezba for a few days at a time, and these days were convenient for her plan to be executed. Vanet learned to dress like Aura, talk like Aura, move like Aura, and behave like Aura.

One day, Aura was away for a mission with the cryptids. Vanet shape-shifted to look like Aura, put on the same clothes Aura was wearing when she left, and went into Dezba and Aura's house. Dezba had been sleeping. Vanet kissed him and woke him up. This time, in his hazy memories, Dezba thought Aura came back early because Vanet looked and acted exactly like Aura. Vanet led Dezba on for sex and succeeded in transferring cancer cells into Dezba's body.

When Dezba was diagnosed with stage four lung cancer, Aura was devastated. The love of her life only had three to six months to live. She took a leave from the cryptids and spent time traveling with her husband.

At Dezba's funeral, Aura was giving an eulogy for Dezba when she noticed Vanet sitting in the audience. Vanet looked blonde, like the first time they met. When their eyes met, Vanet smiled at Aura while changing shape to look like Aura. That was when it occurred to Aura, that Vanet used to give cancer to guys when she was tired of eating them, and enjoyed watching them suffer miserably afterwards.

Aura could see Vanet standing up and leaving the memorial. She ran out after her and tried to capture her, but Vanet disappeared into thin air.

Aura was furious at Vanet. She was angry at herself as well. She felt like her past had finally caught up with her. All the people she killed and all the suffering she had caused came back, and made her beloved Dezba pay. Karma got Dezba because of her.

How was that fair? Aura would rather she die from cancer instead of Dezba. After all, it was Aura who committed these hideous murders, not Dezba, whose only crime was loving her.

She wanted Vanet to pay. She wanted Vanet to know that killing Dezba was the biggest mistake Vanet ever made. She wanted to make sure that the pain that Dezba endured during the last three months of his life and the pain of losing Dezba were not in vain.

What Vanet didn't know was that Aura joined the team of the cryptids after she married Dezba. She views the cryptid team as her chance of redemption. It is her chance of helping human beings in return, instead of killing them like she used to do.

In addition to joining missions, Aura has been the financial sponsor for the cryptids' operations. Dezba owned multiple casinos and other business ventures, so Aura uses a small portion of the money they earn to pay for utilities, vehicles, weapons, and everything else that is needed to run the operations.

"Aura, what's the plan for this demon Vanet? We need to make sure she pays." Saxon asks.

Saxon's question brings Aura back to reality. She looks around the table and sees her team look at her, eager to help in her time of need. At this moment, she feels home. The past few months have drained her energy physically and emotionally. But she is glad she is finally back home.

"Vanet will not be easily located. Plus, she knows I won't let her off the hook after what she did to my late husband." Aura says, "Since she shape-shifts, she can be anyone. The only way we can find her is to lure her out to me."

Nessie asks, "How can we do that? I assume Vanet is intelligent and does not want to be caught."

"We just have to simulate the same situation when I met my husband. She hates it when she sees me with someone and would do anything to get the guy out of my sight." Aura says.

Mei looks at Cole, "Cole, I think you are the candidate. Just pretend you are dating Aura."

Cole nods, "Anything to help you, Aura."

"Thank you, Cole. This might require you to shave your beard." Aura smiles with gratitude, "Vanet knows that I hated the beard on Dezba."

"Done," Cole says.

So, the cryptids, Mei and Cole discuss a plan to capture Vanet.

The next day, Aura goes back home. At night, she goes out to the Moonlit Tree Brewery, where Dezba and her met years ago.

She orders a beer and sits at the bar. She hangs out and observes the room.

The next day, she does the same.

She does this for a week.

On the eighth day, Aura goes to the bar, orders a beer, and looks around.

She sees a good-looking fellow at the other side of the bar. He has short hair, strong, masculine jawlines, and a toned body. He wears a T-shirt and blue jeans.

Aura goes inside the bathroom, changes her clothes to a red T-shirt and blue jeans, and walks out. She makes sure the guy can see her when she walks past him.

And the guy does. He does not move his eyes from her.

He walks over.

Aura has a strange feeling of Deja vu as the guy is walking over. For a moment, she thinks she is seeing Dezba again.

"Hello, do you mind if I sit here?" the guy asks.

"Sure," Aura answers.

"My name is Cole Carter," Cole says.

"My name is Aura," Aura replies.

Cole is charming and honest. He tells Aura that he is a veteran. He tells her that she is beautiful and that he would like to see her again.

At this moment, a beautiful blonde lady walks towards Cole and says, "Hey handsome, want to buy me a drink instead of talking to this boring girl?"

In Cole's earpiece, Chupa asks, "Is this Vanet?"

Cole asks, "I'm Cole. What's your name?"

"Vanet." Vanet proudly says.

At the sound of the name, the cryptids come out of their RV with weapons, surrounding the bar.

Aura says, "Vanet, what are you trying to do, ruin my date like you killed my husband?"

Vanet says, "Hey, Aura. It's a free world. This gentleman can choose whoever he wants for the night."

Cole says, "Let's go, Aura." And then he holds Aura's hand and walks outside of the bar.

Vanet becomes furious. This is another defeat she did not foresee coming. She is charming. She is good-looking. She is sexy. Why is this stupid guy choosing Aura over her, just like what Dezba did? How dare him? She is obviously more attractive than Aura, who is only wearing a T-shirt. So, she runs after Cole and Aura into the parking lot in anger.

That is when Chupa, Saxon, Nessie, Rake, Grey and Mei surround Vanet.

Knowing that she is surrounded, Vanet changes to her true form with blonde hair, pointy horns, sharp teeth and a long tail with an arrow point. "Bitchy bitch! You led me into a trap? I'm not going to be captured."

Aura smiles, "Vanet, let me introduce you to my teammates. We work together banishing demons like you."

Vanet smirks, "How funny! Did you banish yourself?"

Aura's voice rings clear. "Yes. I banished my own demons years ago. This team isn't my disguise. It's my redemption."

Vanet is thinking of ways to hurt Aura the most, "Oh, I remember now, is this what you were doing when I was having hot, steamy sex with your husband, oh sorry, late husband?"

Aura's heart breaks. But she continues to look determined, "You shape-shifted to look like me so that he would mistake you to be me. He did not want you when you looked like yourself, and that makes you pathetic."

"I'm pathetic? You are pathetic! Did he really, truly love you, or did he just like your made-up human look?" Vanet continues to stab Aura in her soft heart with an invisible, sharp stagger made by mean words.

Aura smiles, "Actually, before we got married, I showed him how I truly looked without shapeshifting. He told me I was beautiful. And I told him about my dark past. He was very supportive of me redeeming myself by joining the cryptid team. He indeed loved me for who I truly was."

Vanet is not expecting this answer from Aura. She looks shocked and puzzled.

Aura continues, "Enough talk. Let's fight."

Aura uses her multiple arms to attack Vanet. Vanet swings her tail and fights back against Aura. Chupa uses his break-dancing moves and throws his rope towards Vanet, but her arm grabs it, and she gets loose. Saxon flies up, uses his bow and arrows to shoot at Vanet, but the leather armor she wears deflects arrows to the ground. Nessie uses her flail, and it hits Vanet's waist with scratches and bruises. Grey swings his sniper rifle with a laser blade, cutting Vanet's armor. Rake stabs his dagger at Vanet through the cut of the armor, causing her to have multiple wounds. Mei's sword scrapes off Vanet's skin on the shoulder. Cole pulls the trigger of his gun, and multiple bullets hit Vanet.

Aura takes out the tomahawk that belonged to Dezba and pours Holy Water on it. She feels the presence of Dezba and his ancestors, who passed down the tomahawk to him. She swings the tomahawk towards Vanet and hits her on her head. The tomahawk causes Vanet's head to split in half.

Now Vanet is disabled. Chupa uses his rope to tie her up.

"We need to find her sigil to send her back," Chupa says.

"I know her sigil by heart. Let me draw it." Aura says.

Aura cuts her finger and draws Vanet's sigil using her own blood.

"We need human blood now." Chupa looks at Mei.

"My blood has been working," Mei says, using her sword to cut her finger and smearing blood over the sigil that Aura drew.

"Might I do the honor?" Aura says.

"Of course." Mei steps back.

"I am hereby banishing you back to Hell, Vanet the Succubus." Aura smiles, "See you never."

The sigil turns red, lighting Vanet up with a bloody color. Vanet floats in the air and disappears into the red light.

A drop of tear slides down Aura's cheek as she watches the light of blood and despair disappear.

She wipes blood of darkness and evil off of the tomahawk and says, "Dezba, my love, I have banished Vanet like I promised. And I will never stop until I send them all back."

CHAPTER SEVEN

THE SHERIFF

Noah drives the SUV to the building of the Sheriff's Office and parks it a block away. From the SUV, Big Joe and Noah observe what happens at the building.

Deputy Sheriff Jason Sims, who was following them, has been captured, so Sheriff Hampson may have already been wondering where Deputy Sheriff Jason Sims is and why he hasn't checked in with him yet.

Big Joe and Noah need to find out what car Sheriff Hampson drives. They focus their attention at the entrance of the parking lot behind the building.

Suddenly, a fleet of three cars with Office of the Sheriff markings drive out from the parking lot. One of the passengers is Sheriff Hampson.

Noah starts the SUV and follows the fleet. The fleet of vehicles drives southbound, sounding sirens.

Noah cannot follow the vehicles too closely, but he drives at a safe distance behind them as fast as possible. The sirens provide directions effectively.

The fleet exits Highway 101, and then the sirens stop. It is a rural road, and if they follow the fleet closely, it might alert the sheriffs.

"Okay. Now, how do we find out where they are going?" Noah says.

"Maybe they have a facility nearby. Let's search for anything Sheriff-related by location." Big Joe says.

Noah pulls over. Big Joe scrolls on his phone to search for any facility related to the Sheriff's Office. "There's a facility nearby called 'County of San Cara Justice Training Academy'."

"I think we just hit the jackpot!" Noah says.

Big Joe agrees, "Where else would three vehicles go? I don't think they are responding to a 911 call. This is too far. And why did they stop the sirens when they are still en route? Probably to hide where they are headed."

"Let's go and find out what secrets are buried here, in the 'Justice' Academy," Noah smirks and drives the SUV according to GPS on Big Joe's phone.

"Noah, you are supposed to turn left here." Big Joe says.

"Well, it would be helpful if you had reminded me just now," Noah says.

"The GPS lady mentioned it. And here, the next line tells you what the next move is." Big Joe points to the navigation screen.

Noah's ego is too big to admit this mistake, so he just makes a U-turn and then follows the GPS.

The Justice Academy is in a wooded area within County land. There is a parking lot, but the cryptids choose to park the SUV outside and walk over.

Big Joe and Noah hide behind foliage as they walk towards the buildings. When they approach the parking lot, they see multiple vehicles, including the three marked with the Sheriff's Office shield. Some creatures are seen walking towards the main building. One creature looks like a rhinoceros. The other creature looks like a giant lizard. Another one looks like a giant rat. It seems all the awkward creatures in town are summoned and gathered here.

Big Joe and Noah are hiding behind a tree and focusing on observing the creatures when they hear someone say, "Hurry up!"

They look back and see a deputy sheriff staring at them with an inpatient expression.

Big Joe and Noah are confused, but they start moving per the deputy sheriff's instruction. The deputy sheriff rounds up all creatures to the front of the building, and the cryptids follow the other creatures.

Sheriff Hampson and eleven other sheriffs are waiting for the creatures in front of the building.

The deputy sheriff tells the creatures to line up and stand in front of Sheriff Hampson.

Sheriff Hampson spreads his four-eyed gaze across the line. "Today, you prove yourselves worthy of the Academy. Obstacle, endurance, strength, survival. Pass, or be discarded. Darkness demands only the strongest."

The first event is the Obstacle Course. The obstacle course requires the creatures to start at the starting line, run through the course without touching any obstacles along the way, turn around and sprint through the finishing line. The event is timed, and only the top 50% will move on to the next event.

The giant lizard goes first. He uses his small arms to tuck his giant tail in, but somehow, along the way, his tail falls, hitting a cone. He is immediately disqualified.

Big Joe and Noah feel bad for the creature. Or are they happy that he will not be joining the Demon Academy, a.k.a. the evil side?

Big Joe and Noah use their agility obtained from growing up in forests to move through cones and obstacles like they were running away from predators when they were young. Both make the cut.

The second event is the 666 Yard Run. The creatures will need to run from the starting line along the paved path down to the end of the road and run back across the finishing line. The first 50% pass while the last 50% fail.

The creatures run at the same time. Big Joe and Noah are not the fastest, but they do their best and stay in the top 50% of all creatures.

The third event is the Body Drag. The Body Drag consists of picking up a 666-pound dummy around the chest at the starting line and dragging it for 666 feet across the finishing line.

The creature that looks like a giant rat goes first. He wobbly picks up the dummy and tries to walk backwards towards the finishing line. But after three tiny steps, he falls backwards, and the hard paved road catches him, breaking his back. He is instantly disqualified and tossed out by deputy sheriffs like trash.

Big Joe is getting ready to complete the Body Drag. He is the bulkiest creature among contestants, so no one doubts his abilities in this event. He picks up the dummy with one hand over the chest like it's just a bag of chips, and drags it across the finishing line with ease.

Noah does the same. He is the second largest creature and follows Big Joe's lead. He picks up the dummy with two hands like he is picking up a bag of potatoes.

The fourth and final event is the Wall Climb. The 6.66-foot wall climb requires the creatures to start at the starting line, run to the wall, climb over the wall, and sprint through the finishing line.

By now, there are only Big Joe, Noah and four other creatures left to compete.

The creature that looks like a rhino goes first. He runs to the wall, uses his hands to grab onto the wall, uses his feet to climb up the wall, then he sits on the wall, and plans to jump down. But his nose horns are so heavy that he falls headfirst from the wall. He is immediately disqualified.

It's time for Big Joe to do the Wall Climb. He runs, grabs the 6.66 feet wall, and swings his legs right through the wall, lands like a professional gymnast after a perfect jump with his hands up in the air, then sprints towards the finishing line.

The deputy sheriffs and other creatures give him a round of applause. Big Joe bows like a theater actor towards the audience.

Then it is Noah's turn. He runs towards the wall, steps on the middle of the wall, then uses a tiny force through his wings to fly on top of the wall, and lands sliding down, finally sprinting past the finishing line.

The deputy sheriffs and other creatures have their mouths open, stays silent, then outbursts a storm of applause.

Big Joe, Noah, and a creature that looks like a coyote are the three survivors after four events.

"What are your names, my fellow demon cadets?" Sheriff Hampson smiles and greets the newest recruits.

"Big Joe, Sir."

"Noah, Sir."

"Hunter, Sir."

"Welcome to the infamous Demon Academy. We are the world's largest training academy for demons." Sheriff Hampson says, "You have earned your places as demon cadets by passing the entrance test. For the next six weeks, you will go through the most intense training to become demons. May the evilest win."

"May the evilest win!" The rest of the deputy sheriffs repeat after Sheriff Hampson. This seems to be their slogan.

Big Joe, Noah and Hunter check in to the sleeping quarters of the Demon Academy.

At night, Big Joe, Noah and Hunter are chatting.

"Why do you want to be here?" Big Joe asks Hunter.

"I have darkness and shadows inside that yell at me every day to kill. I enjoy seeing my prey suffer. I want to see more suffering." Hunter replies, then asks, "You?"

Big Joe says, "Same."

Noah nods as well, "Yea, same."

The next day, they are woken up by deputy sheriffs at 3 AM for a morning training session. "Run the 666-yard run for 66 times, now!" The deputy sheriff commands.

Without food or water in their stomachs, Big Joe, Noah and Hunter do not have much energy. But they run like the deputy sheriff commands. As they are running the course, the deputy sheriff keeps yelling at them, "Faster! Faster! You are too slow! Are you pigs? Even pigs can fly!"

Big Joe and Noah look at each other briefly and exchange a few words: "What a jerk."

The deputy sheriff hears them whisper and yells at both, "Hey bulky bricks there, the two of you, keep quiet!"

Hunter is a quiet one. He just keeps silent and takes everything in.

After the morning training, they are told it is breakfast time. As they walk towards the dining table, they see a few pieces of bacon scraps and what looks like one tiny, boiled egg broken into small pieces.

"Hope you are hungry," the deputy sheriff smirks.

Big Joe, Noah, and Hunter look at each other, shrug their shoulders, and pick up pieces of bacon and egg. They feel even hungrier after breakfast.

The deputy sheriff comes in, hurrying them to the strength training court. From there, they are supposed to flip giant tires 666 times.

Already feeling hungry and tired from the morning training, the three of them embark on this new journey. Big Joe, Noah, and Hunter give their best despite being starved and exhausted.

The deputy sheriff yells at them, berates them, and spits at them for being too weak and too slow.

Noah secretly whispers to Big Joe and Hunter during the break, "I guess this deputy is a prison guard?" Big Joe and Hunter chuckle a little bit.

The deputy sheriff hears them and yells, "Chop chop! What are you pigs doing there? The tires are not going to flip themselves, idiots!"

Big Joe, Noah and Hunter shrug and walk back to flip tires.

Soon it is lunchtime. On the kitchen table are 13 pieces of sourdough bread, with nothing else, not even butter.

It is not an appetizing scene, but the three of them are so hungry that they just grab the bread and shove them in their mouths.

The afternoon training consists of weapon practices. In the weapon room, Big Joe, Noah, and Hunter must choose weapons of their own and practice using them.

Big Joe looks around the weapon room and wants to choose something new. A halberd seems interesting. It comes with an axe blade topped with a spike and is mounted on a long white shaft. Big Joe is used to his axe, and this halberd has an additional spike, which comes in handy. And it is longer, which means he can practice long-range attacks compared to short-range attacks using his existing weapon, the axe.

Noah wants to try something different as well. His existing weapon is a spear, which is a long-range weapon. His eyes fall on a warhammer. It has a heavy iron head with a hammer in front and a curved spike on the other side. Noah picks it up, and the white shaft feels good in his hand.

Hunter is not sure what he wants. He has never had a weapon before. He only used his claws and sharp teeth as his weapons in the past. He picks up different weapons and cannot decide which one is good to use.

Big Joe says, "Hunter, use your gut feeling. What feels good? Some are good for long-range fight, some are good for medium range, some are good for close range."

Noah says, "It also depends on what situation you are in for the fight. Do you know if you are better at long range, medium range or close range?"

Hunter is unsure of anything: "I follow my prey around quietly, attack them when they are the weakest, and don't really know if I'm good at anything."

"Well, you passed the entrance test, which means you are better than all the other candidates. I'm thinking you should try the close-range ones since you attack your prey in close range most likely." Big Joe suggests.

"Here, maybe try using this short sword. It comes in handy with close-range fighting." Noah picks up the short sword and hands it to Hunter.

Hunter picks the short sword up and swings it around. The white handle feels good in his hands, "Okay, I like this one."

"Great, you ladies surely take your sweet time," the deputy sheriff says, "These weapons are made of human bones. You better not break them."

Big Joe and Noah glance at each other, and the weapons feel heavier and colder after they are aware of what they are made of.

Hunter has no clue what is going on in Big Joe's and Noah's heads. He simply says, "Cool."

The afternoon training begins. The three of them are told by the deputy sheriff to fight with their weapons among dummies and themselves nonstop for 66.6 minutes.

First, Big Joe, Noah, and Hunter use their weapons to hit the 666-pound dummies. The halberd, war hammer, and short sword quickly make multiple wounds on the heavy dummies, making them fall apart on the ground like helpless dead bodies.

When the dummies become unusable, the three of them start practicing with each other.

Big Joe swings his halberd towards Noah, and Noah uses his war hammer to block the halberd. The force of both parties is so significant that there is a loud slashing sound when the weapons meet, while giving out a powerful vibration. Their hands are seen bruised after the vibration stops.

Hunter slashes his short sword towards Big Joe, and Big Joe blocks it by holding his halberd high. Hunter then quickly moves the short sword back and stabs Big Joe on his shoulder, and Big Joe uses his left hand to grab the blade. The blade made Big Joe's hand bleed, but he was able to stop the attack from Hunter.

Noah waves his warhammer in the air towards Hunter, and Hunter jumps away while poking his short sword towards Noah. Noah changes the direction of his war hammer and hits Hunter's short sword. A loud clang sound is heard, and Hunter's short sword falls on the ground.

The three of them take turns practicing attacks with their respective weapons and quickly get the hang of them.

For Hunter, everything is new and exciting. It is his first time practicing with anyone. All he has is blunt force, without an ounce of technique. But through different moves during practice, he begins to understand the pros and cons of his weapon. The short sword is one of the quickest weapons. The damage of each impact is low, but he can use it to exceed anything if he hits fast. With fast hits, the result of multiple damages can compensate for low damage impacts.

Big Joe and Noah help guide Hunter's moves during practice. For the first time in Hunter's life, he feels mentored and helped, instead of being left alone, fending for himself.

The deputy sheriff yells at them whenever they talk or stop practicing with derogatory terms like "Dumb" and "Pigs". To Big Joe, Noah and Hunter, they feel funny about the term "Pigs" because they have hunted and eaten pigs many times before. "Pork is delicious and sounds great right now." The three of them are so hungry that they have the same thoughts about consuming a pig all by themselves.

That evening, they are given some very watery soup, which barely has anything solid in it. Nevertheless, they devour the tasteless soup like it's the most delicious thing in the world, because they are starving and their stomachs are grumbling loudly, complaining and protesting for lack of protein.

At night, they still feel so hungry that they cannot fall asleep. The stomach grumbling sound is heard one after another, like a symphony expressing how lonely their empty stomachs feel without food.

"Hey, Big Joe, are you awake?" Noah whispers.

"Yep, wide awake." Big Joe says.

"Me too!" Hunter says.

"Let's go get some food," Noah says.

"What about the deputy sheriff who's guarding outside?" Hunter asks.

"That's easy. We can trick him." Big Joe says. He picks up a piece of stone on the floor and throws it on the far side of the room. The deputy sheriff hears the noise and comes to their room. He sees that everyone is sleeping.

Then the deputy sheriff goes back to sit outside.

Big Joe throws another stone. This time, the deputy sheriff goes towards the stone. Big Joe, Noah, and Hunter sneak out. The deputy sheriff comes back after realizing there is no one there, checks on the room, sees the pillows and comforters shaped like Big Joe, Noah and Hunter, thinks nothing of it, then goes back to sit outside.

Big Joe, Noah, and Hunter walk into the dark forest surrounding the Academy. They plan to hunt for dinner.

They quietly observe in the dark and hear something in the distance. It's a deer!

Big Joe's, Noah's, and Hunter's eyes light up. It is a beautiful buck with long antlers. It jumps around among foliage and decides to eat grass.

Big Joe, Noah, and Hunter are experienced hunters. They approach the buck in different directions, keep their bodies low, stay very quiet and hold their breath so they are undiscovered by the buck.

When they become close enough to the buck, they look at each other, and Big Joe mouths, "One, two, three, go!"

The three of them jump up at the same time. Big Joe gets a hold of the antlers, Noah grabs the front legs, and Hunter's teeth break into the buck's butt.

Big Joe and Noah look at Hunter with his teeth inserted into the buck, and they both chuckle a little. This scene reminds them of when they were young.

Big Joe has Deja vu from when he first saw Chupa as well, with Chupa's teeth plugged into a goat.

Hunter sinks his teeth into the buck's haunch, the animal's cry ripping through the trees.

Big Joe's chest tightens. Here is raw instinct, brutal and untempered. He steps forward, ready to show Hunter there is another way. Big Joe says, "Hunter, let me teach you the proper way to hunt. We are not supposed to let prey suffer."

"We are not?" Hunter chews the piece of meat from the buck, and his eyes are wide open from shock.

"It is a part of the wheel of life when we eat other animals. When we die, our bodies become part of the dirt and will provide nutrition to grass, which the animals then eat. And that, my friend, is called the wheel of life." Big Joe explains.

"But we are supposed to be evil and not care about others!" Hunter says.

"Well, rules are rules. When you hunt, you follow the hunting rules." Noah says, then uses his bare hands to break the buck's neck, ending its misery.

"We give our prey a quick death instead of watching them suffer." Big Joe says, "It is called respect for life."

"Okay." Hunter looks confused but continues to eat meat out of the buck's corpse.

Big Joe and Noah join Hunter in devouring the buck.

"You know what would make it taste better? Light up some fire, BBQ this badass to medium rare, and put some salt and pepper." Noah says.

"Oh yeah? I don't know how that tastes. I only had raw meat in the wild." Hunter says.

"Too bad we can't make a fire." Big Joe agrees.

They cannot make a fire because that would make them easily discoverable by the deputy sheriff on duty.

After they finish dinner, the three of them lie on the grass and watch stars in the sky. It is a starry night.

"You see this bright star? That's the Polaris. Polaris indicates the north." Big Joe says, "And these seven stars that form the shape of a spoon are called the Big Dipper. It is part of the Great Bear constellation."

"Bears taste great," Hunter says.

Big Joe and Noah smile as they hear Hunter's remarks.

"Okay, let's go back before they find out." Big Joe says.

The three of them sneak in without being noticed by the deputy sheriff.

The next day, training is tough, food is crappy, and the deputy sheriff is mean. So is the next day, and the day after next. Before they realize, the three of them have been in the academy for five weeks. Every night, they sneak outside to hunt wild animals, devour them, and then watch stars. Big Joe teaches Noah and Hunter about the Little Bear constellation, the Orion constellation, the Canis Major constellation, and the Cygnus constellation.

This is knowledge that Ashley and Alex taught him years ago. Now Big Joe is teaching Noah and Hunter. One word comes to Big Joe's mind. And that word is legacy. He is continuing Ashley and Alex's legacy. He looks up to the beautiful stars and sees Ashley and Alex smiling at him. Two stars in the Great Bear constellation wink at him, and he believes that means approval from Ashley and Alex.

On the first day of the sixth week, right after they walk out of the Academy, Big Joe, Noah and Hunter notice two people sneaking around. They find it interesting and follow them. The two people are wearing all black clothes and have black masks on their faces.

Big Joe, Noah and Hunter approach them from behind like they are prey and tap them on their shoulders.

The two turn around in shock and start throwing punches at Big Joe, Noah and Hunter. But the difference in sheer size alone means there is no chance of the two winning. Before they know it, they have been apprehended by the three.

Noah and Hunter hold the two. Big Joe removes the two suspects' masks and sees that they are two women. One is of African American descent, and one is of Hispanic descent.

"Who are you and what are you doing here?" Big Joe asks.

"What are you? Are you going to eat us?" the African American lady says.

"Don't worry. We are not going to hurt you." Big Joe says.

"I say we just let the deputy sheriff know that we caught these two snooping around. There is no need to question them!" Hunter says.

"How do you explain us being out at night? We should not report them right now." Noah says.

Big Joe turns to Noah and Hunter, "You can let go of their arms."

Noah and Hunter reluctantly take their hands back, letting the ladies loose.

Big Joe continues to question, "What are your names and what are you doing here?"

"My name is Alicia. I'm a deputy sheriff in the County of San Cara," the African American lady says.

"I'm Maria. I'm also a deputy sheriff," the Hispanic lady says.

Alicia says, "We are here to investigate the Justice Academy."

Big Joe and Noah look at each other, both thinking, "Interesting!"

Maria says, "We suspect something foul is going on, because right now there should be no training scheduled. And our suspicion is correct! Look at you!"

"You ladies surely have some great instincts," Noah says.

"We should just kill them, easy-peasy," Hunter says.

"Hunter, not every solution is to kill." Big Joe says.

"What are you proposing?" Hunter asks.

"We have an SUV parked outside the academy. We can hold them there temporarily until we think of a solution." Big Joe suggests.

"Okay." Noah agrees.

And so, the three of them tie Alicia and Maria up, tape their mouths, put them in the back of the SUV, and leave a crack on the car window to allow them to breathe.

By now, dawn is upon Big Joe, Noah, and Hunter. They do not have time to hunt or to eat. They quickly go back to their room.

Another day of starvation, intense physical training, and verbal abuse from the deputy sheriff begins.

By the end of the day, during weapon training, the deputy sheriff is yelling nonstop at them because they do not have much strength left.

"Move faster, you morons!" the deputy sheriff says, "You look like you haven't had lunch!"

Big Joe, Noah and Hunter are all pissed at this moment. In fact, they are hangry: angry at the verbal abuse by the deputy sheriff, and hungry because there was barely any food in their stomachs.

"You, the stupid coyote, move your short ass sword!" the deputy sheriff says.

Hunter is furious. He has never been so hungry before, eating almost nothing for two straight days, and burning calories like crazy. He cannot take the hunger anymore, and he is being yelled at by this mediocre human being using derogatory terms.

Hunter lunges his back, jumps up towards the deputy sheriff with his claws and teeth wide open, and then inserts his claws and teeth right into the deputy sheriff's flesh, causing streams of blood to flood onto the floor.

Hunter tears into the deputy sheriff with terrifying hunger.

Big Joe and Noah freeze, horror tightening their throats. The stench of blood is enough to rattle even them. The blood of the deputy sheriff is calling them, seducing them, and reminding them of how good raw human flesh and blood taste and how good violent killings feel. But Big Joe and Noah resist the urge to join. They resist because they no longer want to go down the dark path of fueling the cruel shadows within.

Suddenly, six other deputy sheriffs show up.

Hunter, with the dead deputy sheriff's meat inside his mouth, has his eyes wide open and gets in his fight position. Big Joe and Noah do the same. They have no idea what will happen next.

The expressions on the deputy sheriffs turn from being serious and mean to smiling, and they start clapping with their hands, "Congratulations, Hunter! You passed the final test."

Hunter is confused. So are Big Joe and Noah.

One deputy sheriff explains, "The final test is for you to eat a human being. The reason why there was not enough food while there were enough verbal attacks, is to push you to your edge, so you eat the deputy sheriff. You have graduated from the Demon Academy!"

Hunter smiles and looks at Big Joe and Noah. Big Joe and Noah feel strange saying "Congratulations!" to Hunter.

Hunter asks, "How do Big Joe and Noah graduate now?"

"Easy," says a deputy sheriff as he points at the door, "Eat them."

They look towards the door, and two deputy sheriffs bring out two human beings.

They are Alicia and Maria.

Big Joe's and Noah's hearts sink to the bottom. Earlier, they had secretly loosened Alicia's and Maria's handcuffs so that they could escape.

The deputy sheriff continues, "We found these two bitches near the Academy."

Alicia spits at the deputy sheriff talking, "Brad, I knew you were part of this!"

Maria curses, "You goddamn demons!"

All the deputy sheriffs laugh as Alicia and Maria struggle to get out of the handcuffs.

Sheriff Hampson walks in and joins the rest of the deputy sheriffs in laughing, "Let's show them who we are."

The Sheriff and deputy sheriffs change their forms from human beings to demons. Sheriff Hampson has four eyes, an elongated neck, long droopy ears, a short beard, and crew cut hair. One deputy sheriff has horns on his head, spikes on his cheek, and claws. Another deputy sheriff has a huge, wide head, a wide mouth with around forty teeth, hair split from the middle, and claws. Another deputy sheriff has spikes on his head as well as cheeks and chin. Another deputy sheriff has long hair, spikes on each side of his head, a mustache, and long teeth. Another deputy sheriff looks like a giant spider, with multiple eyes, legs and arms. The last one has two large horns and fatty egg sacks on its neck with horns.

Alicia and Maria look horrified. But they quickly calm themselves down.

To Big Joe and Noah, this comes as no surprise. They always see demons for how they truly look instead of the human disguise they put on. It is an ability they have naturally as cryptids.

"So what, you are going to eat us now, four-eyed demon, Sheriff Hampson?" Alicia asks.

"Oh, sweetie, no, no, no, we are not going to eat you," Sheriff Hampson says, "They are." He points to Big Joe and Noah.

Big Joe and Noah look at each other. They are not sure what to do. They are surrounded by demons. How can they rescue Alicia and Maria, fight the demons, and get out at the same time?

Hunter's voice cracks, "If you eat them, you'll belong. That's what they want." His eyes flicker between hunger and hesitation, torn between the Academy and the bond he'd found.

"Well, we are going to make this interesting." Sheriff Hampson looks at the deputy sheriffs holding Alicia and Maria, "Release them."

The deputy sheriffs open the handcuffs on Alicia and Maria.

"Alicia and Maria, you have five minutes to run as fast as you can." Sheriff Hampson says, "Big Joe and Noah, you need to capture and eat them, if you want to become one of us."

"Timer starts now." Sheriff Hampson says.

Alicia and Maria start running away from the Justice Academy. They are fit, well-trained deputy sheriffs and can run very fast.

Five minutes later, Big Joe and Noah start running after Alicia and Maria. The demon deputy sheriffs follow them around to ensure they will not escape. When they are running side by side, Big Joe and Noah whisper to each other a plan of rescue for Alicia and Maria.

Big Joe and Noah soon approach Alicia and Maria. As they get closer, Alicia and Maria turn around to fist fight with Big Joe and Noah. Alicia says, "Are you going to let us go again?"

Big Joe and Noah are surprised at how fast the ladies have analyzed the situation, but then it makes sense that the ladies have figured out they are trying to save them because of the earlier event.

Big Joe says, "Glad you figured out we are not with them. Listen, Noah will rescue you while I hold them up."

Noah says, "Correct. You two run towards me on a count of one, two, three!"

Alicia and Maria get close to Noah. Noah quickly holds both ladies with his hands and flies up. As the three of them fly away in the sky, Big Joe turns around to block the deputy sheriffs from chasing after them.

The deputy sheriffs see what happens and immediately start approaching Big Joe. It is a scene of six demons against one cryptid.

Big Joe is not afraid of facing multiple demons. He is the leader of the cryptids and has faced immense hardships before. Fighting six demons is nothing. He uses his size and strength to gain an advantage over the demons. The demons use their claws and sharp teeth to attack Big Joe. Big Joe grabs them, uses his strong muscles to remove them and throws them away like they are smelly, dripping, disgusting trash. But the demons keep coming back like cockroaches climbing a kitchen wall. He is getting tired fighting six opponents alone and is gradually losing his advantage, inch by inch.

This is when Noah flies back and starts to distract the demons. Three demons turn around to attack Noah with their punches, scratches and bites.

Even with Noah back, the cryptids are not holding up as well as they would like to. They barely had anything to eat for the last 48 hours and are fighting far more numbers of demons than themselves.

Then Sheriff Hampson joins the rest of the deputy sheriffs. He is much more tactical in his moves than the deputy sheriffs and quickly shifts the fight in their favor. His four eyes are wide open, and his fists are swift.

Eventually, Big Joe and Noah are captured after a hard, exhausting fight.

Hunter is not sure what he should do. He watches Big Joe and Noah rescue Alicia and Maria, and then watches them fight the deputy sheriffs. He understands that Big Joe and Noah are not here to join the demon team, so he feels betrayed in a way, but the friendship they built over the last few weeks is so real and fulfilling that he cannot force himself to hate them.

Hunter is perplexed.

Sheriff Hampson is angry. He sees Big Joe and Noah as traitors. And traitors deserve the worst punishment. He commands the deputy sheriffs to bring Big Joe and Noah to the indoor training center and to lock all doors. Hunter follows them in.

When everyone is inside, Sheriff Hampson says, "Arrest Hunter."

Hunter is caught off guard. He does not have a chance to fight before the deputy sheriffs apprehend him.

Sheriff Hampson approaches Hunter and uses his claws to cut Hunter's skin on his neck. Blood rushes down from the cut.

Big Joe and Noah look at Hunter, and their hearts break for this young soul.

"You've grown quite fond of this young guy, I heard." Sheriff Hampson says, "And that," he turns to deputy sheriffs, "my fellow demons, is a huge weakness."

Sheriff Hampson commands, "Now, I want you two to fight. Big Joe versus Noah. No joke. No pretending. One kills the other. And then Hunter can be saved. This is the only way to save Hunter. Otherwise, the main artery on Hunter's neck will be cut, and he will die a painful and immediate death."

Big Joe and Noah look at each other. They know they must fight to keep Hunter alive.

Sheriff Hampson asks the other deputy sheriff to throw the halberd and war hammer at Big Joe and Noah.

Big Joe and Noah grab the weapons. And so, the fight begins.

Big Joe starts by hitting Noah with his halberd, and Noah blocks it with his war hammer. The loud bang brings Big Joe and Noah back to when they first met.

It was in 1955. Big Joe was investigating a possible demon sighting in a recently opened theme park called Sunny Funny Land. Visitors to the theme park mysteriously disappeared overnight, leaving local authorities puzzled.

Big Joe walked around the theme park at night. It was dark with limited moonlight. "Where would a demon hide?" Big Joe thought to himself. Then he saw the Haunted Castle. "That's it!"

Big Joe propped open the door to the Haunted Castle and walked around the attraction route. It was designed to be the inside of a medieval castle with scary servants, zombie-looking lords and knights wearing armor and holding weapons.

He walked past the entrance and the Chapel into the Great Hall. A variety of armors are on each side of the hall. At the end of the hall, there was a lone gargoyle, crouching on the floor. The statue was grey-colored like the other armors.

Big Joe walked by the gargoyle and noticed that there was a spot on its foot that was not painted grey. He commented, "I guess the props guy missed a spot on the foot." Then he walked away.

After he turned around to the end of the hall, the gargoyle reached out its hand to a spray paint can hidden inside its wing and hit the button on top. A hissing sound started to come out of the can as the paint sprayed out onto its foot.

It was at night. No electricity was turned on. No sound was around except for Big Joe's footsteps. Then there came the hissing sound.

Big Joe turned around and ran back. The gargoyle's eyes met Big Joe's eyes. Big Joe thought, "Bingo! Here is the demon that had been eating visitors."

The gargoyle, a.k.a. Noah, was going to observe what Big Joe would do as he was undercover investigating the paranormal events in the theme park, but he was now discovered by Big Joe.

Big Joe ran forward and used his fist to punch Noah. Noah flew up, escaping Big Joe's powerful punch. Then Noah charged at Big Joe, using his claws to scratch his face. Big Joe used his arms to block the claws, but his skin was broken during this process. Big Joe saw an armor holding an axe, so he punched Noah and then ran to grab the axe as his weapon. Noah saw that Big Joe got a weapon and flew to another armor to take a spear as his weapon to use.

The two held their weapons and charged at each other. A loud bang was heard throughout the Haunted Castle when the axe hit the spear.

The loud bang at the Demon Academy sounds so familiar yet different.

"Fight! Fight! Fight!" the deputy sheriffs are chanting.

Big Joe and Noah are brought back to reality by the loud chanting noises. They continue to fight. Big Joe jumps up and uses gravity to hit Noah on his shoulder using the halberd. Noah blocks the halberd with his war hammer. Noah flies up and attacks Big Joe with his war hammer, and Big Joe hits back with his halberd. The two use their strength through the weapons confrontation, and separate because one cannot overrule the other. When they separate, both the halberd and the war hammer fall on the floor. Big Joe rolls over, Noah picks up the halberd from the floor and pokes Big Joe repeatedly, but Big Joe rolls fast to avoid being hurt by the halberd. Big Joe jumps up and grabs Noah's warhammer. Now their weapons are switched.

Iron sharpens iron, and one cryptid sharpens another.

Big Joe and Noah are letting out the tension between themselves as they fight. In the years that they have worked together, a dynamic has been building between the two of them. Big Joe's leadership style has been calm and tactical, while Noah prefers blunt force and refers to his style as "No BS".

When Big Joe and Noah let their built-up anger out during this fight, they cannot hold back. Big Joe cuts Noah on his shoulder, and Noah makes Big Joe bleed on his arm.

Hunter looks at Big Joe and Noah fighting tooth and nail and cannot help but feel guilty. They are forced to fight to save his life. If he had not been captured by the deputy sheriffs, Big Joe and Noah might have escaped already. They are not trying to join the demon team, which is obvious, but is that a valid reason to hate them? Look at what Sheriff Hampson did to him, arresting him and hurting him. The demon team does not even care about him. Yes, belonging to something feels great, and that was why he signed up for the Demon Academy in the first place. But doesn't he already belong to something that Big Joe, Noah, and he built over the past few weeks?

Hunter needs to fight for his team. Not the demon team, but the cryptid team. Seeing his teammates, Big Joe and Noah, bleed irritates him and worries him; he gets angrier by the second. Maybe it's the deputy sheriff that he ate, but he can feel his blood boiling. The more he watches Big Joe and Noah fight and kill each other to save himself, the more guilt and anger he feels.

When someone is furious, everything looks red, small and fragile.

Hunter breaks open the handcuffs with sheer strength from his arms and attacks Sheriff Hampson like the mad coyote that he is. His claws feel sharper, and his teeth can penetrate anything. He grabs onto Sheriff Hampson and starts to bite him.

The deputy sheriffs are shocked at what is happening at first, but they quickly jump in to help Sheriff Hampson. With the deputy sheriffs' claws and teeth, Hunter is getting bit and scratched non-stop, causing him to bleed constantly.

Seeing what is happening with Hunter, Big Joe and Noah stop their fight and rush over to help Hunter. But it's the three of them against six deputy sheriffs and Sheriff Hampson. Anger helps them to fight, but they are outnumbered.

Hunter loses more blood. By now, his clothes are soaked with blood. He just wants Big Joe and Noah to leave and live, so he yells at them, "Big Joe and Noah! Let me hold them over! You two go!"

Big Joe will not leave him, "No, Hunter, we are in this together!"

Noah neither, "Hunter, no way! We will not leave you behind!"

Just when they are losing hope, the doors to the indoor training center are kicked open.

In walk Chupa, Saxon, Grey, Nessie, Rake, Aura, Mei, and Cole.

Back when Noah flew Alicia and Maria away, he gave them the keys to the SUV and asked them to reach out to Camp Moonlit Smiles. The deputy sheriffs went through the SUV when they found Alicia and Maria and took away Big Joe's and Noah's cell phones.

As a result, they could not contact the cryptid team remotely. Alicia and Maria drove the SUV directly to Camp Moonlit Smiles and asked the cryptids for help.

So here the cryptids are, saving the day.

The cryptids immediately raise their weapons to fight the deputy sheriffs.

Chupa throws Big Joe his axe, and Rake throws Noah his spear.

Chupa uses his rope to form a knot and aims it at Sheriff Hampson. But one deputy sheriff sees it and grabs the rope. Saxon flies up, uses his bow and arrows to shoot at deputy sheriffs, and the arrows hit three of them, penetrating their arm, leg, and shoulder. Grey uses his sniper rifle with laser blade to charge at a deputy sheriff and is met with gunfire from that deputy sheriff. Nessie uses her flail to hit a deputy sheriff, and it hits the demon's shoulder. Rake uses his dagger to close combat a deputy sheriff. Aura swings her tomahawk towards a deputy sheriff and hits the deputy sheriff with a shoulder wound. She continues to puncture the deputy sheriff with her long nails on multiple limbs. Mei uses her sword to stab a deputy sheriff on their chest, but he moves to the side, so the sword misses him. Cole shoots multiple rounds of bullets at Sheriff Hampson, and the bullets penetrate his shoulders and arms.

Sheriff Hampson and his deputy sheriffs are outnumbered and outgunned.

The tables are turned.

Sheriff Hampson turns to his deputy sheriffs and signals that it's time to flee. His deputies start moving towards him, making a circle. Sheriff Hampson holds Hunter hostage with his claws. Hunter has lost a lot of blood and cannot fight anymore.

"Stop! If you move, I will slit Hunter's throat." Sheriff Hampson yells.

Big Joe signals the cryptid team to stop.

Sheriff Hampson demands, "I will walk out, and none of you can follow me." He walks out with his claws on Hunter, facing the cryptids. The deputy sheriffs surround him and Hunter and walk with them.

Once Sheriff Hampson walks out of the indoor training center, he cuts Hunter's throat and runs away. Hunter falls on the ground. The rest of deputy sheriffs run away with Sheriff Hampson.

Big Joe and Noah immediately run towards Hunter. Big Joe holds Hunter's shoulder while applying pressure on Hunter's main artery. But blood keeps pouring out. Sheriff Hampson slit Hunter's neck with such force that his neck is barely attached to his body.

The rest of the cryptids, Mei and Cole, run after Sheriff Hampson and deputy sheriffs.

Big Joe says, "Hunter, hang on. We are going to get you out of here."

Noah holds Hunter's hand, "Bro, don't worry. We are going to get you medical help."

But the blood floods Hunter's clothes, Big Joe's arms, and Noah's hand.

"It's okay. I know it's my time." Hunter says, "Look, I see the Great Bear." He looks up at the sky, "I bet it tastes great."

Big Joe and Noah chuckle, but at the same time, they are immersed in great sadness. They cannot believe their little buddy is dying. They feel guilty. Maybe if they did not go undercover, Hunter would have lived a long life, albeit a demon's life.

"Thank you for teaching me the right way." Hunter says, lowering his head, "I like it that I belong."

Big Joe and Noah look at Hunter and cannot help but cry. Hunter lies drenched in blood, his young face finally still. The desperate hunger, the searching, the need to belong. All of it ends in silence beneath the stars.

There is something powerful when two bulky guys sob. Big Joe and Noah almost never let their vulnerabilities out, but at this moment, nothing else matters except for mourning for their little bro.

Hunter was young. He was full of hope. But the demons, especially Sheriff Hampson, took that away from him.

The rest of the cryptids are able to capture all six deputy sheriffs. But Sheriff Hampson, the sneaky four-eyed sheriff, the demon that slit Hunter's throat, got away.

Big Joe and Noah are angry, angry that they are not able to capture Sheriff Hampson.

Noah starts to punch the deputy sheriffs non-stop. After a while, Big Joe grabs his arm and stops him, "Noah, that's enough. We need to send these demons back and then plan on how to capture Sheriff Hampson. Let's put our anger towards making it happen."

Noah drags his arm out from Big Joe's hand and hits the floor, trying to calm himself down.

"Let's look for their sigils." Big Joe asks the cryptids.

Chupa and Saxon stay with Big Joe and Noah to keep an eye out for the handcuffed deputy sheriffs. Alicia and Maria come out of the RV now that the deputy sheriffs are captured. Earlier, they were too weak to fight, so they stayed hidden.

Grey, Nessie, Rake, Aura, Mei and Cole spread out to look for sigils.

Usually, the demons have their sigils carved together. Aura finds some sigils in the main office behind a giant Sheriff's Office shield.

There are six sigils, which makes sense for the six sheriff deputies they caught. Big Joe is disappointed that they cannot locate Sheriff Hampson's sigil. But again, it makes sense because the four-eyed demon is as sneaky as a snake.

Same drill. Mei pokes her finger and smears her blood onto the six sigils. The deputy sheriffs are raised up by a bright red light, then they are banished back to the Hell dimension.

After the cryptids get back to the campground, Big Joe and Noah dig a grave by their bare hands to bury Hunter.

"Hunter, my friend. You are home," Big Joe says, "where you belong."

"Rest in power, little bro." Noah makes the sign of the cross using three fingers, touching his head, chest, and shoulders.

From Hunter's grave, the Great Bear is visible all year long. That night, the stars are as clear as can be, shining brightly down.

CHAPTER EIGHT

The Revenge

After wiping their tears off, Big Joe and Noah are ready to take down the sneaky four-eyed demon, Sheriff Hampson. They need a good plan, a plan that is strategic and tactical to banish the demon back to Hell.

Good thing they have Alicia and Maria, who know the Sheriff's Office inside out.

At lunch, Alicia and Maria try Chupa's famous goat chops.

"These are delicious! Chupa, you are a great chef." Maria says.

"I agree, these are some goat chops to die for," Alicia says.

"Thank you! I seriously considered being a full-time chef. But you know, if people see me, they will probably freak out. So that won't work." Chupa says, "Speaking of jobs, are you going back to work now that you know who Sheriff Hampson is, Alicia and Maria?"

"I obviously do not want to work for Sheriff Hampson anymore. I knew there was something fishy about that guy the day he took office." Alicia says.

"Yea there's no way I'm going to work for that four-eyed demon any longer." Maria agrees.

"How about you work for the Navajo Sheriff's Department?" Aura suggests, "You two will be perfect for Navajo."

"Really?" Alicia is intrigued. So is Maria.

"Of course! The fact that you suspected something was wrong, investigated, and fought the demons is enough to show your abilities." Aura says.

"Aura, you think Sheriff Dyami will be willing to hire Alicia and Maria?" Chupa chimes in.

"I can surely put in my recommendation," Aura says.

"You do have a lot of sway in your town." Chupa says, then turns to Alicia and Maria, "I'm sure they will hire you."

"I'm down for it," Maria says.

"Me too." Alicia agrees.

Big Joe and Noah look at each other, and they both look solemn. They know what each other is thinking about.

"Let's go to the meeting room." Big Joe says.

The cryptids, Mei, Cole, Alicia and Maria go inside the meeting room.

"Let's brainstorm some ideas to capture Sheriff Hampson." Big Joe says, "Alicia and Maria, could you tell us what you know about him and the Sheriff's Office? Anything helps."

Alicia says, "Sure. I've been in the Sheriff's Office for a little over seven years. From what I heard, there was something fishy about the previous Sheriff's scandal."

"Tell us more," Noah says.

"The previous Sheriff was Jocelyn Brown. I heard there was a whistleblower report against her for misconduct. The District Attorney's Office was investigating. She was put on administrative leave. But suddenly, she resigned." Alicia says.

Maria chimes in, "There was an article on Neptune News about Sheriff Brown."

Mei says, "Sounds like we need to interview Sheriff Brown on what truly happened."

Big Joe agrees, "Alicia and Maria, do you have Sheriff Brown's contact information?"

Maria says, "I was told to delete her contact information from the County system by Sheriff Hampson. But I took a photo of it before I deleted the page. Let me look through my Cloud storage for the photo."

Cole leans forward, "I'll run a trace. If she's still in your storage, we'll find her." He pulls the laptop open, his fingers already flying over the keys.

And so, with Cole's help, Maria locates Sheriff Brown's contact information.

The cryptids, Mei and Cole, read the article on Neptune News on Sheriff Brown in order to gather more information.

The article indicated, "The former Sheriff of County of San Cara, Jocelyn Brown, resigned amid a scandal. The District Attorney's Office was actively investigating Brown based on a whistleblower report. The report alerted authorities to misconduct by Brown's administration. No charges have been filed against Brown."

"I think the first step is for us to visit Jocelyn Brown. We need to find out what the reason was for the investigation and resignation." Big Joe says.

Mei says, "Agreed. Alicia and Maria, I think it would be great if you two can come with Cole and I to interview Jocelyn."

"Sure!" Alicia and Maria are happy to help.

"While you interview Jocelyn, Big Joe and I can stay in the RV and eavesdrop," Noah says.

Chupa suggests, "Saxon and I can keep watch for the Sheriff's Office."

So, the humans and cryptids decide on the next steps and begin their respective tasks.

Noah drives the RV with Big Joe, Mei, Cole, Alicia, and Maria to Jocelyn Brown's house.

Alicia, Maria, Mei and Cole walk up to Jocelyn Brown's front door. Alicia rings the doorbell.

Jocelyn happens to be home. She opens the door.

Alicia and Maria smile, "Hello, Sheriff Brown! Do you remember us?"

Sheriff Brown is surprised, "Of course, Alicia and Maria."

Alicia says, "These are our friends, Mei and Cole. Sorry to show up unannounced like this, but we are investigating what happened in the Sheriff's Office and need your help."

Sheriff Brown says, "Sorry, I signed an NDA with the County. I can't talk about anything."

Maria says, "Alicia and I discovered what Sheriff Hampson has been doing at the Academy. For the safety of the community, we need to know what really happened with your investigation."

Alicia agrees, "Sheriff Brown, you are the first African American Sheriff elected in the County of San Cara. I'm sure you care about the community that put their trust in you."

Sheriff Brown is intrigued, "What did you discover on the Academy?"

"Sheriff Hampson turned it into a Demon Academy," Maria says.

"Demon Academy?" Sheriff Brown responds, "Well believe it or not, that makes sense. Come on in."

Alicia, Maria, Mei and Cole step into Sheriff Brown's house. It is a simple house. Everything looks clean and sleek.

"What do you mean, 'Demon Academy actually makes sense' ,Sheriff Brown?" Maria asks.

"At first, DA's office informed me of a whistleblower report." Sheriff Brown says, "I did not do anything wrong, so I figured nothing would come out of the report or investigation. Then one day, I was called in to meet the County Executive and the District Attorney. They told me that I was found guilty of corruption. I was utterly shocked. They told me that I had an option to resign and sign the NDA. I was not going to do it. I was prepared to fight."

"What made you change your mind?" Alicia asks.

"It was the night after the meeting. I talked with my attorney and came home. Then I noticed something strange sitting in my living room with its back towards me." Sheriff Brown says, "I immediately pulled my gun out and said, 'Freeze! Who is there?' The thing turned its head over, and I saw a creature with not one, not two, not three, but four eyes! I was shocked and fired at this creature. But the creature was not even bothered one bit by the bullets."

Alicia, Maria, Mei and Cole exchange a look, thinking, "It was Sheriff Hampson, the four-eyed demon!"

Sheriff Brown's voice drops. "It turned its four eyes on me and whispered one word. 'Resign.' The sound wasn't just in the room. It crawled inside my skull. My finger pulled the trigger again and again, but the thing just kept smiling. The creature repeated, 'Resign. Sign the NDA.' I told it that there was no way I was going to resign or sign the NDA. Not only that, but I was planning to fight hard. The creature smirked and said, 'If not, your beloved father will die right now.' Another creature brought in my father, who was already unconscious."

"Despicable!" Maria says.

Sheriff Brown nods, "That was when I knew that I had to sign the NDA. My father is the only family I have. None of my bullets worked against these creatures. I had no defense against them."

"Sorry to hear that. You are the best Sheriff that the County has had. You made a huge impact on the community before you were forced to resign." Alicia says.

"Thank you. That means a lot to me. And now I know that these creatures are indeed demons like I suspected." Sheriff Brown says.

"Yes, they are." Maria says, "Mei, Cole, and their friends have been working on tracking and eliminating these demons."

"Good for you." Sheriff Brown says with her eyes light up for a second, then the light in her eyes dims, "Excuse me, I need to check on my father. He has been bedridden ever since that night."

"Oh my gosh. I'm so sorry to hear that. Of course." Alicia says.

Sheriff Brown goes upstairs to check on her father and comes downstairs, "He is okay. He is asleep." She sits down and looks at Alicia, Maria, Mei and Cole in their eyes with determination and hope, "Destroy these goddamn demons, that's all I ask of you."

Alicia, Maria, Mei and Cole say goodbye to Sheriff Brown and walk towards the RV. Their shoulders feel heavy, as if weights are placed on them. They know that they carry Sheriff Brown's hopes and dreams of justice with them as they walk away.

In the meantime, Chupa and Saxon drive Aura's sedan and arrive outside the Sheriff's Office to keep watch. They cannot drive the SUV because it was seen by the deputy sheriffs, maybe even by Sheriff Hampson, when it was parked at Demon Academy.

They observe cars coming in and out of the Sheriff's Office. There are a lot of cars. All day long, Chupa and Saxon keep watch in the sedan. Then dust falls upon them. There are fewer cars coming in and out.

After midnight, an unmarked truck comes out of the Sheriff's Office parking lot. It is a simple white van like any contractor would drive. The windows in the back of the van are covered. From the front windshield, they see two deputy sheriffs driving. It seems unusual for this white van to come out of Sheriff's Office after midnight.

Chupa drives the sedan to follow the unmarked van at a distance. Chupa turns off the sedan's headlights to stay undiscovered. His night vision helps him follow the van.

The van first drives around the neighborhood in circles.

Saxon says to Chupa, "I guess the deputy sheriffs are well-trained on counter reconnaissance measures."

"Yep, we must be careful. They might be setting up traps for us after Sheriff Hampson was almost captured." Chupa agrees.

The van continues to drive randomly in downtown San Cara. Then it speeds up.

Chupa follows the van, "Good thing I'm a great driver."

The van speeds up and enters the freeway, driving north towards Oasis Moon Bay. "Now they are going somewhere!" says Saxon.

Chupa drives the sedan to follow the white unmarked van. It seems that the deputy sheriffs are going directly towards their destination now, after the initial deterrence. After around 20 miles, the van exits the freeway. It continues to drive for about 10 minutes and arrives at its destination: the pier of Oasis Moon Bay.

The deputy sheriffs park the van near the pier and walk out. Chupa quietly parks the sedan at a distance and walks out with Saxon to spy on the deputy sheriffs.

It is dark and cold after midnight, and the deputy sheriffs stand against the van under the yellow streetlight that is shining down.

A light starts to appear on the water. It comes closer and closer until it docks on the pier. Chupa and Saxon see that it is a two-tiered fishing boat.

The deputy sheriffs walk over to the boat. Three men come out.

They converse briefly, and then the deputy sheriffs walk towards the parked van. One deputy sheriff opens the trunk doors, and the two of them carry out a heavy wooden crate box. They walk towards the boat and hand the crate box to two of the men. The deputy sheriffs continue to carry out four additional crates from the van and hand them to the men. The men then load the crate boxes onto the boat.

Chupa and Saxon look at each other and wonder what is in the crate boxes.

After they load up the crate boxes onto the boat, the two deputy sheriffs close the trunk doors, start the van and leave. The men start the boat engine as well.

Chupa and Saxon choose not to follow the deputy sheriffs. Instead, Saxon flies up to the top of the boat, and Chupa jumps across the water onto the boat.

The three men are all at the wheelhouse of the fishing boat, so they do not notice Chupa or Saxon. Under the darkness of the night, Chupa and Saxon sneak into the cabin where the crate boxes were carried into.

Staring at the wooden crate boxes, Chupa whispers to Saxon, "Here's where my claws come in handy again." He uses his claws to skillfully move around the nail caps and pull them out. Afterwards, Chupa and Saxon lift the cover up.

Inside the crate box are dried yellow straws. Saxon moves the straws away, and the real commodities reveal themselves: weapons. There lie pistols, rifles, shotguns, and grenades in the crate. The weapons look like they are custom-made and have strange, alien-looking features.

Chupa and Saxon check all five crate boxes, and each of them contains multiple weapons.

"Damn," Chupa says, looking at Saxon.

"Yep. I wonder how often they do this and who they sell these weapons to." Saxon says.

Chupa closes the crate boxes. They leave the boat with Saxon flying and carrying Chupa. Good thing the boat has not gone too far from the pier.

Chupa and Saxon drive the sedan back to the Sheriff's Office to continue monitoring. While they wait and observe in the sedan, they call Big Joe up via video conferencing.

By now, Big Joe, Noah, Mei, Cole, Alicia and Maria have returned to Camp Moonlit Smiles.

Big Joe picks up the phone, "Hello, Chupa. How's it going?"

Chupa says, "Good. Saxon and I discovered that the deputy sheriffs sold weapons to a fishing boat."

"Really? Let me put you up on the screen." Big Joe says, signaling everyone to join him in the meeting room, "Hold on, Chupa."

Big Joe continues, "Okay, we are ready. Chupa and Saxon, great job on your discovery. How did you find out?"

Saxon says, "Chupa and I were spying on the Sheriff's Office when an unmarked white van drove out after midnight. We followed the van and noticed that they drove to Oasis Moon Bay."

"The pier where we went to before?" Nessie asks.

"Affirmative. What are the chances, huh?" Chupa says.

"Then two deputy sheriffs came out of the parked van. We noticed a two-tiered fishing boat approaching the pier." Saxon says, "Three men came down from the boat and met the deputy sheriffs. Then they brought five crate boxes from the parked van to the boat."

"Guess what are inside the crate boxes?" Chupa asks.

"If the Sheriff's Office is illegally selling something, it could only be weapons?" Nessie says.

"Yep." Chupa says, "All kinds of weapons. Pistols, rifles, you name it. But the weapons look like they are custom-made and have some strange Alien-looking features."

"Interesting. Great investigation." Big Joe says.

"Are you going to continue monitoring the Sheriff's Office?" Noah asks.

"Yep, that's the plan. We suspect that this is not an isolated incident." Saxon says.

"Folks, what do you think we should do to expose the Sheriff?" Big Joe asks everyone.

"I'm thinking if we can film the transaction and put it online, the public will pressure for a full investigation by a third party," Cole says.

"Agreed. Cole and I can go and work with Chupa and Saxon." Mei says.

Big Joe and Noah also want to go with Mei and Cole.

So, they drive the RV over to meet Chupa and Saxon outside of the Sheriff's Office.

For the next six days, cars come in and out of the Sheriff's Office parking lot, but nothing seems to be of much interest or concern. Most of the cars are marked with the Sheriff's Office logo.

On the seventh day, at midnight, everyone opens their eyes wide to observe. Unlike previous nights of disappointment, an unmarked van is seen leaving the Sheriff's Office parking lot.

Big Joe, Noah, Chupa, Saxon, Mei and Cole get excited.

"Finally, some action!" Noah says and starts the engine of the RV. Cole starts to record using a camera pointing at the white van.

The white van does the same thing as the previous outing, circling around, speeding, and turning suddenly. After the initial efforts of deterrence, the van starts heading north towards Oasis Moon Bay.

Like the previous night, the van exits the freeway and drives towards the pier.

Noah drives the RV to follow the white van closely, but not too close so that the van can discover them.

The white van parks near the pier, and two deputy sheriffs walk out. Everything seems to be Deja vu. The darkness, the coldness, and the yellow streetlight.

A light starts to appear on the water. It comes closer and closer until it docks on the pier. The group sees that it is a two-tiered fishing boat.

Here is where Chupa and Saxon are expecting the three men to come out of the fishing boat, if everything goes the same as the other night. Cole points the camera at the fishing boat.

But something feels odd and different about tonight. Something does not make sense. Something does not add up. But Chupa and Saxon cannot pinpoint exactly what the difference is.

The group notices some movement coming from the fishing boat. Everyone's eyes are laser-focused on the boat.

All of a sudden, five demons in deputy sheriffs' uniforms surround the RV. "It's a trap!" Big Joe yells to the group.

Two more demons burst out of the fishing boat, running towards the RV. The two deputy sheriffs near the white van start charging towards the cryptids, too. The four of them run and join forces with the five demons surrounding the RV.

Big Joe, Noah, Chupa, Saxon, Mei and Cole jump outside of the RV with their weapons, immediately fighting with nine demons.

Big Joe uses his axe to swing at a demon, cutting his arm open while being hit by the demon's sword. Chupa uses his rope to tie a demon's hands together, but the demon is strong enough to break the rope open. Saxon flies up with his bow and arrows, shooting three arrows at once and penetrating two demons' arms and shoulders, missing the third demon because the demon used a khopesh to block it. Noah flies up and pokes a demon with his spear, forcing the demon to block the spear with his claws, making the demon bleed. Mei uses her sword to cut a demon's ear off. Cole shoots holes in the demons.

The cryptids are fighting tooth and nail with the demons. Neither party is winning by an inch.

This is when Sheriff Hampson, the four-eyed demon, comes out of the fishing boat to join the fight. Now the cryptids are outnumbered.

Sheriff Hampson laughs as he fights Big Joe and Noah with his mace, yelling, "One cannot fight evil and win, for darkness consumes all."

Big Joe fights Sheriff Hampson with Noah and says, "Light shines in the darkness, and the darkness cannot overcome it."

Just as Big Joe finishes his sentence, Grey, Nessie, Rake, and Aura come out of a bus parked nearby and join the fight of light shining over darkness.

Back when the cryptids were video conferencing, Big Joe wondered whether the weapons sale was a trap. Aura thought there was a huge possibility that it was a trap set up by Sheriff Hampson to capture them after his last defeat. So, they came up with a plan to fight the demons if it turned out to be a trap. Mei mentioned a Chinese saying, "Tang lang bu chan, huang que zai hou.", which means "The mantis catches the cicada, unaware of the siskin behind; to pursue a narrow gain while neglecting a greater danger."

Now, the siskins are here, right behind the mantises.

Grey carries his sniper rifle with a laser blade. He shoots a round using his rifle, then battles in close range with a demon using his laser blade. The laser cuts the demon's legs, but Grey's skin is wounded by the demon's knife as well.

Nessie swings her flail towards a demon, but the demon dodges it. Chupa sees it and throws his rope to capture the demon, and Nessie swings the flail again, this time hitting the demon hard, causing him a lot of blood.

Rake stabs a demon with his dagger by grabbing the demon's horn. He repeatedly stabs, and the demon tries to run away.

Aura changes shape into a big monster and joins Big Joe in his fight with Sheriff Hampson. She chops a piece of flesh off Sheriff Hampson with her tomahawk, while Big Joe uses his axe to stop Sheriff Hampson's mace from hitting Aura.

Seeing that the demons are surrounded by the cryptids, Sheriff Hampson starts retreating with the rest of the demons. The cryptids will not budge and start doubling down on their attacks.

For Big Joe and Noah, they focus their efforts on capturing Sheriff Hampson. Their eyes are turning red because they want to banish the four-eyed demon, badly, for Hunter's sake.

But the demons are not stupid. They start to gradually surround Sheriff Hampson, who is obviously their boss, shielding his escape.

As the cryptids are fighting the rest of the demons, Sheriff Hampson turns around and runs away to the fishing boat.

146

Big Joe and Noah are tied up in the fight with the deputy sheriffs. Seeing Sheriff Hampson escape, Noah starts to get furious. And so does Big Joe, even though he always tries to restrain himself from anger. With anger as their fuel, both Big Joe and Noah possess joint forces so strong that the rest of the demons are no match. In no time, the cryptids capture all nine demons.

Big Joe and Noah try to chase after Sheriff Hampson, but by now the four-eyed demon has escaped too far for them to reach. The tall ocean waves left behind by Sheriff Hampson are singing a mad song.

The demons are beaten up badly, with black and purple bruises everywhere.

Chupa uses his ropes to tie up all the demons, and Noah locks them up in the bus, the RV and the sedan.

Noah drives the bus, Big Joe drives the RV, and Chupa drives the sedan. The three vehicles head south.

Chupa and Saxon sit in front of the sedan, and the two deputy sheriffs stay in the backseat, tied up like caterpillars in cocoons.

Chupa says, "I want to go grab some goat chops for later today."

"Oh, I could eat some of your world-famous goat chops!" Saxon gets excited, "Let me text the rest of the team that we will be late."

And so, Chupa drives to the butcher they always go to on Farm Way called "Steak Through the Heart Chop Shop".

Chupa gets off the sedan with Saxon waiting and watching the two deputy sheriffs.

Back when Chupa attempted to grab some goat chops without being discovered, he would sneak inside the butcher shop when the butcher was not looking, grab a bag to put all the goat chops in, then leave enough cash on the counter to cover the bill. This happened so many times that the butcher accepted it as the weird behavior of a customer. So, every day the butcher prepared a bag of freshly cut goat chops in his shop, and when the bag was gone, he knew cash would be left on the counter.

Today is no exception. Chupa sneaks in and sees that the butcher has left a huge bag of goat chops for the mysteriously shy customer, a.k.a. himself. Chupa gets excited as he quickly grabs the bag and leaves cash on the counter. He can almost taste the tender, juicy, and savory goat chops, and his mouth starts to water.

Chupa walks out proudly with the bag of goat chops he just bought. When he enters the parking lot, he sees that the three doors of the sedan are wide open. No one is inside. He thinks it's weird, so he yells, "Saxon?"

Chupa hears nothing. He starts to get concerned and looks around for Saxon.

At this moment, Chupa sees Saxon fly towards him.

After Saxon lands, Chupa asks, "Saxon, what happened? I just went to grab this bag of goat chops and suddenly everything changed."

Saxon says, "Just after you went in, Sheriff Hampson drove the white van over and fought me to rescue the two deputy sheriffs. I could not stop him, so I flew away to track them."

Chupa pats Saxon on his back, "Well, at least you are okay. Let's call Big Joe and let him know. We should go back and talk to the group." He gets in the sedan, "And I'm starving! Can't wait to cook the goat chops and devour them."

Chupa and Saxon drive the sedan back to Camp Moonlit Smiles.

At the Sheriff's Office, Sheriff Hampson and the two deputy sheriffs arrive in the white unmarked van.

Sheriff Hampson follows the deputy sheriffs and enters his office.

Deputy Sheriff Miller says, "Sir, what should we do about the upcoming delivery? Should we change location since the creatures found out about Oasis Moon Bay?"

Sheriff Hampson replies, "The most dangerous place is the safest place. The creatures will not fathom that we still dare to transact there."

"Yes, Sir. I will let our contact know that the plan is as-is." Deputy Sheriff Miller says.

Sheriff Hampson says, "Are we ready for the transaction?"

Deputy Sheriff Davis responds, "Yes, Sir. The weapons are ready to be delivered. We have packed all ten crate boxes of ammunition."

"Good. Let's complete the transaction and then deal with the creatures afterwards." Sheriff Hampson says, "How many of us are left?"

"Sir, just you, Miller, and I are left. The rest have been captured by the creatures." Deputy Sheriff Davis replies.

Sheriff Hampson says, "Okay. I'll go with you to seal the deal."

The next day is the planned weapons sale.

At midnight, Sheriff Hampson, Deputy Sheriff Miller, and Deputy Sheriff Davis drive the unmarked white van loaded with ten crate boxes. They are meeting a gang named the Unseen. The agreement is that once the weapons are received, digital currency will be transferred to Sheriff Hampson's digital wallet.

The white van parks at the pier of Oasis Moon Bay. Sheriff Hampson, Deputy Sheriff Miller, and Deputy Sheriff Davis step outside of the van. The three of them wait under the yellow streetlight that is shining down.

Like Deja vu, a light starts to appear on the water. The light floats closer and closer until it reaches the pier dock. This time, instead of two-tiered, it's a one-tiered fishing boat.

Five men in black outfits walk out of the fishing boat. Sheriff Hampson, Deputy Sheriff Miller, and Deputy Sheriff Davis walk up to greet the Unseen.

"You've gotten crate boxes of ammunition?" The shortest man asks.

"Affirmative." Deputy Sheriff Miller replies.

"Let's see them." The short man says.

They walk towards the white van. Deputy Sheriff Davis opens the trunk doors.

The men check all ten crate boxes to ensure each one has weapons inside. Then the short man says, "Your money will be there now."

Sheriff Hampson asks Deputy Sheriff Miller to check that the transaction has been made, then gives ok for the men to take the crate boxes to the fishing boat.

The five men take ten crate boxes to the fishing boat. They make two trips each.

After the transaction is finished, Deputy Sheriff Miller and Deputy Sheriff Davis look at Sheriff Hampson proudly while preparing to leave the scene.

Out of nowhere, Sheriff Hampson yells into the darkness, "You got that?"

The five men are already aboard the fishing boat, but they look back at Sheriff Hampson to see what is going on.

Deputy Sheriff Miller and Deputy Sheriff Davis are confused. They ask, "Sir, what did you say?"

"Yep, we got that!" Someone yells back at Sheriff Hampson in the dark.

Deputy Sheriff Miller and Deputy Sheriff Davis turn around to look in the direction where the voice came from. But they see nothing except for darkness. They turn around and are shocked to see Chupa and Saxon standing right in front of them. Chupa grins wide, showing his fangs. "Well, look who crawled back. Last time you ran without saying goodbye. That hurt my feelings."

Deputy Sheriff Miller and Deputy Sheriff Davis start running away from Chupa and Saxon, but they don't run far before Chupa and Saxon catch up to them and start throwing punches. They attempt to fight back, but since they never fully recovered from when they were captured, they are easily beaten up by the cryptids.

The five men start the engine of the fishing boat and attempt to escape from the chaotic trap. In a flash, one giant brown furry creature jumps onto the fishing boat, and another giant creature with wings flies to the fishing boat.

As it turns out, they are Big Joe and Noah.

The five men from the Unseen feel seen by the two giant creatures. They start using their fists to punch Big Joe and Noah. But the differences in size and strength mean that the men are no match for the cryptids. Before long, the five men are picked up by Big Joe and Noah by their legs like chickens being held upside down.

By now, Chupa and Saxon have tied Deputy Sheriff Miller and Deputy Sheriff Davis up.

Sheriff Hampson walks over. Deputy Sheriff Miller and Deputy Sheriff Davis are hopeful that Sheriff Hampson can rescue them from Chupa and Saxon again.

Boy, are they shocked when Sheriff Hampson high-fives Chupa and Saxon. Deputy Sheriff Miller and Deputy Sheriff Davis look at Sheriff Hampson in disbelief, until they witness Sheriff Hampson change shape into a beautiful lady right in front of their eyes.

Aura winks at the demons.

Mei and Cole walk out with camera equipment.

"We've got the transaction all on video. Sheriff Hampson will be exposed." Mei says and turns towards the two demons and five men, "Welcome to your fifteen minutes of fame. Don't forget to like and subscribe to our TheyTube channel SpiritScouts!"

"Great job, team!" Big Joe says.

"Let's send the demons back," Aura says.

Earlier, Aura had located the sigils for all demons captured in Sheriff Hampson's office. The cryptids bring all the demons captured to the Sheriff's Office under the moonlight. With Mei's blood on the sigils, the demons are banished back to Hell.

The next day, a video of scandalous illegal weapons sale to gangsters goes up on Mei's TheyTube channel. The public is furious about elected official Sheriff Hampson. FBI agents are immediately deployed to the investigation.

Then overnight, five members of the Unseen, tied up, are dropped off in front of the Sheriff's Office while FBI agents are present.

That night, Big Joe and Noah stand in front of Hunter's grave.

"Hunter, we have exposed Sheriff Hampson. He can no longer cause damage here in the County of San Cara." Big Joe says.

"The only thing is, we haven't captured him," Noah says.

"We will. Trust me, we will never stop until we banish him back to Hell." Big Joe puts his hand on Noah's shoulder.

The Great Bear Constellation shines brightly above, twinkling like Hunter's clear, bright eyes.

CHAPTER NINE

THE ALIEN

With a good night's sleep, the cryptids feel energized for the new day. Birds are chirping on trees. Hawks are gliding above the campground.

On a local news channel, the broadcaster is saying that after an investigation on Sheriff Hampson, the FBI discovered that the scandal of the previous Sheriff, Jocelyn Brown, was fabricated by Sheriff Hampson. The County Executive and District Attorney were involved in the scandal after being bribed with a large amount of digital currency. They have been put on administrative leave while the FBI investigates the cases against them.

"Well, I'm glad that Sheriff Jocelyn Brown's name is cleared," Mei says.

Cole agrees, "Hopefully this news brings her some long overdue, and much-needed closure."

Something that has been on everyone's mind is where did Sheriff Hampson escape to?

Cole researches online on possible routes the two-tiered fishing boat could have gone to.

"It is not a big fishing boat, so less fuel is stored onboard. If the boat goes to the north of the Pacific Coast, it will run out of fuel before reaching any major port." Cole says, looking at the map, "So it must have gone to the south. It could have landed in South California, and Sheriff Hampson could have gone to Nevada."

"That's a possibility," Mei says.

Just as they are analyzing the map, Big Joe walks in, "Folks, we received a tip about possible paranormal events happening."

"Where is it?" Mei asks.

"Area 51." Big Joe says.

The name "Area 51" brings back so many memories for Grey, Big Joe and Chupa.

Grey telepathically says to Big Joe and Chupa, "It's been a while."

Big Joe and Chupa look at Grey with emotions boiling under their skin. They know what Grey means. It's been years since they were in Area 51, yet what happened there feels like yesterday.

Grey is brought back to when his memories started.

Ever since he could remember, he was in a room with multiple cells made from iron. He remembered the steel bars were cold, separating him from the outside world.

He was so tiny, cute and playful. A human being in a full hazmat suit came in every day and brought him food and water. He told himself that this human being was his "Mother". He would try to drag her mask down so he could see what she really looked like under the mask. But she always resisted and brought her mask up. She would play with him for a few minutes, but then would refrain from further interactions with him. She took him outside to a white room called a laboratory, where other human beings poked him with sharp needles, took his blood out, and used all kinds of other equipment on his little body. He had scars all over his back and belly. They called him Number 4734679.

No one talked to him. But he had so many thoughts in his mind that sometimes he felt like his head was going to explode. There were also dark shadows within him that he did not know how to handle. The shadows just roamed around his thoughts, adding a shade of darkness and sorrow to his young mind.

One day, his "Mother" came inside the cell and took him outside. He wanted to tell her that he knew she cared about him, but he did not know how to speak. The thoughts inside his brain grew stronger and stronger until he could not contain them anymore. It felt like the thoughts expanded into a bomb, and when the bomb exploded, the thoughts somehow went inside the brain of "Mother". That was when he first telepathically communicated his thoughts to his "Mother".

The lady in the hazmat suit was shocked when she received the telepathic message. Her body language changed suddenly, and Grey knew that she was astonished to hear his thoughts. He himself was surprised that he could telepathically communicate too. He had been feeling the lady's feelings through his abilities, but he never thought telepathic communication was possible.

He continued to telepathically communicate to her, "I have been thinking you are my mother. Are you?"

The lady received his message, had some emotions rampaging under her mask, then stayed silent. Grey was hopeful that she was his "Mother". After all, she did not deny it.

Ever since that day, the lady in hazmat suit started to bring Grey books to read. She read each book to him and taught him how to read.

The lab people would test him on subjects he read, and he would point to the correct answers easily. There were many pages of records of his tests, both for physical and intellectual abilities, stored in the lab cabinets.

Grey suspected that the people in the lab were not aware of his telepathic abilities, as he was never asked about it, nor was he forced to use that ability in the lab. And so, he treated his telepathic ability as a secret between him and his "Mother". He communicated with the lady in a hazmat suit every day, but the lady almost never responded to his messages. This made him sad. The shadows in him amplified the sadness and gave him episodes of depression. When he was depressed, all day long he just sat there and watched sunrise, sunset, and moon rise, moon set through the tiny window above him.

When "Mother" sensed that Grey was depressed, she brought him a book, pointed to a phrase and read, "With great pain comes great wisdom". And then she looked into his dark eyes with so many feelings. The feelings were buried deep under many layers of emotional disguise, but Grey felt every bit of it, thanks to the tiny door that "Mother" opened at that very moment. Right after, she left in a hurry, as if she was trying to avoid being seen by someone.

He grew over the years from being tiny to being tall and skinny. His head was large compared to his arms and legs, probably because of all the intelligence in his possession.

For years, he was the only one in the cell, until one day, two other beings were brought into the room. Each being was put into a separate cell.

Both were beaten up badly. One had brown fur and a very bulky build. The other had black fur, claws, thorns on its back and a smaller build.

Grey was a little excited, for he had never had cellmates before. He felt a curiosity and a strange connection towards the newcomers.

For the first day, the two beings mostly lied on the cold cement floor in their cells. They looked very much injured and exhausted. There were cuts, bullet holes, and bruises everywhere on their bodies. Grey thought they must have been in an intense fight before they were captured. He gave water bottles to the two through the gap of the cells, and they looked at him with gratitude.

The second day, the two beings looked better. The brown bulky being said, "Thanks for giving us water yesterday. I'm Big Joe." The black furry being said, "I'm Chupa. What's your name?"

Grey was not sure if he could trust Big Joe and Chupa, so he did not say anything telepathically.

Big Joe and Chupa thought Grey might not know how to talk. But they continued to talk to him.

Big Joe said, "Do you have a name?"

Grey shook his head.

Chupa chimed in, "Do you want one? Maybe we can pick a name for you?"

Grey nodded.

Big Joe said, "How about Grey? Your skin is grey-colored, and Grey is a unique name."

Chupa said, "Grey? I like it. How about you?" Chupa turned to Grey.

Grey thought this name was cool. It described what he looked like and was not a common name. So, he nodded and smiled.

"Great! You like it. We will call you Grey." Chupa said.

"How long have you been here?" Chupa asked Grey, "A year? A month?"

Grey shook his head and shrugged.

"Oh, you don't know how long? That means you have been here a while." Chupa said.

Big Joe asked, "Grey, have you ever been outside?"

Grey shook his head.

Big Joe and Chupa felt sad for Grey. For one to grow up in a cell without seeing the world and to be deprived of all the possibilities that were beyond cruelty.

Grey could feel Big Joe's and Chupa's sadness towards him through his special abilities. He thought these two new cellmates might not be too bad if they empathized with someone they just met as deeply as they felt.

Big Joe and Chupa told Grey what the outside world looked like. They told Grey how they grew up, what they did, how they met, what adventures they had been on, and how they chased after a lead, stumbled upon Area 51, and were ambushed by military personnel, then ended up in the cells. Listening to Big Joe's and Chupa's stories gave Grey a sense of new hope and curiosity. It woke up something deeply buried inside Grey's heart and soul, like a tiny little seedling that came out of a giant boulder made of dark shadows.

As days went by, Big Joe and Chupa recovered from their wounds and exhaustion. Every day, the lab personnel came and checked whether Big Joe and Chupa were recovering or not. Grey suspected that when Big Joe and Chupa were fully recovered, the lab humans would experiment on them as well, just like they had been experimenting on him.

The lady still came in every day, bringing books for him to read. Big Joe and Chupa saw her and asked Grey who she was. Grey shrugged, as she had never told him who she really was. He hoped that she was his "Mother" and treated her like his "Mother", but ultimately, he did not know who she was.

Big Joe and Chupa wanted to escape with Grey. They told him that the outside world had so much to offer. They promised to take Grey to see mountains high up in the sky and oceans crossing multiple coasts. Grey felt the sincerity in them. He was quite touched by their sentiments. At this moment, he telepathically told them, "Big Joe and Chupa, thank you. I look forward to seeing the outside world and what it has to offer."

Big Joe and Chupa couldn't believe what they were hearing in their heads.

Chupa said, "Wow! I thought you couldn't talk. But this is so much cooler!"

Big Joe said, "Impressive! How do you do that?"

Grey said telepathically, "There are so many thoughts in my head that the strongest thought comes through to you. I guess it's in my genetics."

Big Joe and Chupa felt even more connected to Grey through his telepathic communications. It was like they could feel his exact emotion at that moment when Grey telepathically said something.

The next day, Big Joe and Chupa felt they were almost fully recovered. They had energy to stand and walk around their cells.

The lady in the hazmat suit came in as usual and brought water and food. But something was different that day.

Grey sensed immense stress and fear from "Mother". And so, he asked her telepathically, "Mother, are you okay?"

The lady looked at him with a multitude of emotions. She whispered to Grey, "Run. They want to execute you and study your brain."

Grey was shocked to hear that. After the lab people spent all that time studying him, they must have thought it was time to study his anatomy by killing him. He was a bit scared, too. He had not seen the outside world. And now he was to be killed.

But he was also happy, happy that his "Mother" cared so much about him that she warned him about what was coming. He telepathically said to her, "Mother, thank you for letting me know. But how can I escape? And how about my friends Big Joe and Chupa? Are they going to be in danger too?"

The lady whispered to Grey, "I have the key to your cell and a map of the facility right here." She handed Grey the key and map and continued, "Do you really have to leave with them?"

Grey nodded and telepathically said, "Yes, Mother. They are my friends. I would hate to see them get hurt."

The lady saw Grey's expression and felt the determination in Grey's mind about leaving with Big Joe and Chupa. She sighed a little bit, then said, "Okay. Tonight, I will get the keys to their cells and bring them to you."

Grey was grateful and excited, "Mother, we are going to leave this place and go explore the world! There are so many places I want to go, and so many things I want to do. I can't wait to see the world with you!"

The lady looked at Grey in his eyes with immense love and sadness and smiled. Grey felt strong waves of melancholy coming from "Mother". He did not understand where the sorrow came from.

But he was overwhelmed with the possibility of leaving the cell for a better life, one in which he could explore and experience, one in which he could make mistakes and learn, one in which he could seek a purpose and devote himself.

When "Mother" left, Grey told Big Joe and Chupa telepathically about the plan of escape. The three of them felt hopeful and awaited the lady's return.

And she did. At midnight, she sneaked back into the facility, brought keys to Big Joe's and Chupa's cells and opened the gates.

This time, Grey was finally able to see her face. "Mother" had beautiful straight grey hair, bright eyes, and a face that spoke of kindness.

Grey, Big Joe, Chupa and "Mother" started to run. "Mother" navigated the group because she knew the facility inside out. No guard seemed to have noticed them as they hid when the guards walked by.

Just as they crossed the field and were about to reach the parking lot, an alarm attached to a gate they opened started flashing. This was a new alarm that "Mother" did not know about. The guards from the facility came outside with guns and started shooting at them.

Unfortunately, "Mother" was shot. She fell. Grey was worried. A flood of anxiety submerged Grey's brain. Big Joe picked her up and carried her on his back. They ran for their lives and were able to find shelter behind a hill.

Big Joe laid "Mother" down. Grey was utterly concerned. She did not look good. The bullet entered between her ribs. She was bleeding a lot.

Grey's eyes were dark and full of sadness. He looked at "Mother," and telepathically said, "Mother, please hang on. We will find medical help for you."

"Mother" looked at Grey, raised her left hand, and put it on his face, "My child, I knew I would not survive the run when I decided to rescue you. Don't worry about it. It's okay." She paused as the pain was too intense, "I was never blessed with my own child. In all these past years, I viewed you as my baby. I named you Gregory," She smiled, "which actually works well with your nickname, your friends gave you, Grey."

Grey felt love radiating from mother. It felt like warm sunlight shining through the tiny window of the cell. The cold of darkness at dawn could not block the warmth of love and care from mother.

"Thank you for giving me a chance to be your mother. Each time you called me 'mother', my heart was giggling happily, but I could not show it. If I showed any emotional attachment to you, that would have put you in danger." Mother continued, "My dear Gregory, go explore this wonderful world. I love you."

Then mother smiled and closed her eyes. Her breath became weaker and weaker until she was gone. Grey could no longer feel her heartbeat telepathically anymore.

Grey was devastated. His brain and body were flooded with anger and sorrow. He has never felt such strong emotions from the rampaging waves of losing a loved one. He stood in the eye of the hurricane made from grief and watched years of memories rush by.

And for the first time in his life, he felt streams of warm tears come down from his dark, starry eyes.

Suddenly, Big Joe and Chupa heard some noises around them. They turned around and realized that they were surrounded by military personnel.

Grey was consumed with grief. Big Joe and Chupa yelled, "Grey! Look around us!"

Grey heard a distant noise that became louder and louder. He looked up and saw Big Joe and Chupa yelling something at him. He tried to focus on their voices, but it was hard. After a long minute, he finally made out what they were telling him. He looked around and saw they were surrounded, surrounded by the same people who killed his mother.

Grey's grief turned into anger. Why did these people kill his mother? What did his mother do to deserve this? All she did was rescue them from captivity. She bled so much. The pain caused her pink lips to turn pale. She was so pale. This was so unfair. She could have lived a fuller life with him, her beloved child, Gregory.

Grey was furious. He started to feel a volcano erupting in his mind. The force of steam and gas from the eruption of anger was so strong that Grey saw red color, then black color, and was knocked unconscious by the sudden eruption of the emotional volcano.

He did not know how long he had passed out. When he opened his eyes, he was on Big Joe's back like his mother was right before she passed away.

He saw Big Joe's black and white flannel shirt was covered with his mother's blood. The blood was dry by now, making the shirt feel hard to the touch.

Chupa noticed that Grey woke up, "Grey, how do you feel?"

Grey telepathically said, "My head hurts. It feels like my head literally exploded."

"Do you know what happened?" Big Joe put him on a rock to sit.

"I have no idea. I just remember I was furious while being consumed with sorrow, then I became unconscious." Grey telepathically communicated.

"Your brain wave knocked out the whole group of military personnel! I have never seen anything like that." Chupa said passionately.

"Wow. I have no idea that I can do that." Grey said telepathically.

"We've got to keep moving, Grey." Big Joe said, "There are more people running after us."

"Are you okay to walk?" Chupa asked.

"Yes. I can walk." Grey nodded and said telepathically. He put his hands in his pockets and felt something.

It was the map that mother handed him.

"Grey, do you still have it?" Big Joe asks.

Big Joe's question brings Grey back from memory. Grey knows exactly what "it" means.

Grey nods and takes out a tin box. Inside the box is a piece of folded paper. The edges of the paper are yellowed and show signs of wear and tear. But the owner must have been very careful with this over the years, preserving it to the best of their abilities.

The group comes around Grey and forms a circle. Grey slowly and carefully opens the piece of paper. It is a map of Area 51.

"Do you think they changed the layout of the facility over the years?" Mei asks.

"I doubt it. At least the main structure should still be there." Big Joe says.

"Okay. Let's go." Grey communicates telepathically to Big Joe and Chupa, "It's about time we pay a visit to Area 51."

And so, the cryptids drive their bus to Lincoln County, Nevada. It is quite a change of scenery for them to go from cool beaches in California to hot deserts in Nevada.

Big Joe and Noah take turns driving. Chupa cooks goat chops on the grill when they stop for a break. Grey stays deep in his thoughts during the trip.

One morning, they arrive at Area 51. The cryptids, Mei and Cole, step out of the bus.

Remembering a place is one thing. Stepping into the place is another. Grey, Big Joe and Chupa are hit by the presence of Area 51, and the emotions and memories that charge towards them. Especially Grey. Since he could remember, he lived here.

According to the tip, because of paranormal activities in Area 51, the facility has been shut down. Now, what exactly happened before the military closed the facility? No one knows. The cryptids, Mei and Cole, are about to find out.

Big Joe says, "Everyone, let's look at the map one more time before we go in. We need to be vigilant because there might be demons and traps inside."

After the group reviews the map again, the cryptids are ready to move in. Everyone holds their weapon and rapidly climbs over the fence. The door is locked, so Big Joe and Noah use force to kick the heavy, sturdy steel door open. As the door falls and dust rises, the group runs inside.

Area 51 is a huge facility of highly classified status. There is not much information in public about what might be inside, but Grey, Big Joe and Chupa know. At least they know what was inside years ago.

As soon as they are inside the facility, an alarm starts to sound. "Laser action detection! Watch out, there might be traps." Grey telepathically lets everyone know.

With Grey's warning and holding their weapons up, the group walks cautiously inside.

Lo and behold, rounds of arrows immediately start shooting towards them. Grey swings his sniper rifle like a pinwheel to stop the arrows. Big Joe swiftly moves his axe up and down, left and right, to divert the arrows. Chupa throws his rope in a circular motion to block the arrows. Saxon moves his bow to halt the arrows. Noah swings his spear around to deflect the arrows.

After the arrows stop, the group moves forward. Then, bullet rain starts flying towards them. They run fast and use their weapons to block the incoming bullets. Chupa ducks under gunfire, his voice low and mocking. "Bullet rain. Perfect weather for a hunt." Suddenly, one bullet hits Chupa on the arm, and he's upset, "Man, now I have to use my left arm to grill goat chops!"

The bullets stop. The group continues to go further down the entrance until they see a double-sided door.

The cryptids, Mei and Cole, see a large open floor plan facility when they enter the double-sided door. There are what look like alien aircrafts of different shapes, sizes and textures.

As they are looking around, the speaker starts to sound, "Welcome back, Number 4734679! I have been waiting for you."

Hearing that number in Area 51 immediately gives Grey chills through his bones. In his head, a flashback of all the poking with sharp needles and experiments with different kinds of equipment starts to occupy his thoughts.

The speaker continues, "Number 4734679, here are my welcome gifts. Enjoy."

Hearing the announcement, Grey forcibly pulls himself out of the flood made from miserable memories. He looks around and sees at the end of the facility, multiple creatures that barely look like humans are running towards them. At first, he sees around 7 creatures, then he sees more than 20 of them running fast to attack them.

Big Joe says, "High alert, everyone!"

Noah says, "Let's beat them up!"

A creature with dark green skin and a distorted face wearing a laboratory suit attacks Grey, using a large needle to hurt him. This scene brings him panic attacks from the past. But he takes a deep breath and tells himself that he is no longer the vulnerable small kid he used to be. He uses the laser blade on his sniper rifle and cuts the creature in half.

Big Joe is attacked by a creature that is twice his size with huge muscles in a torn-up suit. Big Joe looks petite compared to this creature with rubbery skin. He uses his axe against the creature, moving swiftly against it. The speed of his movements makes it hard for the creature to follow him, and he hurts the creature in multiple limbs in the process.

Chupa is attacked by a creature that has dark blue skin, large, sharp teeth, and wears a janitor's suit. The creature opens its mouth, bites Chupa on his shoulder, and starts sucking blood.

Chupa laughs, "Really? Blood sucking against me, who has a master's degree in the art of blood sucking?" Chupa uses his claws to slice the creature up like he's slicing goat chops, "Take that from your master!"

There are creatures of every shape and size available to fight. The cryptids, Mei and Cole, are outnumbered. But with their skills and weapons, they are standing firm and making progress.

Mei looks into the eyes of the creature that is fighting her, a short, skinny creature with long hair in an engineering hat and a reflective vest, and she sees nothing. No emotions. Just pure emptiness. The emptiness is so vast that it resembles the ever-expanding darkness in the universe. This creature is no longer human. And that makes Mei sad.

Cole feels the same way. The creature in front of him has a dark blue face, a big belly and wears a doctor's gown. But its face is no longer human, with horns growing outside of the skull. The eyes are very dull when Cole looks at them. There is not even one ounce of humanity in it.

The group fights the creatures off, leaving a trail of disembodied creatures behind them. Once the creatures are cleared, they enter the next room, which is the prison.

The prison cells are all empty except for one. Inside the cell is a small creature with pink skin, two long arms, two additional short arms and two legs. He is around four feet tall.

The creature sees the group enter the prison, waves and says, "Hello folks!" He notices the cryptids, Mei and Cole, looking at his naked body, and frowns, "Hey! Eyes up here!"

When he sees Mei, his eyes light up, "Who's this beauty? How are you doing? My name's Scamp. You like what you see?"

Big Joe says, "Hi, Scamp. I'm Big Joe. How long have you been trapped here?"

"Maybe a few months? One day, I was a happy little guy in the sea, and the next, I was captured by this crazy mental alien." Scamp says.

"The crazy mental alien? Who's that?" Chupa asks.

"He's the guy on speaker earlier, talking about some weird number I don't remember." Scamp replies, "He said his name is Oso and that he is hired by the demons. He looks like an alien. He helps this big-brained demon guy."

"There's another guy?" Mei asks.

Scamp smiles, "Yes, pretty. This big-brained demon said his name is Vogaun."

"What did they do to you?" Big Joe asks.

"Well, they experimented on me. See these scars?" Scamp shows his back.

The group sees scars of various shapes and sizes. One of them looks like a giant centipede that is devouring Scamp.

Grey sees the scars on Scamp and remembers his own scars. He remembers the pain and anger he had when the lab people were experimenting on him. The darkness from the shadowy past starts to consume him.

Big Joe and Chupa notice Grey's energy change. Big Joe pats Grey on his shoulder. And Chupa gives him a pat on the arm, "Bro, we've got you."

Grey is grateful to have friends who have his back. The darkness slowly disappears with the radiance from the solid foundation of friendship they have built.

"Oh, and they experimented on humans too." Scamp says, "And for some reason, the experiments on humans always go wrong."

"Are these weird creatures that attacked us the result of the experiments?" Noah asks.

"Yep. These human creatures are ick." Scamp says.

"What are they trying to do with these experiments?" Cole asks.

"Create demons. They put darkness inside animals and create demons. Or did they say shadows? I don't remember." Scamp says.

"How come you are not a demon?" Chupa asks.

"Yet. I guess maybe they haven't put enough darkness inside me. I don't know. I'm not really a scientist." Scamp shrugs.

"Can we let him out?" Chupa asks.

"I think so." Big Joe says.

Noah grabs the cell door, breaks it, and throws it aside.

"Some muscles you have there, dude. Thanks." Scamp smiles as he steps out of the cell, "Now I can kill you all."

Scamp's grin is wide, childlike. He looks harmless, which somehow makes him even more unsettling.

The cryptids, Mei and Cole, are shocked but alarmed. They raise their weapons.

"Got you! Just kidding." Scamp laughs.

The group feels relieved and awkwardly laughs with Scamp.

Grey telepathically tells the group, "It's time to meet these two. I feel their presence nearby."

"Wait, you can communicate telepathically? That's fire!" Scamp says.

"'That's fire?' Who taught you to say things like that?" Chupa says.

"The entire Gen Z population! And I know I'm slaying it!" Scamp says.

Chupa shrugs his shoulders as he does not "dig" the Gen Z vocabulary.

Grey leads the group to the white laboratory. As they approach the lab door, Grey telepathically says, "I can feel the alien's strong presence. Let's be careful."

Grey opens the door. The group enters the lab.

There are laboratory equipment, transparent tubes, and medical equipment everywhere.

They look beyond the equipment and see the alien Oso and demon scientist Vogaun.

Oso is less than five feet tall, has spotty skin, six horns on his head, horns on his back, and long, pointy nails.

Vogaun is almost seven feet tall, has his brain inside of a glass dome with electrode plugs, four horns on both sides of his head, and wears a white lab coat.

As the group walks closer, they see three giant glass tubes near Oso and Vogaun. The inside of the glass tubes looks dark, so they cannot tell what is inside.

Oso says, "Finally, we meet, Number 4734679. I've read so much about you. There are abundant documents on Number 4734679 in the filing cabinets."

Grey telepathically says, "My name is Gregory. My friends call me Grey."

Oso telepathically replies, "Gregory Grey. Interesting name."

Scamp says, "Hey, strangers! Guess you can't experiment on me anymore!"

Vogaun says, "Glad we don't need to waste time on you any longer. You are not getting anywhere close to the others. You will never be enough."

Scamp says, "Ouch! Way to hurt the little guy!" He pretends to cry, then says, "I don't fall for your gaslighting, asshole! My mental health is more important than your agenda. Mic drop!"

Oso says, "Vogaun, enough talking with the insignificance." He then turns to Grey and says telepathically only to Grey, "Let's see if you can live up to expectations. What are your other friends' names? Let me think. Oh, I remember! Nessie, Rake and Aura!"

Nessie, Rake and Aura are supposed to be standing guard outside of Area 51 in case the demons are to surround the cryptids inside. How does Oso know their names? Why are there three large glass tubes?

Connecting the dots, and now it all makes sense.

Grey starts to get visibly angry, turns to the three glass tubes and tries to open them with his bare hands.

The rest of the cryptids, Mei and Cole, are not sure why Grey is furious.

Oso and Vogaun laugh as Grey punches the glass tubes. Grey's skin on his hands starts to break, leaving blood on the glass tubes.

Oso telepathically says, "Let's see what your anger does."

Grey gets angrier after hearing Oso's comment, and his head starts to feel hot. He lets the anger out, breaking the glass tubes into a million pieces.

Everything happened so fast. The rest of the cryptids, Mei and Cole, use their hands to block the broken glasses that shoot out in a million directions. Then they look at where the glass tubes were.

A fog of darkness surrounds what looks like three creatures with multiple tubes inserted into their bodies. When the dark fog subsides, the group sees who the creatures are.

They are Nessie, Rake and Aura! The three of them have their eyes closed and are taken over by tubes with dark shadows floating inside.

"What did you do to them?" Big Joe asks.

Oso says, "Find out yourselves!"

Then Vogaun presses some combinations on a computer, and Nessie's, Rake's, and Aura's eyes open suddenly.

But their eyes are red.

"Nessie! Rake! Aura!" Chupa calls out to them. But they do not respond.

Oso commands, "Attack."

After hearing Oso's command, Nessie, Rake, and Aura grab the tubes inserted into them and remove them forcibly. Then they get out of the mess and charge at the rest of the cryptid team.

Big Joe, Chupa, Saxon, Noah, Grey, Mei and Cole are forced to defend themselves against Nessie, Rake and Aura.

The three of them have gone mad, attacking their teammates with their claws, hands and teeth. Aura changes shape to have multiple horns and long claws, making her look like a wild animal with many limbs.

The team cannot fight their friends with full force; thus, they have gained some scratches and wounds from their wild attacks. But since the cryptid team outnumbers the three, the team manages to capture the three after surrounding them and attacking them with their weapons. Chupa uses his rope to wrap them up like mummies.

By now, after the mess, Oso and Vogaun have disappeared from the laboratory.

The team searches the parameters, but they cannot locate Oso or Vogaun.

So Big Joe tells the team to be on high alert when they leave the Area 51 building. Noah and Saxon are tasked with flying Nessie, Rake and Aura to safety if the team is to be attacked.

And as soon as they walk out the door, they see the alien and demon they are looking for.

Oso and Vogaun lead a team of demons and surround the cryptids, Mei and Cole. Among the demons with multiple horns and claws, there is a giant demon that must be 12 feet tall. The giant demon has limbs and body parts sewn together from different animals and creatures.

Oso says, "You think we will let you go easily? Attack!"

The demons attack Big Joe, Chupa, Grey, Mei and Cole.

Noah flies up with Nessie and Rake, and Saxon flies up with Aura.

The giant demon sees Noah and Saxon trying to fly away and uses his height to try and grab Noah and Saxon. Noah and Saxon are heavier than normal because they are carrying their teammates. But they change their flying direction suddenly to avoid being touched by the giant demon. Good thing the giant demon moves slower than the flying cryptids.

Big Joe uses his axe, Chupa uses his rope, Mei uses her sword, and Cole uses his gun to defend themselves and fight back at Vogaun and the rest of the demons.

Grey fights Oso. Grey uses his sniper rifle with a laser blade to block Oso's attacks with a battle rifle. But the real battle between them is happening telepathically.

Oso says telepathically to Grey, "Physical fight is boring. Show me what your brain can do."

Grey hears Oso. Oso puts his hand on Grey's forehead. Immediately, Grey feels like his spirit is pulled into a world where there is nothing. Grey looks around and wonders why a world exists with nothing around. Somehow, he sees Oso appear in the world of nothing.

Oso says, "Welcome to the world of telepathy. I'm assuming this is the first time you have been here, judging from your confused facial expression."

Grey does not want to respond. He wonders how he got here and how this world works.

"Nothing is everything." Grey hears a voice in his brain.

Oso raises his hand, and a bunch of pointy red and black rocks appear on the ground, sliding off Grey's shoulder. Grey tries to block the red and black rocks with his hands, and some blue and black rocks appear. In the blue and black rocks, Grey feels a strong presence of his calmness against Oso's fierce attack.

Grey gets excited after his rocks block Oso's. It seems that in this world, he can create things out of thin air with his thoughts and emotions.

Oso pushes both of his hands forward, and a red-and-black-colored wolf with pointy thorns starts to appear and attacks Grey.

Grey uses his hands to block the wolf, and a blue-and-black-colored bear appears. With a push from his hands, the bear rumbles a roar so deep that it shakes the wolf in terror. The wolf growls and targets the bear's neck. With protection of thick skin on the neck, the bear uses its firm claws to grab the wolf and tear it apart.

Oso creates a red-and-black-colored dragon that hisses fire, and Grey blocks the dragon with a blue-and-black-colored serpent spitting water. The deluge of water from the serpent hisses violently as it quenches the blaze, a thick cloud of steam suffocating the last of the scorching red flames. Then the serpent constricts, its powerful form tightening like a magical ivy vine around the dragon's chest, bounding the dragon, each loop a promise of control.

Oso is getting impatient and says, "You think you can beat me? I was born to do this! My species, Chizon, is famous for telepathy. You are just an experiment, Number 4734679! You are only a number. No one cares about you, and you will never be good enough!"

Grey looks at Oso, the lonely alien hired by the demons to create a demon army and somehow feels sad for him. What could have happened that caused him to leave his planet and his species? Was he banished by them? Grey feels a great deal of sorrow and anger in Oso.

Oso pushes his hands forward, and the number 4734679 comes out as three-dimensional red-and-black sharp rocks. Grey uses his hands to push forward too, and three-dimensional blue-and-black letters come out. Grey's letters break Oso's numbers.

Oso is furious, "Number 4734679, that's your identity. I don't see how your letters can beat my numbers!"

Grey's lips trembles into a smile. "Four-seven-three-four-six-seven-nine... It spells Gregory. My mother gave me that name. You call it a number, but it was always love."

Oso hears what Grey says and removes his hand from Grey's forehead. Oso hates to admit that Grey defeated him in telepathy, an ability that Oso is proud of.

Grey comes out from the telepathy world and fights Oso physically. Oso's heart is no longer in the fight. So, he retreats and looks for a way out.

Grey looks around and sees that his teammates have defeated the army of demons. Oso takes this opportunity of Grey's distraction to escape.

Big Joe, Chupa, Mei and Cole tie up Vogaun and the rest of his demon army.

Scamp sees that there's no more danger, so he comes out of the Area 51 door where he has been hiding during the ambush fight.

Scamp kicks Vogaun and pokes him on the glass dome covering his brain, "Now who is poking who?" Vogaun hisses at him and tries to bite him. Scamp moves backwards, barely escaping Vogaun's sharp teeth.

"Now let's find the sigils." Big Joe says.

Grey is seen deeply in his thoughts. He telepathically says, "The sigils are probably in the records room. That's the most secretive place of Area 51."

And the team does find sigils for these demons behind filing cabinets. Mei uses her blood to send the demons back to Hell.

As the team is leaving, Grey looks at Area 51, the place full of memories, tortures, experiments, tubes, and his mother's love. He closes his eyes, and the building collapses behind him as he walks away with the rest of the cryptid team.

A thought lingers in his mind, "With great pain comes great wisdom."

CHAPTER TEN

THE GYM

The cryptid team drives back to Camp Moonlit Smiles.

Everyone is in the Chapel. Nessie, Rake, and Aura are still in their dark demon mode. They growl at the rest of the team constantly, trying to break free from Chupa's ropes.

"How can we extract the darkness out of them?" Chupa asks.

"I'm not sure. I think we need to consult with Bariel." Big Joe says.

The cryptids, Mei and Cole, gather in a circle and close their eyes. By calling Bariel's name in their hearts, a portal is created in the middle of the circle. A bright light starts to shine among them, and Bariel appears.

Bariel says, "My children, why have you brought me here?"

Big Joe says, "Bariel, we are seeking guidance on how we can extract darkness out of Nessie, Rake and Aura. Please help."

Bariel looks at Nessie, Rake and Aura with his eye in the middle, and raises the three of them up.

Nessie, Rake, and Aura hiss and growl at Bariel like wild animals while they are floating in the air.

A sphere of water solidifies in Bariel's hand, glowing like liquid glass. One by one, black tendrils rip from Nessie, Rake, and Aura, screaming as they are pulled into the crystal. When the last shadow is gone, the stone pulses with a light that makes everyone step back in reverence. As the shadows are extracted, Nessie, Rake and Aura's eyes are no longer red. They are then slowly dropped off to the ground.

Nessie, Rake and Aura look around and see everyone staring at them.

"Where am I? What happened?" Aura asks.

"Welcome back! You were taken over by darkness." Chupa says.

"We were attacked by a demon army. And this alien-looking demon used his mind to control us. That's all I remember." Nessie says.

"The alien's name is Oso." Big Joe says, "And Grey defeated him both physically and telepathically."

"Bariel helped extract shadows out of you into this crystal," Mei says.

"Thank you, Bariel," Aura says.

"You are very welcome." Bariel says, "My children, be careful with the crystal. Store it in a secure place. Bye for now."

Then Bariel disappears into the light.

Big Joe takes the crystal and puts it inside a safe in the Chapel.

Rake has not been himself ever since he came back from Area 51.

Noah, his best friend, asks Rake, "What's going on, liberal?"

Rake smiles, "My conservative friend, thanks for asking. When I was trapped in the darkness and shadows, that terrible feeling reminded me of my dark past."

"Sorry you had to go through that. It must have been painful. We all have a dark past. What matters is now. The all-mighty Great Creator guides us through our journeys." Noah says.

"Well, I was trapped in my dark past with nowhere to go. So, I had to relive what I did endless times. It was painful. I did not know when it would end, if ever." Rake says. Then the flood of memories in the past hits him again.

Rake did not remember how he came to the planet. The earliest memory of him was from when he was little. He grew up in a small rural town in Missouri. He remembered searching for food scraps from trash cans.

At night, he watched TV from outside a farmhouse window. He did not stand outside to watch. He crawled on the windowsill to watch. He discovered that he could climb on any surface with his long claws like a spider, and his arms and legs could stretch more than other creatures.

Farmer George was a hulking man with a Confederate flag hanging in his garage, his evenings spent shouting at the TV and muttering slurs between swigs of beer.

George would often beat up his wife, Jane. The reason for violence varied. It could be that dinner was too salty. Or it could be that she was on the phone for too long. Or it could be that she talked to a neighbor in the store. Jane had bruises on her legs, arms, and cheeks. All the time.

Sometimes, little Rake watched George hit Jane. Jane cried and yelled, but George did not stop until he was tired and satisfied. No one came to help Jane.

Rake felt bad for Jane. Jane was a nice lady. She fed the cows, chickens, pigs, and horses every day. But what could he do, a tiny little creature that was trying to survive on food scraps, who had no chance of stopping George?

One day, Jane saw little Rake stealing food from the trash can. The next day, she put a bowl of food near the trash can for this creature. Rake saw what Jane did and went to have the delicious food after she left. And then every day after, a bowl of food was available near the trash can. She did not know what kind of creature Rake was, but she was kind enough to put some food out for him.

One rainy day, Jane put an umbrella over the bowl so that the food she prepared for Rake would not get soggy. George came home drunk, saw the umbrella and the bowl of food, and started to blame Jane for leaving food outside and attracting wild animals. He used his hands to slap her and used his fists to hit her. Jane begged George to stop and yelled for help. But no one was around on this miserable, wet and rainy day. Even if anyone was around, they could not hear Jane's screams because of the loud, pouring rain.

George continued to hurt Jane, with blood coming out of her legs, arms, shoulders, and then her head. Her head was bleeding so much that blood covered her eyes. She could not even see.

Then, Rake came to pick up his food and heard Jane's cries for help.

He climbed on the windowsill and saw that George was beating Jane to death. It looked like George was going to kill her.

Rake was not going to let that happen to such a nice lady. He felt anger burning up in his brain. He jumped inside and used his long claws to scratch George's face. The force was so strong that George flipped to the other side of the room from where Jane was. Jane was falling unconscious, but she saw some creature was scratching George and trying to save her.

George was furious. In his drunken mind, this wild animal came from nowhere to attack him with its long claws. This was all because of stupid Jane leaving food outside. He got up and grabbed a knife from the kitchen. He charged towards Rake, but Rake was very flexible and climbed on cabinets, walls, and sofas to avoid being stabbed.

But George became angrier. He went to his bedroom and came out with a rifle. He started to shoot at Rake, but Rake was fast enough to avoid getting shot.

In his rage, George shot the mirror in the dining room. One long piece of broken mirror fell to Rake's side. He stretched his arm to reach and grab the piece of mirror and used it like a dagger. He poked the piece of mirror right into George's eye.

Rake sliced George up with his long claws and ate him up like he was consuming a cow. He had never been so full before. And the taste of blood woke something inside of him up. Was it darkness, or were they shadows? He did not know. Nor did he care.

This was the first time Rake realized that he had grown up, that he had grown big enough to tackle the previously intimidating human beings.

This also marked the beginning of Rake's hunting endeavor. He started to attack people in the small town, particularly male ones. The town was terrified of this creature that attacked and ate countless human beings. They put up multiple fliers to warn of this monster made of agility and flexibility. And before he knew it, there were not enough people left in the town for him to eat.

One day, he was watching TV through a farmhouse window and saw a piece of news about a music and art fair expected to be attended by thousands of people. He remembered the name was Woodstock. A plan started to form in his head. What if he went to Woodstock? Then he can feast on many more humans.

So, he started to "hitchhike" to Woodstock. He used his long claws to climb on cars and rode on the roofs like a giant spider. Finally, he grabbed onto the rails of a RV heading to Woodstock.

Rake stayed on top of the RV with his claws holding the rails, feeling the wind, pretending to be the king of the world. He looked around at the fields, houses, buildings, and then fields again, as if he was inspecting the vast variety of human beings he would consume as the king of the world. After a while, the RV stopped among hundreds of other cars.

Rake got off the RV and walked inside the venue. All he saw were people, hundreds and thousands of them. This was a scene he had never seen before, coming from a small town in Missouri. He climbed on top of the stage pole and looked down on these humans. All he saw was food in his eyes. He started to get excited about the feast that was about to unfold.

"Rake, did you hear?" Noah asks.

Rake is brought back from his past to reality, "I'm sorry, what was that?"

"Big Joe said that we got a tip about a gym that is haunted," Noah says.

Rake looks at Big Joe.

"There's something different about this gym. Members disappeared for no reason." Big Joe says.

"Where is it?" Rake asks.

"It's located in New York State." Big Joe says, "Near Woodstock."

Rake and Noah look at each other and exchange an expression that only the two of them understand.

"Let's go investigate this gym," Noah says.

And so, the cryptids get on the RV, bus, motorcycle, SUV and head to Woodstock. They drive past fields, houses, buildings, and then fields again. Before long, the vehicles are parked three blocks from the gym.

The gym is called Iron Beast Gym. Mei and Cole go to interview local businesses in the same plaza and find out that this gym is owned by two bulky guys named Astraz and Ozgad.

As soon as Rake hears these two names, he is thrown back into memory lane.

Back in Woodstock Music and Art Fair, Rake enjoyed capturing humans while they were captivated by music. When the attention was focused on stage, it was a piece of cake for Rake to climb near the humans and slash their throats open with his sharp claws.

Oh, how much had he feasted. His belly was no longer hungry. There were plenty of people with limbs, guts, and bellies to consume from.

But he started to notice some bones lying on the grass that he did not recognize. Besides him, who could be eating human beings and spitting these bones out?

He became curious. So, he started to observe what happened at the concert instead of actively hunting for himself.

That was when he noticed two demons with gigantic muscles that he had never seen before. One demon was taller with two horns on his head and eight different-sized horns on his chin. The other demon was shorter with seven horns on his head, two horns as his ears, and multiple small horns on his chin that looked like a beard made from horns. The demons hunted as a team. One kept watch while the other approached humans quietly and snapped the victims quickly. The two then share the humans by splitting them evenly in half, starting from the head down to the legs.

The demons noticed Rake too. The one keeping watch signaled to the other, and they both came over to chase after Rake.

Rake was not sure what the demons' intentions were, so he started running away. He utilized his agility to zig-zag his way around the trees at the border of the concert. The two creatures kept chasing after him. Rake did not have as much muscle strength as the two creatures. Before long, the two caught up to him.

Rake stopped running and turned around, "Hey, I don't know what you want from me."

The demons laughed, and the taller one said, "Obviously not for muscles!"

The shorter one said, "We noticed you have been eating humans. Your agility is impressive. Do you want to hunt together?"

Rake felt relieved that the demons did not want to hurt him. He had never been asked to join anything before. So he said, "Sure. I've never hunted in a group before."

The taller demon said, "Great. I'm Astraz." He pointed to the shorter demon, "This is Ozgad. What do you call yourself?"

Rake said, "The farmers that saw me, they called me Rake."

"It's settled then, Rake. You can help us by keeping watch and identifying easy targets. Astraz and I can hunt." Ozgad said.

Then the trio started to hunt as a team. Efficiency and accuracy were achieved by their teamwork. They ruled Woodstock and ate many, many humans.

The demons amplified the darkness inside of Rake. He felt that the shadows within him were consuming him, making him more violent and eager for blood. Every human he consumed made him hungry for even more. It was as if he could never be full. One by one, the demons and Rake killed and ate human beings.

"Rake, aren't these demons the ones you were hanging out with back in Woodstock?" Noah asks Rake, which brings Rake back to reality.

Rake looks at Noah, "Yep, Astraz and Ozgad."

"Wait, you know these demons?" Chupa asks.

"Yea. Way back then, before I met Noah, I used to hunt with these demons." Rake says.

"This would be a good opportunity to learn more about the demons' operations." Cole suggests.

Big Joe agrees, "Rake, how was your relationship with these demons when you parted ways?"

This question brings Rake back to the final day of Woodstock.

Astraz, Ozgad and Rake were in the middle of devouring an overweight human being when they were attacked by a creature with two horns on forehead, long claws, wings, and a bulky build. What was weird and interesting was that this creature was wearing an American flag T-shirt.

The creature held a long spear as his weapon. He flew in from the sky and used the spear to pierce Astraz in the back.

Astraz, Ozgad and Rake were shocked. Ozgad and Rake looked up with their mouths full of blood and flesh. Astraz cried out loud and cursed while meat and blood fell out of his mouth.

Ozgad and Rake started to use their fists and claws to fight the creature.

The creature pulled the spear out of Astraz and used the spear to slice Ozgad up. But the creature seemed hesitant to hurt Rake, which was strange.

Rake saw the hesitation in the creature's eyes and used it against the creature. He fiercely swung his claws towards the creature's head, and his claws landed near the creature's horns. The creature used his left claw to grab onto Rake and tried to pull him away, but Rake deeply planted his claws into the creature's skin and stuck to the creature like a fishhook hooked onto a fat fish's lip.

When the creature realized that he could not forcibly remove Rake, he let go of his spear.

The creature surprised him. Instead of striking, its claws traced maddening circles beneath Rake's arms. The sensation broke his grip with humiliating laughter, an absurd weakness in the middle of blood and battle.

The creature took this opportunity and grabbed Rake using his claws, unplugging Rake's claws from the creature's skin.

The bulky creature held Rake like a bear held salmon.

The creature opened his mouth, and Rake thought his life was over.

To his surprise, instead of eating him, the creature said to Rake, "Look, your demon friends left without you. And, of course, they took my spear."

During the time when Rake was fighting toes and nails with the creature, Astraz and Ozgad took the creature's spear and took off without Rake.

The creature continued, "Don't worry, buddy. I won't hurt you. My name is Noah. I can see you are not a demon. You are the same as me."

Rake looked at the creature's horns, wings and bulky muscles, and looked at his skinny body. He was not sure that he was the same kind as this creature.

"We don't look alike, but I can feel that we are the same kind. There are shadows within you that pull you to the side of darkness, right?" Noah asked.

"Yeah, I guess. How do you know?" Rake asked.

"Because I have shadows too. That's what I mean by us being the same." Noah said, "What's your name, buddy?"

"They call me Rake," Rake replied.

"Rake. You have a very fitting name. Do you know why I chose my name as Noah?" Noah asked.

"I assume you did it based on the Bible?" Rake said. He heard Jane read the Bible before, so he knew some stories from the Bible.

"Correct. The Great Creator will forgive our sins and wash us clean. The shadows within us will be gone." Noah continued, "We are called cryptids. We work for an angel and fight demons."

"I am a cryptid?" Rake asked.

"Yes, you are. There is a team of cryptids that hunt demons. And we are drawn to each other when we see a cryptid. Do you feel the connection?" Noah said.

Rake did feel a strange connection to Noah, the bulky creature, who was staring at him with an eager and silly smile. But he did not want to confirm Noah's theory, so he stayed silent.

Rake continued to think about the situation he is in. Astraz and Ozgad ran away without him, leaving him to die with Noah. Noah could have eaten him or beaten him to death, but he chose to tell him who he was. It seemed to be an easy choice.

"Okay. Can I see the other cryptids?" Rake asked.

"Sure. Let's go. We have our headquarters in California." Noah said, "Hop on my motorcycle."

And so, the road trip to California began. On the way, Noah told Rake about his past life full of darkness and killings. Noah told Rake how he found the Great Creator and chose a life of redemption. Noah told Rake that if he chose to, he could redeem himself too. Noah also talked to Rake about his conservative political views and that he believed in traditional values.

Noah told Rake, "If you want, you can be our family. You will be my little brother. Us against the demons. Us against the world." Noah paused and joked, "You do still owe me a spear, though."

Rake heard many a liberal value at Woodstock, so he did not agree with Noah's conservative values. But over the days, he grew fond of Noah. To him, Noah was the big brother he never had. Growing up, Rake wished he had a big brother there to protect, teach and guide him. Now he finally found one.

Rake argued back and forth with Noah about political views, but in his heart, he knew differences in politics wouldn't impact the friendship and trust they were building. Different political views are different perspectives on life and should not break friendship or family.

"Rake, did you hear the question?" Chupa asks.

Rake looks at Chupa, Big Joe and Noah, and says, "They escaped without me when I was attacked."

"Then that's perfect! You can probably play with their guilt and get information." Mei says.

"Well, I doubt that the demons ever feel any guilt. But sure, I can try." Rake says.

That night, the cryptid team strategically discussed what information Rake could pry out of the demons.

The next day, Rake walks inside the Iron Beast Gym. The logo of the gym is a spear, and the letters of the gym name are giant red colored wild writings. As Rake enters the doors, he sees a spear hung up on the back wall.

Under the spear sits a bulky demon with horns on its arms and sharp teeth. For human beings, they see the demon as a regular, bulky guy. But the cryptids can see demons as they naturally appear.

The demon speaks, "Welcome to the Iron Beast Gym. My name is Shane. How can I help you?"

Rake looks at his muscles and says, "My name is Rake. I'm tired of being skinny. I would like to build more muscles and am not sure where to start."

"Rake, my man. Of course! You have come to the right place. We can provide you with a free trial pass today. I suggest a private trainer service so that you can be guided and trained the correct way from the beginning." Shane says excitedly.

Rake says, "Sure, I'm open to that. Who are your private trainers?"

Shane says, "Our co-founders, Astraz and Ozgad, are the most highly rated private trainers. They are under high demand, though. I can try to see if they are available to help you today."

"That'll be great. I appreciate it, Shane." Rake says.

"We do have some forms for you to fill out today," Shane says, and hands Rake a tablet.

As Rake is filling out the forms on the tablet, Shane goes inside the office to find Astraz and Ozgad.

Then Rake hears a familiar voice from memory years ago. "What's up, Rake?" Astraz says while reaching out for a handshake.

Rake looks up and sees Astraz and Ozgad standing in front of him, looking confused first, then shocked, "Oh damn! Rake! Good old Rake! I know that name sounds familiar." Astraz says, looking at Ozgad. "Rake! My buddy! Where have you been?" Ozgad asks.

Rake acts shocked, "Astraz and Ozgad! No way! Long time no see."

Astraz and Ozgad give Rake fist bumps. Astraz says to Shane, "Rake is an old friend. We'll take care of him." Then he says to Rake, "Bro, come over to the office."

Rake follows Astraz and Ozgad to their office.

"I see you kept the spear from that fight," Rake says.

"Yep. Gotta remember the pain and humiliation from that asshole." Astraz says.

"How did you get away from that jackass?" Ozgad asks.

"Well, I was seriously hurt. That bastard poked holes everywhere in me. I must have passed out, and he thought I died, so he left me in a garbage bin at Woodstock." Rake says with a miserable face.

"Wow, sorry to hear that, bro," Ozgad says.

"That asshole. He penetrated me with that spear of his." Astraz says while showing his scar made by Noah.

"What happened to you all these years, Rake?" Ozgad asks.

"I've just been rolling solo, hunting and stuff." Rake says, "You two have done well here. It's an impressive gym."

"Thanks, man. It is a great money maker and brings in our food source if you know what I mean." Astraz says.

"Smart! Food just comes in automatically." Rake comments.

"Yep. It helps with ranking up too." Astraz says.

"Ranking up? What do you mean?" Rake asks.

"Recently, we found out that someone is organizing demonic activities. We were told there are different levels for demons. To rank up to legion status, we must consume more souls. The more, the better, the faster we can climb the ladder." Ozgad says.

"Interesting. Can I rank up too if I consume enough souls?" Rake asks.

"Why not? If you roll with us, you will probably get there sooner." Astraz says.

"Sounds good. Thanks for taking care of me, bro." Rake says.

"No prob, bro," Astraz says.

"Do you know who organizes and where?" Rake asks.

"We don't really know. We are not ranked high enough to know that information." Astraz says.

"Although, didn't we hear something about Highway 66?" Ozgad says.

"Oh yeah, that's right. Highway 66 was mentioned. Something about an abandoned town." Astraz says.

"I'm hungry. Do you want to start our lunch?" Ozgad has his hand on his grumbling belly and asks.

"Sure. Rake, you want to join us?" Astraz says.

"Of course!" Rake gets excited, "How do you operate? Who do you decide to eat? If you eat everyone, how do you make money?"

"We have demon members and human members. But we mostly eat the trial pass holders." Astraz says.

"There are quite a few of them today. Let's go." Ozgad says.

Astraz and Ozgad lead Rake to the gym. Astraz says, "Mary, Cane and Mike, please come to the office."

An Asian lady, a Caucasian guy, and an African American guy look up from their diligent work out sessions on the treadmill, weightlifting and planking. They stop what they are doing and walk over.

"Since you are trial pass holders, we have a special promotion today with private trainers. Please follow us to the office." Astraz says.

Mary, Cane and Mike follow Astraz, Ozgad and Rake back to the office.

Astraz says, "Ozgad and Rake, let's help one each. I'll take care of Mike, and Ozgad can take care of Cane. Rake, you can take care of Mary."

Rake understands what Astraz means. These are directions for killing human beings.

"Let's go!" Astraz commands.

Astraz grabs Mike's shoulders, but all of a sudden, Mike changes from an African American man to Aura, moves down to avoid being touched by Astraz's hands, and uses her multiple fists to punch Astraz.

Ozgad punches Cane, but his fist is somehow deflected by Cane's hand. Cane, who is actually Cole, punches Ozgad in the face.

Rake punches with his fist towards Mary, then his fist turns into a high five. Mary is indeed Mei.

Astraz and Ozgad glance at Rake and understand that their little bro is not on their side.

When Shane hears the fighting noises, he realizes that the hunt has gone south. He runs into the office to help Astraz and Ozgad.

The other cryptids arrive at the gym too.

The fight moves from the office to the main gym area. Demons and cryptids fight.

Astraz says to Rake, "Rake, I can't believe you betrayed us. These friends of yours cannot even lift 500 pounds, I bet!"

Noah says, "Oh yeah? Catch this!" He jumps out of the fight zone, puts 1000 pounds of dumbbells, lifts them with ease, then throws them towards Astraz.

Astraz tries to catch and hold the dumbbells, but he ends up being pinned down by the heavy weight, "You asshole!"

Rake pulls the spear from the wall and throws it to Noah, "Here's the spear I owe you. Now we are even."

Noah laughs, catches the spear, and uses it to fight Ozgad.

Before long, the cryptids are able to capture the demons.

Ozgad spits, "Rake! You are a damn traitor! You betrayed your own hunting group."

Rake says, "You left me to die when we were attacked years ago. You betrayed me first. I'm just returning the favor."

The cryptids look for the sigils of demons in the gym. The sigils are carved into the logo in the office. Mei smears her blood onto the sigils.

Rake says, "I hereby banish you back to Hell."

As Astraz, Ozgad and Shane are captured in the red light, they yell towards Rake, "You will be defeated! You are weak!"

"You left me once," Rake says, voice steady. "But I found a family who never will. My strength is not from demons. It's from my cryptid brothers and sisters."

And then the demons disappear into the red light.

CHAPTER ELEVEN

THE HIGHWAY

C hupa is whistling the song of great goat chops while grilling a new batch of goat chops at a campground near the entrance of Highway 66.

The cryptid team is en route to investigate demonic activities further based on tips from Astraz and Ozgad. According to the demons from the Iron Beast Gym, there is an abandoned town near Highway 66 that holds more answers to the recent surge of demonic activities. Who is summoning all the demons? Are they successful in creating more demons? If so, how are they able to create a demon from a creature on Earth? These are questions on the cryptids' minds.

Cole researches on the laptop while eating a goat chop, "Remember, last time when we were trying to determine where the two-tiered fishing boat could have gone to, we concluded that it could have gone to South California or Nevada."

Mei says, "Yes, I remember that."

"Looking at Highway 66, the overlap with South California and Nevada is the last part right here. So, we need to be on high alert after we pass Utah." Cole says, "And we can continue to research on which abandoned town it might be."

"Great work, Cole." Big Joe says.

After lunch, the cryptid team drives their RV, SUV, motorcycle and bus onto Highway 66.

Of the cryptids, Saxon knows Highway 66 the best. He grew up on this route.

When Highway 66 was first built, Saxon was just a little kid. He did not remember anything before then. All he knew was that he grew up on Highway 66.

As a little mothkid, he found the days to be long and nights to be even longer. He walked along the highway and picked up scrap food containers and things thrown out of car windows. He ate mice and other animals that were hit by cars while crossing the highway. Day by day, he grew bigger. He started to catch raccoons and other small animals that happened to run along the highway.

One day, there was a car accident where a huge truck full of groceries crashed, dropping everything onto the highway. Saxon took a bunch of food and hoarded them. Shortly after, he learned that he could use human food to lure animals. That was when he taught himself to set up traps for animals using nets he found along the highway. Trapping made his hunting life much easier. He was able to catch more small animals in less time.

One time, he set up a trap. A few birds flew in for some grains. He ran to the birds and tried to catch them. But the birds flew away quickly. Saxon felt frustrated, and he vowed to capture the birds and continued to set up traps for them. Each time, he did not run fast enough to capture the birds.

As a result, Saxon was even angrier and more determined to capture the dumb birds. He set up one more trap. He was ready to run as soon as the birds landed. And the stupid birds came. Just as the birds were landing, Saxon ran out to capture them. The birds were on high alert and flew up immediately after Saxon moved from where he was hiding. He jumped up and tried to grab their feet, but he couldn't reach them. The dark shadows inside him started to fire up, making him more angry at the birds. He jumped up again, and the anger did something to his body. He noticed he was getting higher up in the air.

That was when Saxon realized that he could fly. His wings were flapping in the sky. He struggled to change direction to catch up to the birds. The anger lit by the darkness inside of him was powerful.

Fueled by the shadows within, he pivoted, turned, sped, caught the birds, and ate them like a monster that ate its appetite away.

Then he felt invincible on Highway 66.

At first, he went after small animals like rabbits and raccoons. Then he wanted something bigger. So, he hunted deer and mountain lions along the highway. But that did not entertain him for too long. So, he started to think about hunting something more challenging: human beings.

He observed human beings on the highway. Cars were too big and too heavy to mess with, for he did not have that much strength to lift them up from the ground. But motorcyclists seemed to fit his needs. They have minimal coverage and protection from air attacks.

Then he waited patiently on a tree near the highway and observed like a lion that was eyeing its prey. A single motorcycle was fast approaching.

Saxon could feel the darkness inside him getting excited and amplified as he waited for the perfect moment to attack. And it was time! Saxon quickly flew off the tree, aiming for the motorcycle, and precisely snatched the human on the bike. The motorcycle slid to the middle bump of Highway 66 and on the way, hit several cars, causing a massive chain of accidents. Saxon then snatched the human beings who were injured from their cars.

How satisfying it was when his plan worked.

Ever since then, the shadows within grew bigger every time Saxon consumed a human being.

The darkness was consuming him too. He felt like he was covered by solid black shadows even in the middle of a summer day with scorching sunlight burning the asphalt road to a boil.

Life continued as he hunted for motorcyclists along the highway. But with every human he captured and ate, there was less and less excitement in him. There was no joy nor challenge. He started to feel bored. Somehow, endlessly consuming was no longer satisfying or fulfilling. It seemed that nothing could fill the emptiness in his heart that was scooped out by long, slim, shadowy hands made of endless darkness.

Then one day, his boring human-eating life was interrupted by just another motorcycle.

Noah and Rake, sitting on the motorcycle, wave at Saxon, "Saxon, remember this was where we met?"

Saxon comes out of the past briefly and sees the road sign that Rake is pointing towards. It says, "Petrified Forest Park".

Yes, he remembers that day like it was yesterday.

Saxon was near the Petrified Forest Park waiting for his prey when he noticed a motorcycle fast approaching. There was a bulky creature with horns and, interestingly, wings too, wearing clothes with an American flag printed on them. Behind this creature was another skinny creature with long silver white hair wearing a black skinny shirt and black skinny jeans. They were both riding on the motorcycle.

Saxon was intrigued, for he had never seen creatures like these before. He started to get excited.

As the motorcycle came closer, Saxon flew up from the abandoned car he was hiding behind and then flew down to capture the skinny creature. He grabbed the skinny one from the back and flew up.

The bulky creature heard and felt the commotion, drifted with the motorcycle and came to a sudden stop on the highway. He looked up and saw Saxon flying away with the skinny creature.

The bulky creature immediately flew up and chased after Saxon in the sky. Saxon was dragged down by the skinny creature's weight in the air. The skinny creature was using its claws to fight Saxon, which made it harder for Saxon to balance while flying away.

The bulky creature had larger wings, bigger muscles and flew faster than the burdened Saxon. When the bulky creature caught up to Saxon, he attacked Saxon using his fists. Saxon fell lower in the sky and struggled to hold on to the skinny creature while flying. The skinny creature took this opportunity and broke free from Saxon and skillfully fell to the ground with a perfect gymnast landing.

Saxon and the bulky creature fought in the sky. Saxon was more agile because he weighed less than the bulky creature, while the bulky creature had more muscle strength.

The bulky creature threw powerful punches at Saxon. Saxon stopped flapping his wings, which caused him to free-fall. As a result, he dodged the bulky creature's punches.

As Saxon was lower than the bulky creature in the air, he punched the bulky creature in his private part. The bulky creature yelled, "Damn bastard!" The bulky creature looked pissed, and he let out fire from his mouth.

Saxon was shocked to see fire coming out of the creature's mouth. In his panic, he tried to fly away and avoid the fire, but his hair was already burnt by the flames, making him look bald in the middle of his head.

Saxon was angry. How dare this goddamn bulky creature burn his handsome hair? He started to kick the bulky creature, aiming for his face. But the bulky creature used one hand to hold Saxon's foot and used his other hand to hug Saxon's body into his shoulders.

Now this looked awkward and embarrassing. From the outside, it looked like the bulky creature hugged Saxon tightly and slowly flew down from the sky. To any passerby, the two might have looked like lovers locked in a slow, swirling embrace. An intimacy born of violence rather than affection. The only thing missing was some computer-generated images of cherry blossoms floating in the air as they gracefully turned around in the air.

Saxon struggled to stretch out of the bulky creature's arms, but the bulky creature was too strong.

Now they were both on the ground. Saxon said, "You pervert! Let me go!"

The bulky creature said, "You can try to get away, but don't worry, I'll catch you again, buddy."

Saxon was angry, so he bit the bulky creature on his arm. The bulky creature's muscles were tough, and Saxon was not able to bite deep. But the bulky creature let out a scream, "Hey! Stop biting! I won't hurt you."

Saxon looked at him and did not believe him.

The skinny creature walked over, looked at the situation of Saxon and the bulky creature, and laughed, "Wow, you two are really getting intimate. Get a room!"

The bulky creature said, "Rake, shut up!"

"The skinny creature's name is Rake." Saxon thought.

Rake said sarcastically, "Oh, I'm so scared, Noah!" Then Rake looked at Saxon, "I'm just kidding. Noah's the soft-heartedest ever. What's your name?"

Saxon answered, "I'm Saxon."

Noah said, "Saxon, nice meeting you. I'm going to let you go. But don't try to escape, because we can and will capture you again."

Then Noah loosened his arms, and Saxon walked out.

Saxon said, "What are you going to do to me?"

Rake said, "Saxon, don't worry. We are not going to hurt you."

"Then what do you need from me?" Saxon was confused.

"Fundamentally, we are the same," Noah said.

"We all have shadows within us that dictate our desires. Do you feel that?" Rake said.

"How do you know? I do feel the darkness inside eating me away." Saxon said.

"Because we are the same. We call ourselves cryptids. Noah said the Great Creator made us." Rake said, "Just a week ago, I was like you, hunting and eating random human beings to fill a hole within me that kept getting bigger and yelling for more. Then Noah helped me."

Saxon seemed to be in his thoughts.

"Saxon, there are more cryptids like us. Don't you want to meet your brothers and sisters?" Noah said, "You are welcome to join us. And we can fulfill our purpose together. There's a reason why we are here on this Earth. We are meant to do something great."

Saxon looked at the two cryptids in front of him and wondered what decision he should make. If he stayed, life would have been the same. Day in and day out, he would be hunting, eating, sleeping, pooping, then hunting again. But if he chose to go with Noah and Rake, there would be no telling how his life would be changed and what challenges he could face. And change sounded scary.

But change could be good too. He was feeling bored. He was faced with no challenges for a long time. He was young and still wanted to see more of this world. Outside of Highway 66, there were more things to experience, more places to explore, and more creatures to meet.

If he never tried it, how would he know whether it would work out or not?

And so, he made his decision. It was not a decision to be comfortable but an uncomfortable decision to make. It was a decision to chase after something he had no idea about. It was a decision to trust someone he knew nothing about. It was a decision of immense risk, but to him, he had to take this risk. His life and soul called for it.

He did not want to regret and wonder what his life would have been if he went with the cryptids. He refused to let life slip by in the shadows of what could have been.

So, he said, "Let's go." And that was the start of something new, scary, hard, and wonderful.

Saxon looks at Noah and Rake on the motorcycle, the two best friends with diametrically opposed political views, and smiles.

All these years of friendship, camaraderie and purpose fulfilled the empty hole he had inside that was skillfully scraped out by the dark shadows. If he must do it all over again, he will still choose to join the cryptids. All the doubt, worry, concern, and stress are part of growing pains that he had to experience. Growth is painful, but satisfyingly fulfilling.

The cryptids ride along Highway 66, like what Noah, Rake, and Saxon did years ago. Only time has passed.

They drive past Arizona and cross the border into California.

"Hey folks, we need to stop," Saxon says suddenly.

The team stops the vehicles.

"Something is not adding up. We drove past this bar at least three times in the last 30 minutes." Saxon says and points to the name of the bar, "The Whispering Serpent".

"I was wondering about that too." Chupa says, eating a goat chop, "That's an interesting name for a bar. It sounds sneaky."

"My instinct tells me something strange is going on." Big Joe says, "Let's try one more time and observe what happens."

The cryptids drive the RV, the SUV, the bus, and the motorcycle forward from the Whispering Serpent. As the vehicles move forward, the Whispering Serpent moves back from their view. Then the cryptids see the Whispering Serpent in front of the road again.

Interesting. They have to stop the vehicles and investigate.

"We might be trapped in a time loop." Grey telepathically says to the group.

"Damn! It might be some magic spell!" Scamp says.

"Or it has something to do with this slimy bar," Chupa says.

"Let's go inside the bar and see what's going on." Big Joe says.

"That's right, Big Fur!" Scamp says.

Big Joe frowns after hearing Scamp's newly picked nickname for him.

Big Joe, Chupa, Saxon, Mei, Cole, and Scamp walk inside the bar while the rest of the cryptids stand guard outside.

As they enter the bar, the sign of the bar secretly flashes a dark green light.

"Hello! Welcome to the Whispering Serpent," the bartender says. To the cryptids, the bartender looks like a demon with green horns. To Mei and Cole, the bartender looks like a human being with an undercut hairstyle wearing a green velvet suit. Big Joe nods to Mei and Cole, indicating this bartender is a demon.

"My name is John. I'll be your bartender today," the demon continues, "The Whispering Serpent is a neutral ground where no violence is permitted. Do you acknowledge and commit to this requirement?"

"Sure, John." Big Joe says, "I think you are aware of the reason why we entered your bar. We want to know why we cannot drive forward from the bar."

"Of course, sir." John says, "Please follow me upstairs." Then John hands everyone a pair of green sunglasses, "Please wear these sunglasses at all times after you enter the room."

The cryptids, Mei and Cole, think this requirement is strange. But they put on the sunglasses as requested.

The stairs and floor have green velvet carpet on them, which makes every step feel expensive.

There are two snake-looking demons wearing green sunglasses and velvet green suits standing outside the owner's room. One is a bald male. The other is female with buzzcut hair. When they see the cryptids, Mei and Cole, arrive, they open the heavy black door and lead the way, "Welcome. Please follow us."

The cryptids, Mei and Cole, walk in following the two bodyguards. It is a large office with green and black colored furniture inside. Green velvet drapes fall from the ceiling to the carpet, stopping every inch of sunlight from coming in. They see a wide, dark green office desk and a light green office chair with its back turned towards them.

The female bodyguard says, "Ms. Medusan, they are here to see you."

The chair turns around, and the cryptids, Mei and Cole, see a lady with green snakes for hair. She is wearing a black leather jacket and black leather pants.

The lady smiles and says, "Welcome, Big Joe, Chupa, Saxon, Mei, Cole and Scamp, to my brokerage."

The cryptid team feels shocked that this lady already knows their names.

The room is filled with awkward silence.

Scamp, bothered by this uncomfortable moment, jokes, "The past, present, and future walk into a bar. It was tense."

"Aren't you a jokester, Scamp." the lady says.

"How do you know our names?" Big Joe asks.

"My dear, of course I know. I deal with information. It is my business to know." the lady says, "My name is Virginia Medusan. And I know you have questions for me."

"Hi, Ms. Medusan, why do we keep driving back to this bar? How come we cannot go forward?" Big Joe asks.

"There is a spell cast on this section of the road that prevents vehicles from passing through," Virginia says.

"What can we do to go past it?" Mei asks.

"It's interesting that you are the one asking for a solution. That's going to cost you." Virginia says with an evil smile.

"How much?" Mei says.

"I take different types of payments for each transaction. For this one, I will need your blood. One vial for each vehicle." Virginia says.

"Four vials of Mei's blood? Why?" Chupa asks.

"I'm afraid that is not something I can share. You should only care that I am providing a solution and the only solution for your little situation." Virginia says, "You have 5 minutes before you lose this deal forever." Then she puts up an hourglass for 5 minutes.

The cryptids, Mei and Cole quickly form a circle to discuss.

"I don't think we have another choice at this point. I'll just give her my blood." Mei says.

"But what if she does something evil with your blood? Then more damage is coming." Saxon says.

"That's a good point. But we must get to the abandoned town to stop the four-eyed demon from creating or summoning more demons. If we are not fast enough, soon we will be outnumbered by demons and cannot succeed in stopping Sheriff Hampson." Big Joe says.

"Weighing the two options, we should probably just give her the blood, that is, if Mei is still okay with doing it," Cole says.

"At least she is not a demon. I've donated more blood than four vials. Let's do it." Mei says.

"Time's up! What's your decision?" Virginia asks.

"I'll give you my blood," Mei says, rolling up her sleeve.

"Fabulous!" Virginia says, smiling. She swings her hair, and four snakes stretch from her head, aiming for Mei's vein. The snakes bite Mei on her artery and start sucking blood. Before long, the snakes have enough blood in their mouths and spit the blood into four green glass vials with snake patterns.

"Good girl, Mei." Virginia says, holding and admiring the vials of blood, "Would you like a cookie or a juice box?"

"I'll take a cookie!" Chupa says.

"I'll take a juice box!" Scamp says.

"I held up my side of the bargain. Now, are you going to break the spell?" Mei says.

"Oh dear, the spell cannot be broken," Virginia says.

Mei, Cole, and the cryptids start to get anxious. They get ready to fight.

"You can try punching, but this bar is a neutral zone protected under a spell." Virginia smirks.

Big Joe tries to punch Virginia, but for some reason, his fist would not move forward to hit Virginia, no matter how hard he tries.

"Don't worry. I'm a businesswoman after all and have a reputation to keep." Virginia says, signaling to her bodyguards.

The male bodyguard brings out a green tray. The female bodyguard takes four stones from a snake-shaped cabinet and puts them on the tray. The male bodyguard then hands the tray to the cryptids, Mei and Cole.

The four stones have green sigils carved on them. Mei picks them up from the tray.

"Put these in your vehicles and you shall pass," Virginia says, then turns her chair around.

The bodyguards have their right hands pointing towards the door, "Thank you for your business."

The cryptids, Mei and Cole, walk out behind the bodyguards and then downstairs to the bar.

John sees them and says, "Please leave the sunglasses in the bin." He points to a green velvet bin on the bar table.

As the team puts their sunglasses in the bin and walks out, John waves, "Have a great day."

The cryptids, Mei and Cole, go back to the rest of the team and explain what happened at the Whispering Serpent.

Aura says, "We need to figure out why Virginia Medusan needs Mei's blood."

"Yes. Probably also why Mei's blood works for banishing demons back to Hell." Nessie says.

"We can talk to Bariel to find out." Big Joe says.

So the cryptids, Mei and Cole join their hands together and use their thoughts to call Bariel.

But this time, Bariel does not appear. Instead, his voice is heard, "Nothing before its time. All shall be revealed."

Big Joe opens his eyes, "Interesting. This has never happened before."

"I guess it's not time for us to know yet," Noah says.

"Or maybe we are meant to find out ourselves." Big Joe says, "Now let's find the abandoned town."

They put one stone on each vehicle and start driving the RV, the SUV, the bus and the motorcycle.

This time, after they leave the Whispering Serpent, they do not come back to the same place anymore, thanks to the stones with green sigils.

The team continues driving on Highway 66 towards California.

Cole says through the speaker system installed by Grey on all four vehicles, "According to my analysis of the map, we are entering the likely area of the abandoned town."

Big Joe says, "Let's be on high alert, everyone. We might be attacked."

Just as he finishes his sentence, they hear loud popping engine noises.

On the windshields of the RV, the bus, the SUV, and the motorcycle, a computer Heads-Up Display appears, warning, "13 demons are approaching on motorcycles."

Grey telepathically says to everyone, "Folks, I've made some improvements on the vehicles, which you can see on the windshields." He continues telepathically, "Artificial Intelligence assistant Glorixian will help us with gadget and weapon deployment."

Chupa looks at the windshield and says, "Cool!"

Scamp says, "Damn, telepath and technology, way to go TNT!"

The cryptids look forward and see a gang of 13 motorcycles driving fast towards them. There are 13 demons wearing leather jackets and leather pants on the motorcycles. On the front and back of the leather jackets, there are writings of "Hellion Riders".

The demons surround the cryptids' four vehicles on Highway 66.

The demon in the middle has brown skin with lava burning on it. He has horns on his head and looks handsome with a clean haircut. He says, "My name is Calderas. You cannot cross this part of the Highway."

"What if we must?" Big Joe asks and continues to drive the RV forward.

"Then we will not hold back. Let's go!" Calderas says and signals to his motorcycle gang.

The 13 motorcycles drive forward, closing in on the cryptids' vehicles.

Four motorcycles approach the four vehicles, attempting to hit them sideways. Glorixian suggests, "Demon motorcycle collisions forecasted, deploy magnetic landmines?" Big Joe says, "Go ahead."

The sides of the RV, the bus, the SUV and the motorcycle closest to the demons' motorcycles open small doors and launch magnetic landmines towards demons' motorcycles.

The magnetic landmines roll on the highway towards the wheels of the four demons' motorcycles, and as soon as they are close enough to the axles, they latch themselves on, causing the motorcycles to go out of balance and fall to the ground.

Before the demons' motorcycles fall, the four demons jump on top of the RV, the bus, the SUV, and the motorcycle.

The demons on top of the RV, the bus and the SUV climb onto the windshields to block the view of the cryptids and start punching the windshields to gain access to the inside of the vehicles. The vehicles are reinforced by titanium; thus, they are bulletproof, and the windows are made with multiple layers of glass and plastic, so they are extremely hard to break. But the multiple punches by demons are starting to cause some damage to the windshields.

Big Joe says, "Glorixian, can you take over driving?"

Glorixian says, "Yes, of course."

Big Joe climbs out of the RV. The demon on the windshield is Calderas. Calderas sees Big Joe climb out and starts punching him, "I only fight with the leader. Show me what you've got!" Big Joe swings his axe towards Calderas, and Calderas uses his hands to hold on to the handle of the axe. Now the two leaders of their respective groups are pushing each other's limits on the axe. Big Joe's strength is unmatched, but Calderas' strength is nothing short of impressive. They push each other's limits, and finally, Big Joe pushes Calderas off, and they climb towards the roof of the RV.

Calderas says, "Not bad, big furry guy." He then throws heavy punches against Big Joe. The two are in a close fight, like they are competing against each other in Ultra Brawling Championship.

Cole drives the bus. Nessie climbs out of the bus to fight the demon on top of the bus. She swings her flail and hits the demon on his face. The demon jumps up to the roof and uses his sharp claws to scratch Nessie.

Aura drives the SUV and swings it around to get rid of the demon. The demon holds on to the side mirror. Saxon climbs out and flies in the air, drags the demon by his feet and swings him away to the back of the highway.

Noah rides the motorcycle, and Rake sits in the back. The demon jumps on top of the windshield, standing on the side view mirrors and blocking Noah's view. Noah asks Rake to take over the motorcycle while he flies up, punching the demon on his head and dragging him off the side view mirrors.

Another three demons surround the RV, another two demons surround the bus, another two demons surround the SUV, and another two demons surround the motorcycle.

Glorixian suggests, "More collisions forecasted. Turn on Holy Water sprinklers?"

Chupa says, "Coolio! Proceed."

Skinny and long sprinkler tubes are raised up from the vehicles through tiny doors that open on the roofs and motorcycle handles and start sprinkling Holy Water like lawn sprinklers watering the grass, except that the grass gets burnt by the water. As soon as the Holy Water is sprinkled on demons, their skins burn like human skins that have encountered acid.

This diverts demons from approaching the vehicles, but not for long.

Glorixian suggests, "Laser tire slashing?"

Aura says, "Yes, please."

The vehicle's tire axles shoot laser beams out, slicing the tires of demons' motorcycles in half. The motorcycle crashes on the side of the highway. The demons attempt to jump up onto the roofs of the RV, the bus, the SUV, and the motorcycle.

Three demons jump onto the RV. Chupa climbs up the roof and utilizes his kicks against a demon. Grey joins Chupa on the roof and shoots bullets at the demons with his sniper rifle. Scamp hides inside the RV under the seat.

Two demons land on the bus. Cole and Mei climb up to fight the demons with Nessie. Mei swings her sword towards a demon, cutting the demon's arm off. Cole uses his gun to hit a demon in the head and shoots another demon with a bullet penetrating his head.

Saxon, flying above the SUV, stops one demon from reaching the SUV roof by kicking him in the face mid-air. The other demon lands on the roof. Saxon, hovering over the demon, shoots an arrow towards him, hitting him in the shoulder. A bulky demon jumps from the bus to the SUV. Aura asks Glorixian to take over driving and climbs up the roof to fight the demon. Aura uses her tomahawk against the bulky demon while changing herself to look like a monster with huge muscles.

Noah flies in the air and uses his spear to puncture a demon mid-air when the demon attempts to jump onto Noah's motorcycle. Rake, asking Glorixian to drive the motorcycle, uses his dagger to stab a demon in his gut.

The fight between leaders continues for a while before Big Joe uses his full strength to kick Calderas on the chest, causing him to fall to the ground. Chupa sees that, jumps off the RV and uses his rope to tie Calderas up. The cryptid team sees Big Joe winning, and the team morale is boosted up. They fight with more confidence, and before long, they have the demons defeated and tied up. Several demons escape from the end of the fight, running away.

The cryptid team stops the vehicles, gathers up the demons, and questions the demons for information.

Big Joe asks Calderas, "Why do you want to stop us from going forward?"

Calderas smirks and says, "We are contracted to protect the entrance."

"Entrance to what?" Mei asks.

"That I can't say," Calderas replies.

Noah lifts Calderas up by his collar and punches him, "Answer the question. Entrance to what?"

Calderas spits out blood and says, "You will have to find out."

Noah gives out more punches to Calderas, but Calderas just laughs.

Seeing that no further information will be obtained, Big Joe says, "Noah, that's enough."

"We just need to keep moving forward and see, I guess," Mei says.

"Now what do we do with these demons? There are no sigils here, and I doubt that the demons will let us know where and how to find their sigils. So how do we send them back?" Chupa says.

Grey telepathically communicates, "Hell Fire. The vehicles can shoot out Hellfire. We can see if Hell Fire works for these demons, like when we used Hell Fire against Zorzulith."

"Brilliant! Let's do it." Aura says.

So, the team gathers all demons who are tied up like mummies by Chupa's Holy Water-dipped ropes and lays them in the middle of Highway 66. They have four vehicles lined up against the demons, get on the vehicles, and simply command Glorixian, "Hell Fire, now."

The vehicles open doors from their exhaust pipes, and then flame throwers slide out of the exhaust pipes to shoot Hellfire towards the demons. The demons burn like flame-grilled chicken. A red light intensifies, and the demons are banished back to Hell.

As the Hell Fire burns, the cryptid team drives the RV, the bus, the SUV and the motorcycle away like cowboys leaving a duel with victory.

CHAPTER TWELVE

THE GHOST TOWN

" **T**hey will be ready for us." Big Joe says, "The demons from Hellion Riders that escaped are probably warning them right now."

"We need a good plan," Aura says.

The team huddles and brainstorms a plan of action before they arrive at the abandoned town.

The abandoned town is called Gold Valley. It used to be a mining community with thousands of residents until the gold ran out. The gold miners then abandoned the town, leaving buildings, houses, and stores behind, attracting erosion, rust, and ghosts that are searching for places to haunt.

The cryptid team drives the RV, the bus, the SUV, and the motorcycle to the town. The entrance to the town is an arch made of wood with a hanging board. On the board spells the weathered and barely recognizable town name, "The Gold Valley".

Big Joe, Chupa, Saxon, Noah, Grey, Nessie, Rake, Mei, and Cole walk outside of the vehicles holding their weapons, while Scamp hides in the RV.

They shoulder their weapons and begin to sing "Yankee Doodle", voices loud and mocking. It isn't for pride. It is to rattle the demons before the first strike.

The demons are surprised at the cryptid team's move and come out from their hiding places and traps.

"Hello, demon maggots. Your favorite patriotic American Cryptids have arrived at the scene!" Big Joe says.

Sheriff Hampson walks out from the town hall wearing a cowboy hat and a Gold Valley badge, "Howdy, Big Joe and Noah. I see you brought your cute little friends. Are they here to join the academy?"

"Unfortunately, no. The academy has not been proven to be effective." Noah says.

"You mean it didn't work on your little buddy? What was his name? Oh right, Hunter!" Sheriff Hampson says.

Big Joe and Noah are brought back to the time when Hunter was alive. The feeling of sadness mixed with guilt and anger consumes them for a moment. They quickly shake off the emotional distraction.

Big Joe and Noah look towards Sheriff Hampson, and are shocked when they see, in the background, Hunter walking out from the town hall. He looks different, with two large bolts holding his neck together and numerous stitches holding his limbs together. He is wearing welded chest armor and shoulder pads.

How can Hunter be alive? Big Joe and Noah look at each other and think to themselves. His throat was slit by Sheriff Hampton. They buried him at the campground. He lies under the stars. How did he get here? Is he truly the Hunter they know? Or is this someone who merely looks like him?

Then they see Deputy Sheriff Jason Sims walk out of the town hall. Now it all makes sense. The Deputy Sheriff must have escaped from the underground prison and informed Sheriff Hampson of the campground location. Then they found Hunter's tomb and somehow brought him back.

Sheriff Hampson says, "Hunter, do you remember these two?" He points to Big Joe and Noah.

Hunter's red eyes look at Big Joe and Noah without any emotion, "Nope. Who are these clowns?"

Big Joe and Noah are heartbroken to hear Hunter's voice again. Oh, how much they have missed him? Yet he sounds so different, so cold, as if he has no feelings or hope.

And Big Joe and Noah cannot feel anything else other than the dark shadows inside of Hunter. There is not an ounce of soul nor warmth from him. Instead, they can only feel an emptiness filled with darkness, like a black hole sucking any life that is left of Hunter.

Sheriff Hampson commands, "Hunter, kill them."

Hunter hears the command, and an evil smile comes to his face. He holds a short sword like he did in the academy and charges towards Big Joe and Noah.

Big Joe and Noah do not want to hurt Hunter. How can they hurt their little buddy who died because of them? They block Hunter's attacks, which are much more deadly and powerful than before. Hunter is ferocious. He keeps scratching and slicing Big Joe and Noah. The more blood he sees, the more excited and aggressive he gets.

"That's enough!" Nessie says, joining the fight and attacking Hunter with her flail. The rest of the demons and cryptids move in.

Big Joe fights Sheriff Hampson. Noah fights a demon named Torath. Torath wears a cowboy hat and a cape and looks like a skeleton with bare muscles, two large horns and huge ears. Rake fights a demon named Mizgozud wearing a deputy sheriff's hat, a confederate flag, and round glasses. Mizgozud has four pointy ears and large pointy teeth. Chupa fights a demon named Golgathan with goat horns, large, long eyes, sharp claws, wearing a black furry collar and a black leather coat. Saxon fights a demon named Charro with a third eyeball on his forehead, wearing a sombrero, riding on a horse. Grey fights a demon made of shadows named Sonnun. Mei fights a previous deputy sheriff who was sent back to Hell but returned. The demon's name is Jurnin. He has unique round eyes and two pointy horns and wears a deputy sheriff's uniform. Cole fights Deputy Sheriff Sims.

Everything seems to be similar to the previous fight at the Demon Academy. Yet, this time, the cryptid team is outnumbered and outgunned.

Besides the demons fighting the cryptid team in close combat, there are other demons holding firearms that shoot out Brimstone projectiles with green fire towards the cryptid team. The demons also have guns that shoot out shadow bullets. When the shadow bullets hit the cryptids, shadows are injected into cryptids and their souls are corrupted, causing them to lose their purpose and strength.

Big Joe and Noah see the cryptid team suffering and losing, and they are worried that the shadow bullets will weaken their souls. So Big Joe and Noah shout, "Retreat!"

The cryptid team hears the command from Big Joe and Noah, and they know what they need to do. As they discussed beforehand, Big Joe and Noah will hold the demons over, and the rest of the team will retreat.

Scamp watches the fight in the RV, hears the magic word and talks to Glorixian, "Azen fog release!"

Long, curvy transparent tubes come out from the exhaust pipes of the RV, the bus, the SUV, and the motorcycle, and a blue-colored fog quickly occupies the arch area and then expands to the whole town.

The Azen fog slows the demons down by blocking their visions while the cryptid team retreats to their vehicles.

Big Joe and Noah hold over the feisty demons, including Sheriff Hampson and Hunter. The fight is so intense and hard that Big Joe and Noah are not able to leave. Big Joe and Noah are covered with wounds and blood and have been hit with multiple rounds of shadow bullets. Their spirits are weakened so much so that they cannot fight with their full mental strength.

The vehicles that hold the rest of the cryptid team drive away while Big Joe and Noah are fighting with the limited spirit and power left in them.

Then they are captured, tied up, and brought to a prison cell inside the abandoned mine.

Big Joe and Noah are so beaten up and exhausted that they immediately pass out in the prison cell.

The next day, when they wake up, they are tied up on two large wooden crosses.

"Wakey wakey, sleeping beauties!" Sheriff Hampson says.

Big Joe and Noah look around and see Sheriff Hampson staring at them. Hunter, Torath, Mizgozud, Golgathan, Charro, Jurnin and Deputy Sheriff Sims stand beside Sheriff Hampson.

The shadow demon Sonnun stands right in front of them.

"Now that you are awake, the process can begin." Sheriff Hampson says, signaling to Sonnun.

"What process?" Big Joe asks. But no one responds. Big Joe and Noah struggle to get out of the chains that tie them up, but the chains do not budge.

Sonnun is made of shadows. When he fought with Grey, every time the laser blade cut a part of him off, the lost shadow part reattached back to Sonnun immediately.

Sonnun lifts his hands up, and shadow balls are formed from his body. There is at first one shadow ball floating in the air, then two more are formed, then there are twenty-six shadow balls flying around him. He uses his right index finger to push the balls gently, and the shadow balls fly one by one to surround Big Joe and Noah.

Sonnun holds up both of his hands vertically and pushes them forward abruptly. The thirteen shadow balls surrounding Big Joe and the thirteen shadow balls surrounding Noah enter Big Joe's and Noah's bodies, respectively, after Sonnun's powerful push.

As soon as the shadow balls touch Big Joe's and Noah's skin, an intense burning sensation starts to hit them hard. The more shadows enter their bodies, the more painful it gets. Big Joe and Noah let out loud cries like they are experiencing slow and excruciating deaths. For these two tough guys to cry out loud, the pain must be unbearable.

While Big Joe and Noah are tortured by the shadow balls inside their bodies, Hunter watches them without any emotion. But in an instant, he feels like his head is splitting with a crack in the middle. The pain feels like lightning has struck him, burning his head up where the crack is. Hunter is not sure why he is experiencing this heartbreaking pain. But he pretends nothing is bothering him. If there is one thing he learned from following Sheriff Hampson's leadership, it is that the weak are not tolerated. Once weakness is shown, one is thrown away like unwanted trash.

The shadow balls break inside Big Joe's and Noah's bodies. Their eyes open with anger, pain and sorrow. Then their eyes change color like solar eclipses. Shadows gradually cover their eye retinas until they are fully dark. Then their eyes are closed, only to open five seconds later with a terrifying color of blood.

The moment Big Joe and Noah open their red eyes, Hunter feels his heart ache like never before. It feels like a cold, sharp knife with salt on it has punctured through his soft, sensitive and vulnerable heart.

"The shadow corruption is complete. Now they have been transformed fully into demons." Sonnun concludes.

"Excellent work." Sheriff Hampson says, looking at and admiring Big Joe's and Noah's red eyes, "Big Joe and Noah, welcome to the House of Colath." He pauses, "We are legion for we are many."

The four-eyed demon, Sheriff Hampson's real name is Colath.

Colath continues, "Now, Big Joe and Noah, you will be led by Hunter to capture the cryptids that escaped."

Big Joe and Noah do not have any expression on their faces or eyes and respond, "Yes, Colath."

Hunter looks at Big Joe and Noah with disdain, "Really? These two newbie morons?"

Colath looks at Hunter, "Yes. Do you have any issues?"

"No, Colath." Hunter looks at Colath, then turns to Big Joe and Noah, "You two, come with me."

And so, the journey begins of Hunter, Big Joe and Noah tracking the cryptids. They use their sense of smell to track the cryptids like a tiger traces its prey in the wild.

The cryptids seem to be very good at hiding their smell, as Hunter, Big Joe and Noah can only locate certain spots they have been to. It is not easy to connect the dots and figure out where the cryptids are headed. Some of the leads are even completely wrong.

But day and night, the group of three diligently hunts for the cryptids under Colath's orders.

They only rest a little bit around midnight. When they lie on the trees, the Great Bear constellation shines brightly above them. Hunter, Big Joe, and Noah stare at the Great Bear and wonder why the constellation feels so close to their hearts, as if there is somehow a close connection between them and the constellation.

They don't talk much. Mostly, they only communicate about hunting directions.

To them, the world looks dark and red. There is no hope nor purpose inside their empty hearts. The only thing left in them is a desire for destruction. To kill and destroy everything seems to be the sole direction. No need for compassion. No need for morality. No need for ethicality. The world is a cruel place, and they must return the cruelty to survive.

Along the way, there are no towns or human beings, so they rely on hunting wild animals for food. There is something familiar about hunting as a pack. They work smoothly as a team. With one look at each other, they know what to do, whether it's to block a prey's way of escape or to move around the prey to attack on the other side. The three of them understand each other without saying a word. There seems to be a tacit agreement between them. Or is it some kind of connection in their past lives?

This is strange for Hunter. He does not understand why the Great Bear feels like a part of something inside him that is connected to these two newbies. He does not understand why the three of them have so much unspoken understanding of each other. He does not understand why he had a headache and a heartache when the shadow balls corrupted Big Joe and Noah. To him, it feels like there is a history among the three of them. But he does not remember. No matter how hard he tries to search in his brain, nothing comes up in his memories. Everything in the past is blocked by dark shadows.

Big Joe and Noah are confused as well. There are shadows blocking their memories of what happened in the past. They do not know who they were or where they came from. All they know is that there is a lot of anger and hate inside of them, wanting out. It seems that the world has done them wrong, and now they are here to take revenge. Every animal they kill, they kill with violence, without mercy. It is their way of taking out on this dark and bloody world. At the same time, they feel the connection between themselves and Hunter. The interactions they share are evident that they somehow know each other from the past. But nothing comes up when they try to remember. It is like they type "Hunter" in the search engine of their brains, but a "404 error (not found)" returns.

As Hunter, Big Joe and Noah spend more time together, they get more comfortable with each other's presence. Every hunt feels like Deja vu. Every conversation feels familiar. Every interaction feels like it had happened before, maybe in another life.

Soon, they start to talk about how the hunt went. They share a joke or two. They smile a little at each other. They chat about how they are feeling that day.

They begin to share grins after the hunt, brief jests whispered under their breath. Each laugh is a hairline fracture in the armor of shadows. Even though the crack is so small that it is skinnier than a single piece of hair, the warmth of the crack melts the sorrow and pain away, just a little bit at first, then a little bit more, and a little bit more.

One day, the three of them come across a piece of bone that smells like it used to be a lamb chop.

Big Joe and Noah both feel a strong connection to the piece of bone that they are holding. In fact, before they realize, they both have their tongues out and lick one side of the bone each. Then they realize that this looks ridiculous and quickly retrieve their tongues that are hanging out on the bone. They have drooled uncontrollably as well, so they must wipe their mouths.

"Are you guys hungry or something?" Hunter asks while being confused about the situation in front of him, "Does this bone really taste that good?" He licks it, and there's something about the sauce that makes the bone taste delicious.

"Guess this chef must be very good at cooking lamb chops." Big Joe says while scratching his head and feeling embarrassed, and Noah agrees, "Very flavorful sauce."

"Wait. This smells familiar." Hunter says, trying to figure out what the smell is.

"The cryptids!" Hunter, Big Joe, and Noah all speak at the same time.

Finally, they have found something they can track the cryptids with. The bone is still fresh, so the cryptids have not traveled far from the location.

Hunter, Big Joe and Noah search the area for the cryptids. After a day of searching, they notice some smoke coming from the middle of a cactus forest.

"Interesting. It smells nice." Hunter says.

"This might be the cryptids cooking dinner." Big Joe says.

"Let's go check it out," Noah says.

The three of them lower their bodies, hide behind cactuses and approach the source of the smoke. And their suspicion is correct. It is the cryptids.

Chupa is grilling some goat chops and singing his Song of Great Goat Chops, "Goat chops, goat chops, you are the best. World-famous goat chops made by the best." Smoke comes from the charcoal grill, and the sizzling sound of goat chops harmonizes with Chupa's singing.

"So, it was a goat chop, not a lamb chop." Big Joe whispers to Noah and Hunter as they are watching the cryptids. "We've got to get the recipe somehow," Noah whispers in reply while drooling. Hunter smiles as he hears this conversation.

Grey is inventing, experimenting and making new weapons in the lab on the bus. Suddenly, Glorixian says, "Big Joe, Noah, and Hunter are detected nearby. But the initial scan shows that they are covered with dark shadows."

Hearing this, Grey gets off the bus and sees Big Joe, Noah and Hunter come out from the cactus they were hiding behind, holding a halberd, a war hammer, and a short sword, respectively and ready to fight.

Chupa holds the grilling tongs and looks up, sees Big Joe, Noah and Hunter, smiles, and says, "Hello folks, you are just in time for a new batch." But soon he realizes that they are not here for BBQ.

Big Joe, Noah, and Hunter start charging against Grey and Chupa. Saxon, Mei, Cole, Nessie, and Rake hear the commotion and join the fight. They are surprised that Big Joe and Noah are fighting them without reservation. The cryptid team sees that Big Joe's and Noah's eyes are red, just like Hunter's eyes. They understand that Big Joe and Noah have been corrupted by the demons.

Grey analyzes the situation and decides to try and use his telepathic abilities to talk to Big Joe and Noah. To show them what happened in the past, Grey needs to put his hand over their heads.

Grey jumps up from behind Big Joe and grabs his neck with his left hand, and uses his right hand to touch Big Joe's head. Big Joe fights Grey telepathically. The dark shadows within Big Joe amplify Big Joe's fear. The fear of losing loved ones and the fear of failing as a leader make Big Joe throw strong, icy punches at Grey telepathically. Grey sees the fear within Big Joe and blocks it with the love he received from his mother and from the cryptids, which becomes fire that melts Big Joe's cold, icy punches. The fear that comes with the ice is shattered into pieces. With strong determination, Grey forces Big Joe's mind into his brain to see past events. Grey shows Big Joe the time when he first met Big Joe and Chupa at Area 51, how they bonded, escaped, and then how the cryptid team found their purpose, met Angel Bariel and fought demons. Big Joe, blinded by the dark shadows, at first resists seeing anything that Grey shows him. But Grey uses his strong, powerful mind to force Big Joe's eyes open. Then Big Joe sees all the past events. A drop of tear falls from Big Joe's eye as he sees the bond the cryptids share and the hard, exhausting battles they fought to become who they are now. Big Joe finally realizes where he came from and who he is. He understands that he is a cryptid and that he has a mission. Grey telepathically talks to Big Joe, "Big Joe, I sense some demons closing in. They might be sent by the four-eyed demon to spy on you. We need to keep your identity under cover. So, keep fighting us."

Big Joe grabs Grey's arm and throws him onto Noah.

Grey takes the opportunity deliberately given by Big Joe, grabs Noah by his horn, and puts his hand on Noah's head. Grey sees that the shadows have corrupted Noah's soul and fed Noah enormous anger. Telepathically, Noah's angry fireballs hit Grey fiercely and continuously. Grey fights Noah's angry fireballs with agility and calmness. Noah's anger keeps on shooting out fire while Grey's calmness and love become a shield around him. Grey uses his strong mind and pushes the shield of peace and kindness forward. The shield shatters and becomes heavy rain, extinguishing Noah's fireballs. Then Grey opens his mind to Noah telepathically and shows Noah when they first met, the journey the cryptids had been on, the bond the team shared, and the support Noah received from and gave to the team. Noah's shadows gradually break open, with his soul shining through the cracks of shadowy darkness. Grey then tells Noah about the mission he is on and suggests that him and Big Joe stay undercover.

Noah picks Grey up and throws him onto Hunter. Grey puts his hand on Hunter's forehead and fights Hunter telepathically. Hunter's mind is wild and bloodthirsty. Hunter charges towards

Grey with a fierce animal instinct that turns Hunter into a large, shadowy monster with a bloody mouth. Grey uses his internal mindfulness to form giant calming hands that capture Hunter, and comforts Hunter by slowly and gently petting him on the head and on the back. Hunter bites the hands at first, but when he feels the immense love with comforting warmth, he slows down and enjoys the gentle strokes on his fur. He leans into the giant warm hands. Grey invites Hunter inside his mind and shows Hunter the memory of when he was fighting with Big Joe and Noah against Sheriff Hampson. And then Hunter sees the memory of when his throat was slit by Sheriff Hampson, and how sad Big Joe and Noah were. Hunter sees Big Joe and Noah burying him under the Great Bear constellation and smiles. Tears drop off from Hunter's cheeks. The memories finally have come back to him. He remembers why the Great Bear feels so close to his heart and why his heart and head ached so much when Big Joe and Noah were corrupted by shadows. Grey telepathically says to Hunter, "Hunter, my friend. Big Joe and Noah care a lot about you. They were devastated when you were killed by Sheriff Hampson. And it is even more painful to see you working with the demons now. Big Joe and Noah are on a mission to send the demons back, including the four-eyed demon, Sheriff Hampson. Now that you know who you are and what happened before, I hope you can make the right decision to help Big Joe and Noah. More demons are close to us as of right now, so be extra careful with Big Joe and Noah, my friend."

Hunter nods to Grey and then fights him off.

Then Hunter looks at Big Joe and Noah, and their eyes meet. An abundance of emotion is boiling under their calm expressions. They cannot let any feelings show.

Torath, Mizgozud, Golgathan, Charro, Sonnun, and Jurnin show up. They have been following Hunter, Big Joe and Noah to ensure they do not derail from the task given by Colath, the four-eyed demon and leader of the Gold Valley. Now that the cryptids have been located, the demons decide to show themselves and help Hunter, Big Joe and Noah capture them.

Chupa, Saxon, Grey, Mei, Cole, Nessie, and Rake fight the demon team, which consists of Hunter, Big Joe, Noah, and the other demons that have just shown up. The cryptid team is outnumbered again.

Glorixian suggests, "Holy Water spray?" Scamp, hiding inside the bus, watches the fight and says, "Holy shit! That's a lot of demons. Yes, Holy Water!" Glorixian says, "Sure, Scamp." Just like what happened on Highway 66, skinny, long sprinkler tubes are raised up from the vehicles through tiny doors that open on the roofs and motorcycle handles and start sprinkling Holy Water. The only difference is that another set of long sprinkler tubes is raised up, with Holy Water mist spraying out, not only burning the demons' skin, but also blocking their views.

The cryptid team is not affected by the Holy Water, so they quickly retreat into the vehicles and drive away while the demons are burned by the Holy Water spray and mist.

Hunter, Big Joe and Noah return to the Gold Valley with the other demons.

Before Hunter, Big Joe and Noah started their mission of capturing the cryptids, Colath informed the other demons to follow and observe the three to confirm if they had truly turned into demons. Now that they have witnessed the fight, and there were no questionable interactions between the cryptids and the three, the demons' mission is complete.

When Hunter, Big Joe and Noah are back in the town hall, Colath meets them and greets them, "Hunter, Big Joe and Noah, I am delighted that you have truly become one of many."

Hunter, Big Joe and Noah say without any expression on their faces, "We are legion for we are many."

Colath says, "Meet your orientation leader, Sonnun. He will show you around and get you trained on processes."

Sonnun comes forward, "Hey, newbies. Let's go. We have a well-developed program for new demon recruits. Here's an agenda."

Sonnun hands Hunter, Big Joe and Noah three pieces of paper with Latin letters written wildly all over them.

"The first item on the agenda is Legion Overview. Then we will go through our Vision Statement, Mission Statement, and your Job Role, Introductions and then the Gold Valley Tour." Sonnun reads the agenda.

"Sounds great." Big Joe says.

"Looking forward to learning," Hunter says.

"Can't wait," Noah says.

And so, the orientation begins. Hunter, Big Joe and Noah learn that Colath is a legion status demon. The legion is called House of Colath, named after the four-eyed demon. Their Vision Statement is "To destroy the world with no mercy." Their Mission Statement is "To kill and eat each and every human being on planet Earth." The three of them are part of the Brute Force Team within the House of Colath. They have already met their teammates, who are Sonnun, Torath, Mizgozud, Golgathan, Charro, and Jurnin. Their probation period is 666 days.

Then there's the final agenda item after a quick fifteen-minute break, the Gold Valley Tour.

The town hall of Gold Valley is the office and meeting room for Colath's core operations. From the town hall, he controls the ghost town.

In the abandoned gold mine, there are tunnels leading to different rooms. There is a weapons room where firearms that can shoot out Brimstone projectiles and guns that can shoot out shadow bullets are stored. Traditional weapons like halberds, war hammers and maces made from human bones are on display as well.

There is a room closed with a black iron door. On the door are statues of the tortured in Hell. What is interesting is that the statues move and scream in pain as they are tortured. This room can only be accessed by high-ranked demons. Two demons guard the door at all times.

"Now that we have finished our agenda for orientation, you can walk around and familiarize yourselves with the facility."

Sonnun says, "Tomorrow is our all-hands-on-deck meeting called the Meeting at the Town Hall. Our leader Colath, will give a speech followed by team building exercises."

"Do we have meetings often?" Big Joe asks.

"Yea. Meetings keep us motivated for our grand mission. You will get used to this in no time." Sonnun replies, "The three of you will be introduced to the legion as new demon initiates during this meeting."

"Oh, that sure sounds uncomfortable," Hunter says, as he hates the thought of being stared at by a bunch of demons.

"You'll survive." Sonnun says, "Now you can feel free to roam around the town."

Hunter, Big Joe, and Noah inspect every inch of the town. As they are entering the mine, a demon wearing a leather jacket walks towards them. This demon looks familiar. He is Calderas from the Hellion Riders.

Big Joe and Noah remember Calderas, who was banished back to Hell. How is he here again?

Calderas sees Big Joe and Noah, and starts to talk, "What's up, guys?" But his voice is not a male voice but a female one.

Big Joe and Noah understand now. They do not have their full memories back yet, and that's why it took them a minute to figure things out.

"Aura! Good to see you." Big Joe says, lowering his voice.

"Let's talk in private," Aura says.

So, the four of them sneak into the dark, shadowy part of the mine.

Aura is surprised to see Hunter here, but quickly figures things out. "Did Colath resurrect you?"

Hunter says, "Yes. Then Sonnun corrupted me with dark shadows. But Grey showed me the past, so I know better now."

"Good, Hunter." Aura says, "I've been undercover for a while now. Do you know what's inside the Gate of Hell?"

"No. We are trying to figure out a way to get in. But we are not ranked high enough." Big Joe says.

"Easy. Follow me." Aura says.

Aura leads the way. As she walks, she changes her shape into a higher-ranked demon, Jurnin.

The four of them arrive at the Gate of Hell.

Two demon guards see Jurnin with Hunter, Big Joe and Noah.

Jurnin says, "I've been ordered to show this room to these new recruits under special orders from Colath."

The guards do not question Jurnin, who is a staple on Colath's core team.

The Gate of Hell opens. Bright red light shines through the gate. Jurnin, Hunter, Big Joe and Noah walk inside while the tortured on the Gate of Hell are attempting to grab them with their hands and drag them into the black iron gate.

The gate closes behind them.

The room is made up of rocky walls from the gold mine. As they enter the room, they see an arch made of dark shadows and dried blood that morph into moving sigils. There must be more than a hundred sigils moving around. On top of the arch, Latin letters are written, "House of Colath." The letters are made of blood, human bones and dark shadows that morph constantly. There are six crosses on the left of the room. Each cross has a human being tied to it. Hunter, Big Joe and Noah check on the human beings tied to the crosses. All are deceased except for one. He is covered in blood and passed out.

"Hello?" Big Joe asks.

The man wakes up and looks at Big Joe, Noah and Hunter, slowly turning his head. He sees Jurnin and starts to freak out.

Aura changes back from Jurnin to herself, "Hey, it's okay. We are not demons."

The man looks surprised to see Aura's shape shift.

Noah says, "What did the demons do to you?"

The man is very weak. He turns to Noah slowly, "Blood. They kept cutting me up for blood to smear onto the arch."

"How about the other five?" Big Joe asks.

"I don't know them. I was kidnapped separately and brought here by Jurnin. The demons tried their blood, but it didn't work. Fortunately, my blood worked, so they kept me alive." He pauses to gain energy, "My name is Ben St. James. If I die, please tell my daughter I love her. Her name is Rebecca St. James, and she goes to St. John Catholic School." Ben says.

"Ben, we are not going to let you die," Noah says.

Ben feels a little relief after hearing Noah's words. He has lost hope in the past few days, but now he has a reason to be hopeful again.

"Ben, what happens when they put your blood on the arch?" Aura asks.

Ben says, "They call it the Demonus Arch. My blood is smeared, then demons come out of that. I noticed the symbol changes when each demon crosses the arch."

"I've been here once before. But there were many demons, so I could not ask questions. Like I suspected, Colath and his legion are using the portal to transport demons from another dimension to here." Aura says.

"I'm guessing every time a demon comes through, the sigil is imprinted on the arch." Big Joe says.

"That makes sense. Judging from the sigils, Colath has a legion of at least a hundred demons." Noah says.

"We need to alert Grey and the rest of our team to this information. Not sure if Grey can invent that many weapons to fight a hundred demons in a short amount of time." Big Joe says.

"I'll change back to Calderas' shape and drive the motorcycle out of town to inform them," Aura says.

"Ben, we will be back to save you." Big Joe says, "Until then, stay hopeful."

"Thank you. Because of you all, I will." Ben says.

Aura, Hunter, Big Joe and Noah say goodbye to each other.

The next day, all the demons gather in the town hall.

Golgathan is the moderator for the Meeting at the Town Hall, "Good morning, fellow demons, demon initiates, and demon familiars. Welcome to another Meeting at the Town Hall. We are legion for we are many."

The audience chants, "We are legion for we are many."

"Now, the first item on the agenda is an introduction to the new demon initiates. Let's welcome the new recruits: Hunter, Big Joe and Noah!" Golgathan says.

Hunter, Big Joe, and Noah stand up. The audience cheers.

"Hunter is a resurrected addition that completed a full shadow transformation. Big Joe and Noah are additions from our rivals. They also completed a full shadow transformation." Golgathan introduces them.

Hunter, Big Joe and Noah wave to the audience and quickly sit down.

Golgathan continues, "The second item on the agenda is from our very own supreme leader, Colath!"

Colath steps onto stage and waves to the audience, "What's up, my fellow demons?"

The audience cheers, claps, and whistles like concertgoers responding to a superstar.

Colath continues, "Today, inspiration is a word that is on my mind. So, I'm going to share something personal with you. For centuries, I have worked hard, killed countless human beings, and dreamed about the day when I will have my very own legion. 'House of Colath' seemed like a distant dream. I was a demon initiate like you, Hunter, Big Joe and Noah. Other demons told me it was impossible to shake the status quo, that I started too late, that I would never be bad enough to reach legion status. They told me to stop trying and give up my dream. But I did not listen to them. In my head, there was a voice telling me that if I tried hard enough, eventually I would make it. I persevered through hardships, through setbacks, and through difficulties. Then our dishonorable prince started to notice my disrespectful work and put his distrust in me. Before long, I was granted legion status."

Colath looks at the crowd from his house proudly and says, "Today, I look at you and know that it's all worth it. We are legion for we are many."

The audience chants, "We are legion for we are many."

At this climax of a moment, a loud boom is heard overhead. The demons look up, thinking it might be fireworks for Colath's monumental speech.

But instead of fireworks, it is a bomb. The bomb blows up, breaking the roof of the town hall. As the roof collapses, another bomb arrives, blows up, and splashes a type of liquid everywhere. The demons are seen burnt by the liquid.

Ah, the liquid is Holy Water.

The once grand town hall is filled with terrifying screams from the demons.

Colath is mad. Who dares to interrupt his perfect speech? Then he sees the cryptids arrive.

Saxon flies in. Chupa, Grey, Mei, Cole, Nessie, and Rake arrive in the vehicles. They are wearing shiny golden armors and holding different kinds of firearms than the traditional weapons they used to carry before.

Saxon shoots four arrows from his new mechanical bow towards Hunter, Big Joe, Noah, and Aura, who is disguised as Calderas. The arrows touch their bodies and spread into armors that cover their bodies using nanotechnology. Saxon shoots another set of four arrows towards Hunter, Big Joe, Noah and Aura and the arrows land in their hands and spread into firearms.

The armors were forged in Hellfire and submerged in Holy Water before they were put to use. As a result, the armors can provide protection against brutal force and shadow bullets.

Colath sees this and understands that somehow Hunter, Big Joe and Noah managed to clear the shadows out of themselves, and that Aura has been undercover as Calderas. He becomes furious, for betrayal is his worst enemy and loyalty is his highest priority.

The vehicles continuously shoot out Holy Water towards the demons, damaging some and killing some. Big Joe, Noah, Hunter, and Aura utilize their firearms to shoot Hellfire towards the demons around them in the town hall. Saxon, Chupa, Grey, Mei, Cole, Nessie, and Rake use their firearms to shoot out Hellfire towards the demons outside of the town hall.

Colath, Torath, Mizgozud, Golgathan, Charro, Sonnun, Jurnin, and Sheriff Sims charge towards the cryptid team. Like a recurring nightmare, they fight in close combat again.

Big Joe fights Colath. Noah fights Torath. Rake fights Mizgozud. Chupa fights Golgathan. Saxon fights Charro. Grey fights Sonnun. Mei fights Jurnin. Cole fights Deputy Sheriff Sims. Aura fights a deputy sheriff who was banished to Hell and came back named Fifith. Fifith has two large horns on his cheeks, two long horns as his chin, and multiple horns on his head. Hunter fights another deputy sheriff who was banished to Hell and came back named Solya. Solya has four small horns, two each as his cheeks. On his head are six horns, with two giant horns in the front and four smaller horns in the back.

Colath is furious at Hunter, Big Joe and Noah, so he takes it all out on the leader of the cryptids, Big Joe. He swings his mace fiercely at Big Joe. Big Joe moves left and right, using his firearm with an axe on it to block Colath's attacks. Big Joe uses his firearm to hit Colath, but Colath uses his hands to hold on to Big Joe's firearm. Colath fuels his strength with anger. It is hard to defeat Colath by Big Joe alone.

Torath shoots shadow bullets towards Noah. Noah flies up and dodges the bullets. Noah takes his firearm with a spear attached and charges against Torath. Torath uses his guns to shoot at Noah while dodging the spear. The spear barely misses Torath's head and slices his shoulder.

Mizgozud throws heavy punches at Rake. Rake uses his agility to get away from the punches, jumps up, and grabs onto Mizgozud's neck. "Confederate flag, isn't it too outdated?" Rake says, indicating the Confederate flag T-shirt that Mizgozud is wearing. Mizgozud gets angry and says, "Punk! I will squish you like a pumpkin!" Rake stretches his arms long to circle around Mizgozud's neck multiple times, and tightens the grip, "You can try, but can you breathe?"

Chupa looks at Golgathan and says, "My favorite goat chops! Come to papa!" Chupa pulls the rope tight to create a small and large hole, slips the rope over Golgathan's nose and ears, pulls out any slack, keeps the loop down on Golgathan's muzzle, and grabs the rope with his thumb. Golgathan is mad and humiliated because he is muzzled like a goat, so he uses his claws to try to untie the muzzle. But he cannot. Chupa uses this opportunity to tie his legs up, and Golgathan struggles to stand up and falls.

Saxon flies in the air to shoot arrows towards Charro. Charro uses his sombrero to block the arrows. Charro whistles, and his demon horse runs towards him. He jumps up the horse and uses his higher height to fight Saxon. Charro grabs onto Saxon and throws punches at Saxon. Saxon swings left and right, using his wings to dodge Charro's punches, and returns the favor by punching Charro on his face.

Sonnun puts his hands together and pushes a flood of shadows onto Grey. Grey uses his firearm to shoot out Hell Fire, which burns the shadowy flood and makes Sonnun go "Outch!" as the shadows are a part of Sonnun. Grey uses the laser blade on his firearm to cut Sonnun up into pieces. The shadows that make up Sonnun's body are temporarily separated, then they combine to form Sonnun's body again.

Mei uses her firearm with a sword to attack Jurnin. The sword gets stuck on Jurnin's horn, so Mei jumps up and grabs Jurnin's horn and forces the sword out of Jurnin's horn. Jurnin grabs Mei's legs and drags her down, but Mei already has her sword freed, and she uses the sword to poke into his chest.

Cole and Deputy Sheriff Sims fight fist to fist. It is like a combat between Cole's military training versus Deputy Sheriff Sims' academy training. They fight punch by punch, representing their respective backgrounds. Jab, cross, lead hook, rear hook, lead uppercut, rear uppercut, you name it, and they are using it.

Aura changes into a giant monster while she fights Fifith. She uses her giant claw to grab Fifith's long chin and punches Fifith. Fifith uses his claws to cut into Aura's giant claw, making her bleed. Aura uses her other giant claw and grabs Fifith's waist, and throws him into the crowd of demons being burnt by Holy Water.

Hunter leans into his training from the Demon Academy to fight Solya. Solya is bulkier than Hunter, but Hunter is more flexible and faster. Hunter swiftly moves around when Solya hits him with a hammer and uses his firearm with a short sword to cut and swipe Solya.

Scamp shoots Hell Fire balls at demons using his crossbows from the sunroof of the bus. He is scared for his life, but with the protection from the bulletproof bus, he feels safer and wants to help.

The fight is exhausting and long-drawn-out. The cryptids are sweating, bleeding, and running out of energy. They continue to fight the good fight. Not because it is easy, not because they think they can win, but because it is what is right.

Gradually, the cryptid team defeats demons, demon initiates, and demon familiars one by one. The demon team is admitting defeat by getting captured or fleeing the scene.

Then there is only one demon left to fight, the four-eyed-demon, Sheriff Hampson, Colath.

The cryptids surround Colath.

"Your legion is gone. You should give up." Big Joe says, holding his firearm.

"You have no idea what legion means." Colath laughs, opens his shirt, and the cryptids see that his belly becomes bigger and bigger until a smaller deformed demonling with long neck, sharp teeth and four eyes, around three feet tall, steps out. Then, more and more smaller demonlings, in different shapes and sizes, looking like deformed Colath, jump out of Colath's belly.

"Demonlings, attack the cryptids!" Colath commands as more and more demonlings come out of his belly.

Around a hundred demonlings charge towards the cryptid team. They are ferocious like untamed wild animals, biting, eating, and scratching everyone on the cryptid team.

The cryptids drag the demonlings off, then more demonlings climb on them. It starts to feel like a never-ending battle. The cryptids, Mei and Cole, are submerged with demonlings and can barely breathe.

Hunter sees Big Joe and Noah buried by the demonlings. For a moment, he is out of air and sees the Great Bear constellation coming down, extending a giant furry paw, and picking him up. He is afraid, afraid to lose Big Joe and Noah to the shadows again. He is angry, angry that Colath is winning with shadowy darkness. The fear of losing his cryptid brothers amplifies his anger. He knows that if he does nothing, everyone will die at the hands of Colath. There is no way he is going to let the same fate that happened to him happen to Big Joe and Noah. The anger helps him fight off the demonlings, but the love and concern he feels for Big Joe and Noah fuel him with unparalleled strength.

"None of you can stop us. We are legion. We are many." Colath laughs, enjoying the scene of the cryptid team struggling.

Hunter tears free of the swarm, his sword blazing in the torchlight. He lunges and draws the blade across Colath's throat, echoing the wound he once suffered. The legion's laughter dies with him.

"And we are cryptids. We are family." Hunter says.

The light shines in the darkness, and the darkness has not overcome it.

The demonlings disappear as Colath's throat is slit.

The cryptids, Mei and Cole, can finally breathe. And they breathe heavily, while looking at Hunter. Chupa ties Colath up with his ropes.

Hunter, Big Joe, Noah, Chupa, Saxon, Grey, Mei, Cole, Nessie, Rake, Aura, and Scamp take Colath inside the Gate of Hell. Noah helps untie Ben from the cross.

In front of everyone is the Demonus Arch.

"Well, having all the sigils on the arch makes our job easier," Aura says.

"Good thing I had plenty of goat chops before the fight." Mei says while cutting her hands and smearing her blood on the sigils on the arch.

A bright red light shines from the sigils, dyeing everyone and everything the color of blood.

"Hunter, would you do the honor?" Big Joe says.

Hunter nods.

He picks up Colath's cowboy hat on the ground, wears it on his head and adjusts it to fit, and says, "I hereby banish you demons back to Hell. Especially you, Sheriff Hampson, four-eyed demon, Colath."

Colath and the other demons are absorbed by the bright red light into the Demonus Arch.

Before Colath disappears into the red light, he laughs, "Sending me back won't do you any good. He will know I failed him. He will be coming for you."

"What is that supposed to mean?" Chupa asks.

"We'll figure it out later. We always do." Noah says.

"We must destroy this town so that other demons cannot come over and use the arch." Big Joe says.

"I made Hell Fire missiles that can be targeted at the Demonous Arch," Grey says.

"Let's do it," Aura says.

And so, Big Joe, Hunter, Noah, Chupa, Saxon, Grey, Mei, Cole, Nessie, Rake, Aura, Scamp and Ben walk away to the vehicles, while a missile hits the Demonous Arch, blowing up Hell Fire everywhere and destroying the Gold Valley.

A week later, the cryptid team is home at Camp Moonlit Smiles.

Big Joe is writing and sketching everything that happened over the last few months.

Mei and Cole are reviewing and editing video clips they captured.

Aura, Nessie, Hunter, Saxon, and Grey are watching TV.

Scamp, Rake, Noah, and Chupa are playing a game of dominoes.

A TV commercial comes on, "Elect Charles Kiley, the obvious winner for Mayor of San Rosa."

Grey looks at the TV screen and sees Zorzulith the Head disguised as a human being in the TV commercial. Father Devin, the evil priest, stands beside Zorzulith as his Policy Aide.

At the campground, a portal opens and out steps Jackson Jackelope with an automatic rifle strapped on his shoulder and a mystical trinket in his hands while being chased by three demons.

TO BE CONTINUED.

CAMP MOONLIT SM

BUNKER CENTER
& AURAS RESIDENCE
& BUNKER ENTRANCE #2

SAXON'S COMMUNICATION
TOWER RESIDENCE

FLOATING
CROSS
MONOLITH

TRANSPORT
SIGIL SITE

CHU
& GOA

RICHARD'S
CABIN

NESSIE'S DOMAIN

KOI'S
CABIN

RECREATION
CENTER &
BUNKER #1

CAMPING
AREA #2

MOONLIT
LODGE

DORMS

SHOPPING
CENTER

GIFT
SHOP

CAMP ENTRANCE

GROCERY
SHOP

CAMPING
AREA #3

GAS STATION

HWY 7

ES
MOONLIT CRESCENT CAVE
DEET'S CABIN
EO'S HUT
RAL'S CABIN
PORTAL SITE
NOAH'S CHURCH RESIDENCE
SE
WEEP'S HUT
BIG JOE'S CABIN
JACKSON'S CABIN
RAKE'S CABIN
VALKO'S HUT
FAITH CEMETERY
SCAMP'S HUT
ZAT'S CABIN
ALL
CAMP OFFICE
SHEPHARD'S CABIN
CAMPING AREA #1
PIP'S CABIN
ECURITY
PARKING LOTS

7″0″
6″9″
6″6″
6″3″
6″0″
5″9″
5″6″
5″3″
5″0″
4″9″
4″6″
4″3″
4″0″
3″9″
3″6″
3″3″
3″0″
2″9″
2″6″
2″3″
2″0″
1″9″
1″6″
1″3″
1″0″
9″
6″
3″
0″

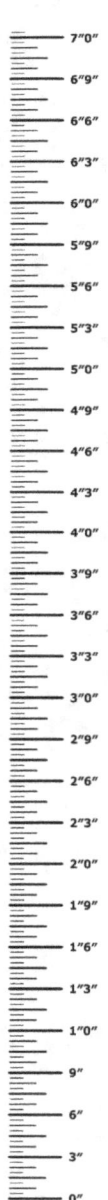

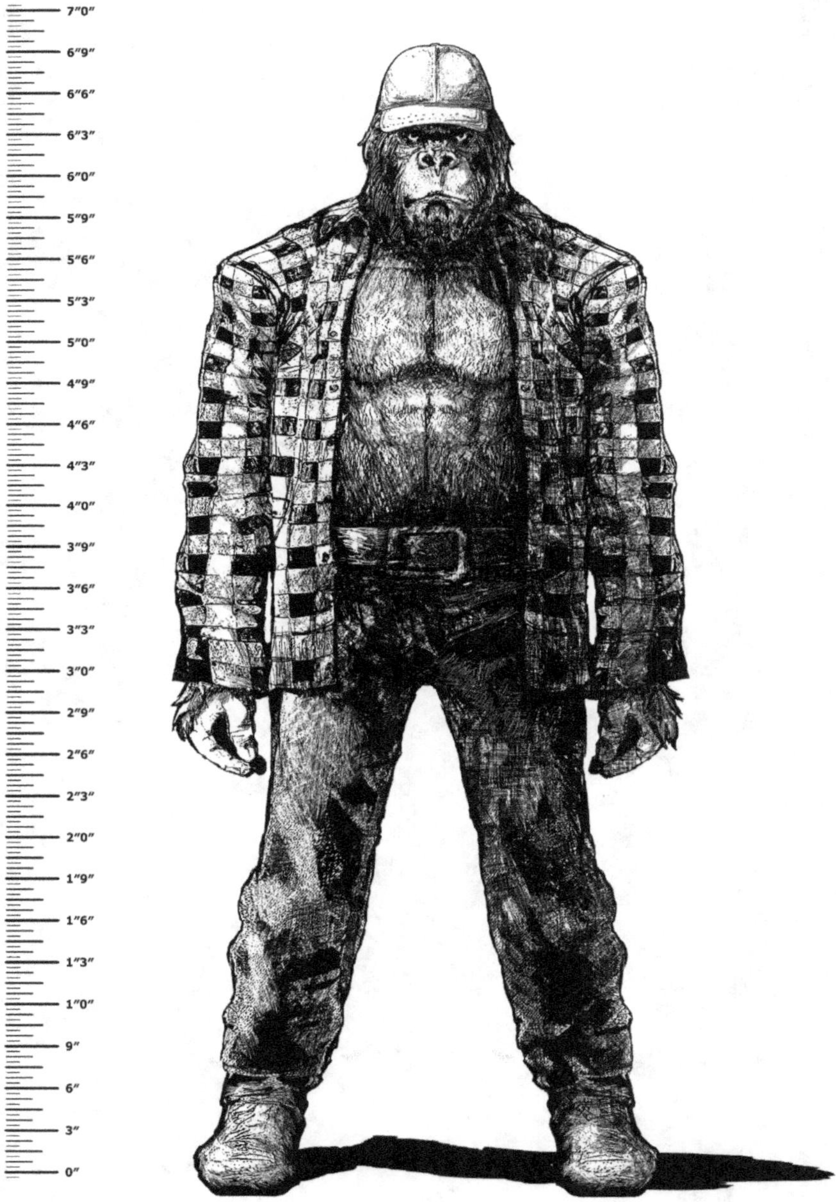

BIG JOE

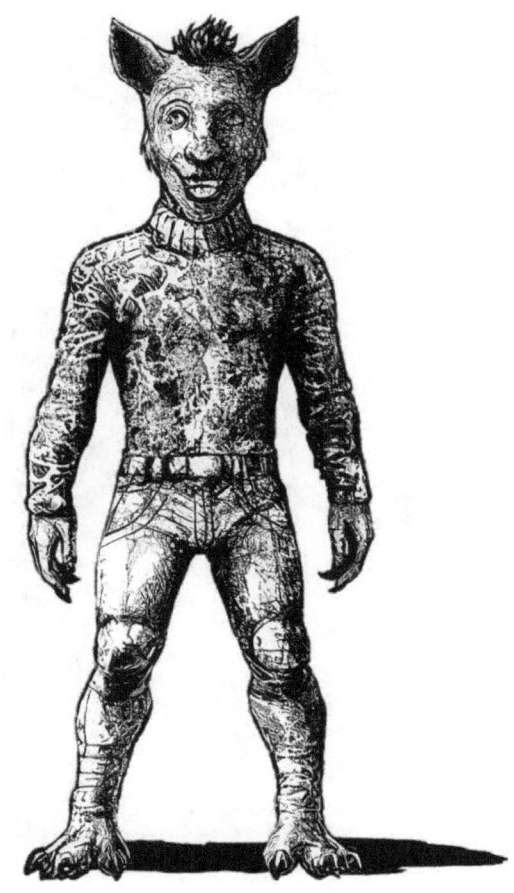

CHUPA

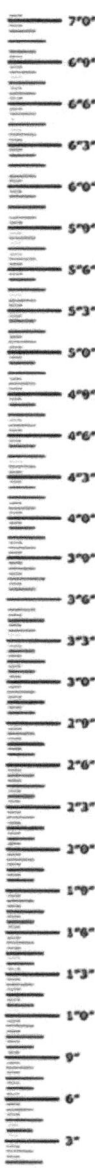

SAXON

NOAH

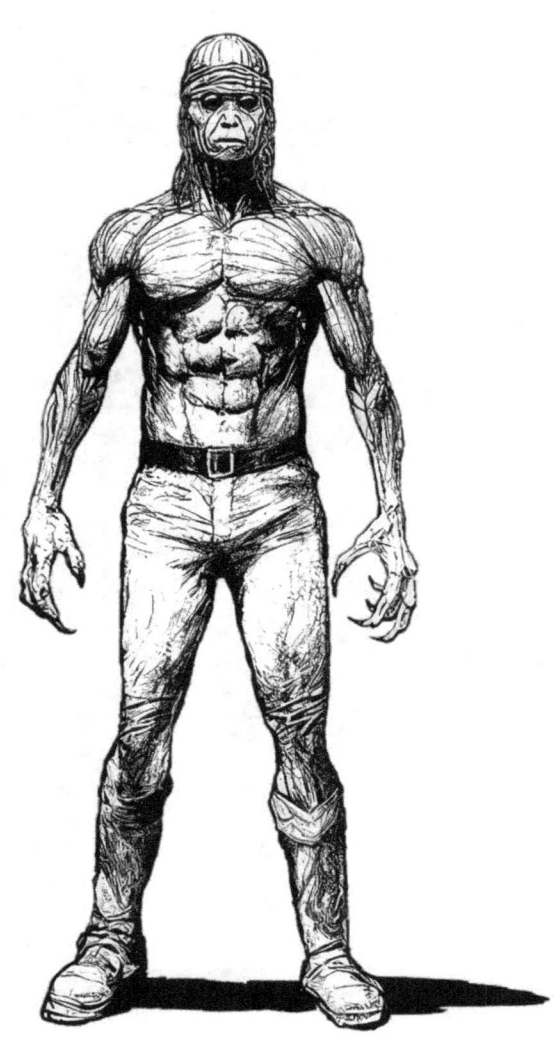

RAKE

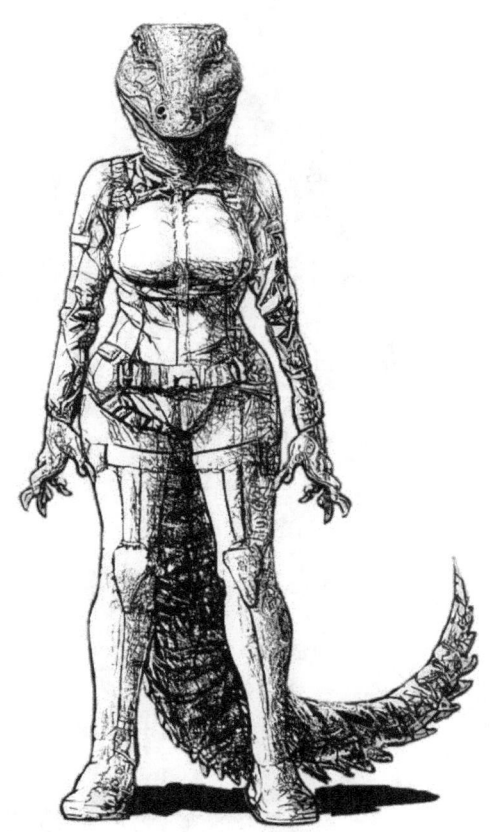

NESSIE

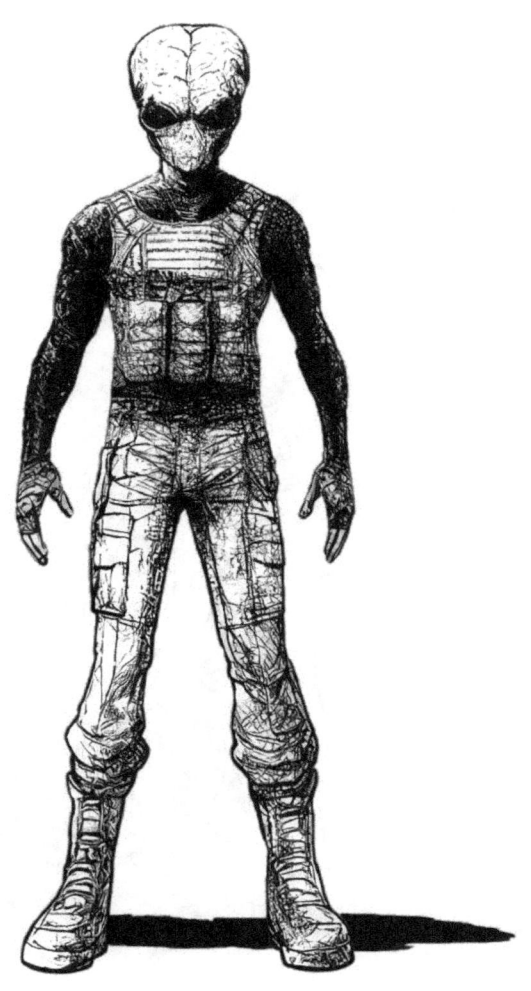

GREY

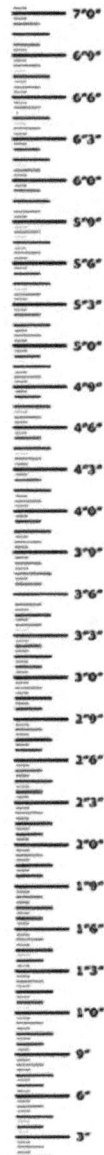

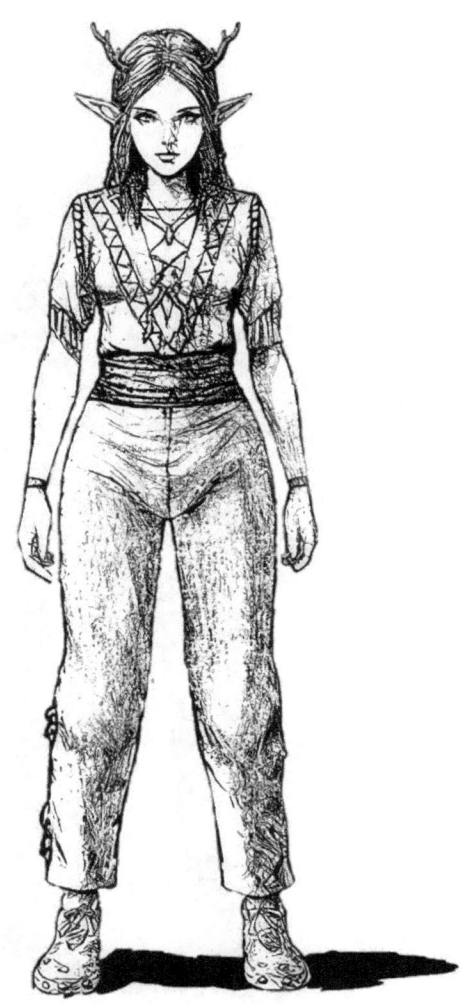

AURA

HUNTER

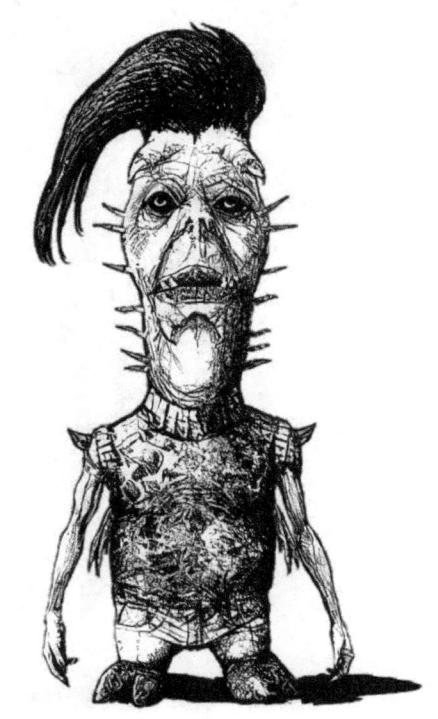

SCAMP

BARIEL

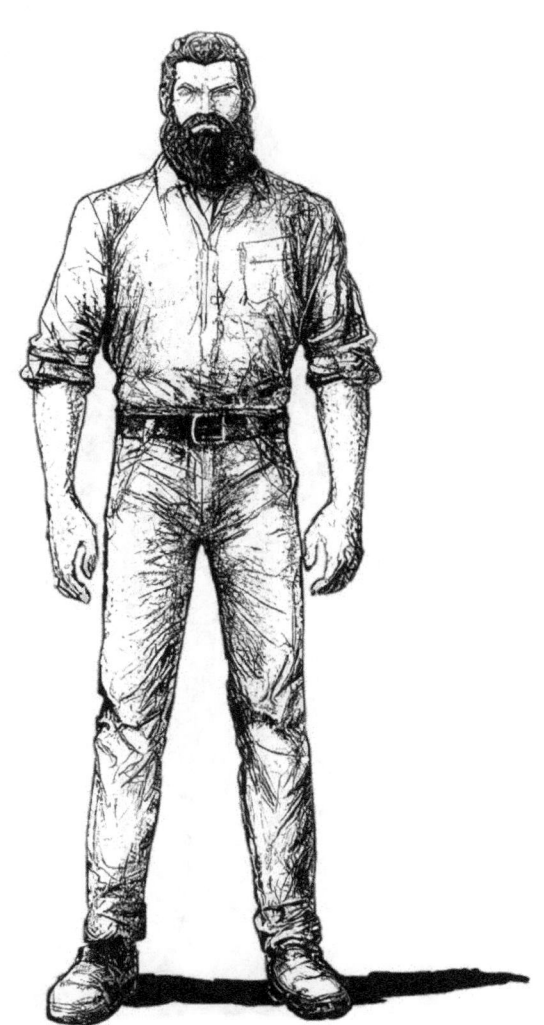

COLE CARTER

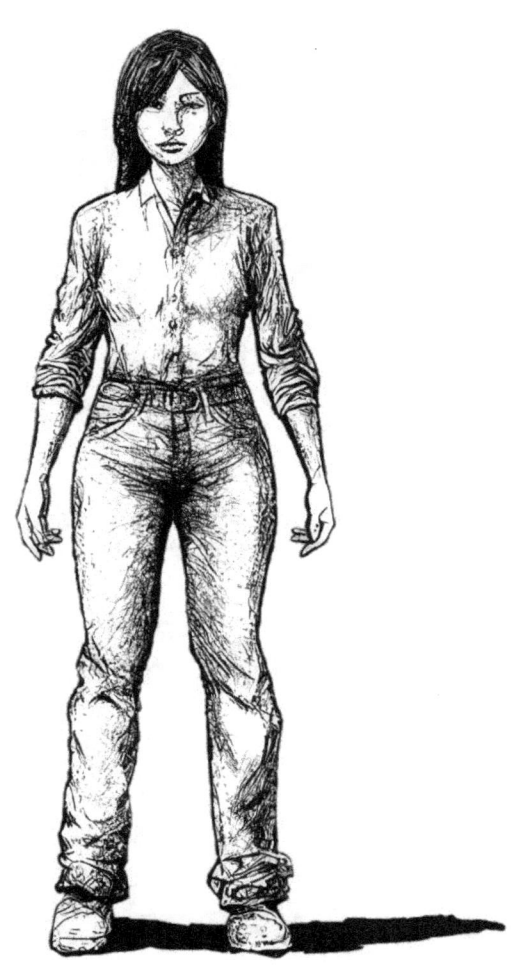

MEI HE